CLOUD REBEL

R-D SERIES, BOOK THREE

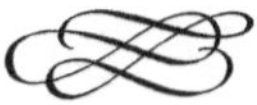

CONNIE SUTTLE

Print Second Edition (2018)
Print ISBN: 1-63478-061-2
Print ISBN-13: 978-1-63478-061-2
eBook ISBN: 1-93975-999-4
eBook ISBN-13: 978-1-93975-999-3

Published by:
SubtleDemon Publishing, LLC
PO Box 95696
Oklahoma City, OK 73143

Cover art by Renée Barratt @ The Cover Counts

To Walter, Joe, Larry, Lee, Dianne, Sarah and Mark.
Thank you.
And for my sisters Kathy and Beth—you are my heroes.

ACKNOWLEDGMENTS

As always, this book is the result of collaboration. If it weren't for the support of my editor, my cover artist and my beta readers, it would be less than it is. All mistakes, as usual, are mine and no other's.

About the Author:
Connie Suttle lives in Oklahoma with her husband and a conglomerate of cats. They have finally banded together to make their demands, which has proven disconcerting to all humans involved.

You may find Connie in the following ways:
Facebook: Connie Suttle Author
Twitter: @subtledemon
Website and Blog: subtledemon.com

High Demon Series:

Demon Lost

Demon Revealed

Demon's King

Demon's Quest

Demon's Revenge

Demon's Dream

God Wars Series:

Blood Double

Blood Trouble

Blood Revolution

Blood Love

Blood Finale

Saa Thalarr Series:

Hope and Vengeance

Wyvern and Company

Observe and Protect*

First Ordinance Series:

Finder

Keeper

BlackWing

SpellBreaker

WhiteWing

~

R-D Series:

Cloud Dust

Cloud Invasion

Cloud Rebel

~

Latter Day Demons Series:

Hot Demon in the City

A Demon's Work is Never Done

A Demon's Due

~

Seattle Elementals Series:

Your Money's Worth

Worth Your While*

~

BlackWing Pirates Series

MindSighted

MindMage

MindRogue

MindMaster*

~

Black Rose Sorceress Series

The Rose Mark

Rose and Thorn

Black Rose Queen

Queen of Thorns and Roses

Future Wars Series

Buffer Zone

Black Zone*

Other Titles from SubtleDemon Publishing:

Malefactor

Transgressor

Underhanded*

by Joe Scholes

*Forthcoming

CHAPTER 1

Ilya

"You wanted to see me?" I asked. I stood before Colonel Hunter's desk after James ushered me inside and closed the door, leaving us alone.

"I did. Sit down," he gestured with a hand. "Want coffee?"

"No, thank you."

"At least sit down."

"Of course." I took the offered chair and attempted to make myself comfortable.

"We think we have a sighting—in Vancouver." Colonel Hunter released a sigh before shaking his head. "I wanted it to be a fake, but the photograph appears to be genuine."

"Let me see," I said, leaning forward to take the offered tablet. If this were a drug survivor, he had successfully stayed hidden for more than a year.

That's how long it had been since the attack at the White House. Forcefully shoving that memory away, I studied the grainy photograph on the tablet.

"This looks very much like," I began.

"Those lizard fuckers who hit us at the White House," Colonel

Hunter agreed. "Matt's seen it—he thinks the same. If this image is real, we don't need those scaly bastards showing up here a second time."

"At least we understand better what the scaled woman was early on—the one who attempted to take me and—well."

"I know. It's poetic justice, I suppose, that some of the drug survivors would be of that race."

"You want me to track this one?"

"I want you to go to Vancouver and see what you can find—if anything. The address of the man who took that photograph will be sent to you when you arrive. He's agreed to an interview. Find out what you can and get back with me. The President wants us to be discreet."

"Of course. When do I leave?"

"Tomorrow morning. Take that tablet—it's all on there. Do you need funds?"

"No."

"Let me know if that changes."

"I will."

∼

Reth Alliance Founder's Chambers

Ildevar Wyyld, Founder

"Deonus, they went without my permission, which brands them rogues," Geethe Cheriss, Prime Potentate of Lyristolys, whined. At least he appeared humanoid instead of changing to the scaly alter ego of his kind.

Lyristolyi were related to Sirenali in some way, but Lyristolyi didn't possess the ability to place obsession. If they fought or wanted to appear aggressive, they wore their scales. For everything else, they were humanoid.

"While I'd like very much to believe that, I have my doubts," I snapped at Geethe's excuse. "This was too well-coordinated and too many of your trackers were involved, I think. You know the rules—if any non-Alliance world has a government, or in this case, many governments, they must be approached by an envoy from the Reth Alliance. This was not done."

"I understand the rules, Deonus Wyyld. I stand by my statement—these were rogues. Punish them, not Lyristolys."

"Except we can't find them—those who survived, that is," I thundered. "Your rogues killed nineteen world leaders and hundreds of others, sending that planet into near-chaos. I want those rogues caught and delivered to the ASD for prosecution."

"Yes, Deonus." Geethe bowed as low as he could without toppling over.

"Leave my sight. I want updates every eight-day on your search for these rogues."

"Yes, Deonus."

Geethe scurried backward, never taking his eyes off Ildevar's boots, until he was through the wide door and away from the Founder's Chamber. Ildevar heard running after that.

"Did you light a fire beneath that pretentious ass?" Norian Keef, Director of the Alliance Security Detail, asked quietly as he turned away from a nearby window. He'd heard the entire conversation with Geethe—who'd likely fled to get away from Norian as much as to escape Ildevar.

"He'll never openly admit that he sent that army of trackers to Earth," Ildevar snorted. "He's lucky he's still alive to lie and place blame. My question is this—did they get all the drug and its survivors, there? You know a survivor is just as dangerous as that infernal powder ever was—they can infect others with the same type of blood, after all."

"I know." Norian shook his head. "Want me to send someone?"

"I'd appreciate it," Ildevar replied. "Perhaps more than one. Make sure they speak at least one of the languages where they're dropped, too."

"I know the routine, Deonus," Norian jerked his head. "I'll see who I have to send."

~

Corinne

More than a year has passed on Earth. That meant nothing to me where I was. Actually, it meant nothing to me *when* I was.

I was four hundred years in the future, still waiting for a decision to come from the Larentii Council.

To show how little they thought of my talent and power, they left me to wander wherever I wanted, although I was expected to spend my nights at the Larentii Archives. The Archives had become my home, once I'd arrived on the Larentii homeworld.

The Archives had been uninhabited most of that time, so I'd wandered through them, reading, listening, watching, studying—any form of learning or information was stored in the Archives, including a history of Earth.

The Larentii version of that history was far more detailed and accurate than anything actually produced on the planet in question. I'd only read up to the time when I'd been pulled away from Earth— what was the point in depressing myself more than I was already?

Instead, I turned to other worlds and read their histories.

Yes, Larentii can bend time as well as fold space. If I'd known that when I was still on Earth, I might be in a lot more trouble than I was already.

At first, a few Larentii came—mostly curious to see the one who'd become Larentii after getting the drug. When they learned their staring upset me and made me shake, they backed off.

At least they were a polite race.

I'd seen, too, in the ones who'd arrived to study me, that female Larentii were quite rare. I understood much from those meetings, and wondered whether they knew I could read them as easily as I'd read humans (and others) on Earth.

I'd learned a new word, too—*Sirenali*.

That's what President Phillips had become after getting the drug. Capable of placing obsessions that would remain with the recipient until death, the Sirenali were supposed to be extinct.

I didn't want to bring up that bit of history with any Larentii, because they refused to discuss it, most of the time.

I was deep into the history of Le-Ath Veronis when the Archivist and one of his sons arrived one sunny morning.

"Do you know who I am?" The Archivist peered over the book I held open and floating before me with power. I didn't want to put my fingers on anything, in case the item in question was fragile.

I was Larentii, after all, and had more than enough power to hold something in front of me—even while sleeping if I wanted.

"Nefrigar. Chief Archivist for the Larentii," I spouted after lifting my eyes from the book and seeing his face.

"Ah. So wonderful," he smiled. "Welcome. I'm sorry we were out when you arrived. This is my second son, Valegar," he introduced another Larentii who resembled him greatly. "My eldest, Serrigar, is still out gathering information with my two youngest."

I stared at Valegar as a slow and magnificent smile came. His hand took mine and he kissed it, while his eyes glowed a very bright blue.

"Is this?" Nefrigar's voice sounded far away and faint as I blinked at Valegar.

"Yes, Father," Valegar replied as my consciousness fled.

Larentii Council Chambers

"Is that what you were waiting for? To see whether anyone might have a M'Fiyah with her?" Breanne studied Kalenegar. "If that's true, then I may have to amend my description of you—from heartless bastard to merely bastard."

"My parentage is known and recognized, therefore, that word does not apply," Kalenegar huffed.

"I know—I just wanted to jolt you out of that pretentious shell you wear." She smiled to let him know she was teasing.

"I received mindspeech from Nefrigar moments ago, that's why I sent for you," Kalenegar ignored Breanne's remark. "You have no idea how many Larentii went to see her—most of them shielded heavily so she wouldn't see—we learned it upset her greatly to be under such scrutiny."

"She wasn't born Larentii, and she still has all those memories of living among humans, so that's not a surprise. Who has the M'Fiyah with her?"

"Valegar," Kalenegar offered a slight smile. "I worried that the Archivist's sons would never agree to have their children."

"So they want their children to have love from both parents, I take it?"

"I believe that to be true, yes."

"He still needs to ask her, you know. I don't want her knocked up and finding out later."

"I believe Nefrigar and Valegar will prevent that from happening," Kal sniffed.

"When will you tell her? Do those filth from Lyristolys know to stay far away from her?"

"In this timeline, they should know better. Four hundred Earth years have passed since their brutality was visited upon that planet. Many died who should not have. Ildevar threatened to remove them from the Alliance shortly after for their mistakes."

"Speaking of that," Breanne began.

"What do you want, love of my heart?"

"I want a lot of things. Mostly, I want to send Corinnelar back to Earth in the past—there are things which require her attention."

"Are you giving permission?" One of Kalenegar's dark-red eyebrows rose in curiosity.

"I am."

"I doubt Valegar will allow her out of his sight so soon."

"Look, I know he's an Earth scholar and understands the excrement happening in the past four hundred years. I'll give him permission to go as well. I believe those two can be trusted to decide when to intervene and when not to."

"You've studied her, haven't you?"

"Yes. It's all I can do to hold back from introducing myself. Who knew there'd be two Vhanaraszhes?"

"The drug," Kal snorted softly. "You and I know it for the abomination it is, as it interferes with all timelines."

"Yes, but this time, I believe it has worked to our advantage, rather than our disadvantage. Here's my question, though."

"What question is that?"

"Do you have a M'Fiyah with her?"

"I have muted it. Now is not the time, if ever it will be."

"Now I know why you didn't influence the Council to kill her outright."

"She is Larentii, no matter how she arrived at that state."

"Sure. That's your excuse and you're sticking with it."

"She may not understand the concept of multiple mates—that is foreign to her in her other existences."

"I understand that. Let's see how it works with Valegar. I may consider dealing with the problem experienced by her previous mate —should I find him worthy."

"That is my desire," Kal agreed. "To see that he is worthy, before offering relief from the obsession and a place among immortals."

"Just keep those trackers away from him until I make a decision," Breanne said.

"I will inform Valegar."

"Thank you."

~

Notes—Colonel Hunter

"Did you receive the number and address from James?" I asked. Rafe had reached Vancouver and was now checking in.

"I have them," Rafe acknowledged. "It's late—I'll contact him in the morning."

"Good idea. Let me know what you've learned after talking with him."

"I will."

~

Vancouver

Ilya

Something about this assignment worried me. No—not from Colonel Hunter's standpoint—the name and phone number concerned me.

A great deal.

That's why I wanted to wait until the following day; I could plan my moves in case this turned out to be a trap.

I'd seen too many similar cases in my past to believe otherwise.

It made me wish for *her*—and *her* talents—to tell me whether the contact was a safe one. Instead, I found myself boarding a tourist bus headed for Stanley Park that afternoon, so I could clear my head and think.

~

Larentii Archives

Corinne

"Your acceptance was never in question," Nefrigar explained. "I am sorry you believed your life in danger at any time."

"But he said," I began. I felt like crying. Tears, when I hadn't taken in anything but sunlight for more than a year, were more than difficult to make. I wanted to cry them anyway.

"I know—and perhaps he meant those words when he first came upon you," Nefrigar replied. "I believe his mind was changed moments later. Perhaps he will explain that to you himself, someday."

"I don't expect the Head of the Larentii Council to waste his time on a drug survivor," I muttered, turning away.

Before our private meeting, Nefrigar had to chase Valegar away—Val was determined to see to my every need for some reason.

"Ah, but you are quite special. He should have explained that to you at the beginning," Nefrigar smiled gently. "I do not wish to upset you, but someday, I hope he takes time to tell you how special you truly are."

"If he doesn't intend to kill me, then he doesn't have to waste his time," I said. Yes, I felt shaky—a throwback to my previous lives that at times I couldn't dismiss. I wasn't sure any naturally born Larentii ever suffered from permanent emotional or psychological problems.

"I can tell you this much—every Larentii who sees you knows it," Nefrigar's smile widened. "You are an unreadable. Unless you expend a certain type of energy, as you did on Earth, or send mindspeech to one of us, we cannot locate you. That's how special you are."

"Then what's to keep me from just disappearing from here?" I asked.

"You have the tiniest of chips implanted—Kalenegar saw to that himself at the beginning. He will be able to find you, and now, because he has given permission, Valegar and I can find you as well. If anyone intends you harm and you are unable to protect yourself, we will know."

"Why tell me all this?" I hunched my shoulders.

"Because he has received word from one of the Three," Nefrigar beamed. "You and Valegar have been given permission to go back to Earth in the past and sort the difficulty created by the Lyristolyi and their drug."

"I'm not endangering Ilya," I said.

"Ah, but you will be in a position to protect him," Nefrigar said. "I believe that's the intention—I hear that those remaining are to have their blood neutralized of the drug—Valegar knows how to do this— in order to allow them to live their lives without fear of reprisal or of someone obtaining their blood for illicit purposes."

"So Val will be going, too?"

"I don't believe he can be torn from your side for long," Nefrigar chuckled.

"I don't believe this," I dropped my face in my hands. "What about Auggie and the others?"

"By all means, approach them if you want, merely explain that your doings are controlled by you and no other. You may take his suggestions under advisement, but your decisions will be your own."

"I want to kick Matt Michaels' ass," I said.

"Tell him that," Nefrigar said. "Although I doubt you'd follow through with that threat."

"He could have done something to protect Nick and Maye. He didn't lift a finger," I huffed. I was still angry—and sad—about that.

"It is often that way—when the powerful are undecided as to what to do in such circumstances. Whether their interfering will alter the timeline too greatly and affect everything adversely afterward."

"I still think he's a schmuck."

"As I said, tell him so. I believe he may be more troubled by the events of that day than you realize."

"Right. I'll be sure to look him up for a philosophical discussion. When are we leaving—Val and I?"

"You may leave anytime—Val is more than adept at bending time to arrive on a selected date."

"When does he want to leave, then?"

"Why don't you ask him? I believe he would like time alone with you."

"Nothing's going to interfere with this," I touched the ring on my left hand. I'd had to enlarge it, but it was there.

"He has no desire to interfere with that, unless that one places your life in danger," Nefrigar reassured me. "We have no jealousy. Surely you've discovered this for yourself?"

"I know I don't feel it, but Ilya sure did."

"Perhaps it would be best to stay out of his way, while this obsession plagues him," Nefrigar cautioned.

"Yeah. I get that. If I see him, he won't see me."

"That would be best, although it could prove painful for you."

"I know."

"Allow Valegar to help you through this—he is more than fond of you already."

"You'll have to explain that to me, someday."

"Let him—eventually. When you're ready."

"All right. May I take an hour for myself? This is a lot for me to process," I said.

"Take your hour. I warn you, Valegar will be counting the nanoseconds and will know exactly when that hour is over."

"Right."

Falaca, a herd of wool-bearing animals, nibbled grass about me as I sat on a hillside near the equator of the Larentii homeworld. I could see why the animals liked it here—plenty of grass, tasty flowers and no predators.

Occasionally, a woolly head butted against my arm as I sat there; friendly falaca were asking for an ear scratch. I obliged.

"We remove the wool without harming or frightening the animal, and then weave it for our clothing, whenever clothing is required," Valegar sat beside me. His father was right—he'd counted every second until the hour was up.

"So—everybody runs around naked?" I turned to him. So far, everyone I'd seen had been dressed. For the most part. Val smiled.

"I understand that nudity is unnatural to you in your past lives— those that you recall," he said. "To us, it is easier to soak up sunlight if all our skin is exposed."

"I get that, it just feels strange to me—to wander around with all the naughty bits exposed."

"Naughty bits," Valegar laughed. "There is nothing naughty about any of your bits."

"You find that amusing?"

"I am an Earth scholar. I understand a great deal from those cultures."

"Well, you're probably way ahead of me, then. Some of that stuff I may never understand."

"It only seems overwhelming, because to your past selves, it was. Now, you are Larentii. That is likely no longer true."

"Yeah. I'm tall. I'm blue. Woo-hoo, woo-hoo."

I'll admit, I'd never seen a Larentii lose it before. Valegar practically fell over laughing. He'd almost recovered when a falaca bleated in his face. That brought on a new round of chuckling.

Yeah, it made me laugh, too.

I studied him as he reached out to stroke the falaca's head. For a blue man, he was beautifully made. Not an ounce of fat anywhere, and the corners of his eyes crinkled nicely when he smiled or laughed. I almost reached out to touch the curve at the end of his lips before pulling my hand back.

"You may touch me anytime," he said. He'd read my desire—likely in the movement of my hand.

"I'll have to get used to that," I said.

"I know. If you'd been born Larentii, we'd have had energy sex already."

"Okay, you'll have to explain that to me. Not now," I held up a hand when he opened his mouth. Instead, he took my hand and kissed it before setting it back in my lap.

"When do you wish to leave?" he asked. "I will allow you to choose clothing and shoes for me, as we must disguise ourselves to fit in."

"Okay. I have a question."

"Anything, Lara'Kayan."

"Uh—will Ilya only try to kill me if he recognizes me?"

"I believe that's the way the obsession works. Remember, he has seen you in all three incarnations."

"Yeah. I get that. How should I disguise myself, then?"

"I'll take care of that. All will see you as you desire; only your Ilya will see you differently."

"You can do that? That's outstanding."

"I will do anything for you, my love."

"Wow, that was fast," I said.

"It's the way the M'Fiyah works," he shrugged.

～

Vancouver
Ilya

The meeting was set at one that afternoon, after I'd had a phone conversation with the informant during breakfast. I'd gotten an e-mail from Giovanni Carano, too, at an alternate e-mail address. I asked him to check on the villa—I wanted to buy it if the owner were willing to sell.

He asks for a million, U.S., Giovanni informed me.

Tell him yes, I responded and turned off my phone. My bank account had been increased exponentially, shortly before her disappearance. It's as if she'd known, somehow, that she would no longer need money. It was one of many gifts she'd given me, and all I could do was bring her death if I ever saw her again.

My visit to Stanley Park the day before had mired me in melancholy. *She* was dead. There was no other explanation, yet the obsession persisted. I should have killed the bastard who placed it when he stood in front of me. Instead, I'd allowed him to speak and he'd ruined my life.

I'd watched him die, though, and took much satisfaction from that. *She'd* kept a promise—one made to me. The manner of his passing, however, had been much too painless for my liking.

If I could, I'd bring his worthless body back to life and beat that life out of him this time. Just as he'd intended for me to beat—*her*.

Fighting back nausea, I shook myself and turned to other subjects. I had a rental car—the informant's address was on the eastern edge of Vancouver and I had no desire to depend upon a taxi or other transportation to get me there on time.

After driving through a tall gate, I parked in a circle drive outside a two-story brick house. Shoving a Glock into the back waistband of my jeans, I adjusted my jacket and opened the car door.

It was risky not employing my shield, but even more dangerous to fire my weapon with a shield in place, which would likely result in death by my own ricocheted bullets. No, this time I chose to rely on my skill and reflexes.

The front door opened before I arrived to knock. I barely had time to turn and fire at the man who'd appeared at the side of the house, a rifle in his hand.

That left no time to shoot back at the armed man standing in the doorway, who'd fired at me at the same moment the one at the corner had. My shield would have protected me from outside bullets while my own did the damage. They'd planned this carefully; I was a dead man and I knew it.

Except that wasn't what happened.

The bullets from the rifle dropped to the ground halfway between my intended assassin and me. The rifle in his hands began to glow red until he dropped it with a yelp amid the scent of burned flesh.

The one at the corner? I'd killed him cleanly. Someone stepped over his body to take his place.

"Time to stop shooting." Two people I didn't recognize appeared feet away from me. "Go ahead," the male nodded to the scaled creature who aimed a gun at me. "You have been warned. You will die if you fire."

He fired. His bullets never left the gun. Instead, he had the strangest expression on his face as he died, dropping as if he were boneless, to the ground.

The man in the doorway attempted to run. I shot him in the shoulder, bringing him down. He lived because I had questions to ask. Not just of him, but of the two who'd appeared to help me.

"I am Valegar," the blond man nodded without my asking. "This is Rinnelar," he indicated the red-haired woman beside him.

"That's that fucker Merle Askins," Rinnelar exclaimed as she walked toward the scaled man. "Val, I'm surprised he chose scales instead of a more normal appearance."

I barely heard her; lifting handcuffs from a jacket pocket, I jerked the survivor's burned hands behind his back and secured him while he shuddered in pain. "Colonel Hunter," I said the moment I had a hand free to dial his number, "this was a trap. Two are dead; one is alive but wounded. Do you have a team to send?"

"They're on the way," he said, his voice stern, his words clipped.

≈

"I had no idea you'd be my backup," I said when Opal climbed out of the van ten minutes later. My rescuers—Rinnelar and Valegar—had disappeared the moment I'd called Colonel Hunter. I should have photographed both; they were strangers, although they'd done me a favor. I was at a loss to explain any of it.

"Who's lizard man?" Opal asked as two agents followed her and took charge of the survivor. She'd gone to examine the dead attackers while the survivor was loaded into the van.

"Two strangers arrived to help—the woman claimed the scaled one was Merle Askins."

"Seriously? Two strangers came to help? Did they identify themselves?"

"The man called himself Valegar. The woman was Rinnelar."

"Well, well, well," Opal sighed. "You've been saved by Larentii."

≈

Notes—Colonel Hunter

"What the hell are you talking about?" I shouted. "Opal said what?"

"Colonel Hunter, I'm right here and I can hear you clearly." Opal had taken the phone away from Rafe.

"Two Larentii were there? What did they look like?" I demanded.

"Colonel, you should know as well as I do that they can look any way they want." Her voice was dry.

I took a moment to consider that. "Yeah, I suppose you're right," I mumbled. "Where are they now?"

"How should I know? Rafe said they disappeared right after they pulled his fat from the fire."

"That brings me to my next question," I said. "Why did they pull his fat from the fryer?"

"I said fire, and I have no idea."

"Does Rafe have injuries?"

"None that I can see."

"Good. Are you riding back with him or in the van with the prisoner?"

"I'll ride back with Rafe—I've already sent the prisoner on—he has a bullet in his shoulder and his hands are burned, so he needs medical treatment."

"How did his hands—never mind. Ask Rafe to write a report and send it in, including all details on Larentii help."

"I will. Do you want to talk to him again?"

"No. Just—have him send the report."

"All right."

I ended the call and set my cell phone on my desk. Yes, I was thinking about having a cursing fit. Instead, I blinked as two people appeared before me. One of them, I recognized.

"Hello, Auggie," she said.

CHAPTER 2

otes—Colonel Hunter

"Rinnelar is a nickname of sorts—we call her Corinnelar—it's an honorific as denotes her position as a member of the Larentii race. I am Valegar," the man—*Larentii*—said. At least they looked human as they sat on my guest chairs—which helped to keep my panic under control.

"I don't work for you anymore, Auggie," Corinne said bluntly. I blinked at her for a moment. The last time I'd seen her, she was eight feet tall and blue-skinned. Now she looked just the way I remembered her before that, with blonde hair and bright-blue eyes.

"How did you keep Rafe from—you know?" I asked.

"He didn't see me this way. I was disguised so he wouldn't recognize me."

"That probably saved both of you," I sat back in my chair and studied my guests. "Tell me, why are you here? I see they let you live."

Valegar snorted at my statement. I didn't ask him to explain his reaction. Truthfully, I was too afraid to ask him to explain it. I knew what Corinne could do. The man who sat beside her—I got the idea he might fry anybody who took advantage or thought to harm her.

"Frying is never an option," Valegar plucked those thoughts from my mind as easily as a child could pick raisins from a cake. "We release particles," he added.

"Auggie, we have permission to do a bit of cleanup," Corinne explained. "But we may not be the only ones here."

"What's that supposed to mean?" I asked. I was getting a headache trying to stretch my mind around what sat in front of my desk.

"It means that the ASD may have sent trackers. Not only will they attempt to find any drug survivors, but any remnants of the drug. You understand that drug survivors are just as dangerous as the drug itself?"

"Yeah. I sort of figured that out," I said, dropping my eyes. He was right. Even one drug survivor could make endless copies of himself—all he needed was a busload of people with the same blood type. "What about Rafe?" I began.

"We can neutralize his blood so the drug won't carry over to any recipients," Valegar explained. "He will have to be made aware of it, however, and grant permission."

"If he doesn't give it?"

"Then we step aside and allow the ASD to do their work."

"What—exactly—is the ASD?" I asked, reaching into a desk drawer for the bottle of ibuprofen I kept there.

"Alliance Security Detail," Valegar explained. Corinne watched him as he spoke—something was between them, that much I could see. Shaking three tablets into my hand, I reached for my cup of cold coffee to down them.

"They'll be asking for your permission to track any survivors from the U.S. Program," Corinne said. "I'm asking you to deny that request. They'll also approach the Russian government for their permission. I don't give a damn what they say. If they say no, Valegar and I will track them anyway."

"I've often wanted to speak as humans do," Valegar offered Cori a blinding smile. "Perhaps I will attempt it and you can tell me if I err."

"Honey, I think you can do anything you want," Corinne smiled back.

"I think I need more ibuprofen," I grabbed the bottle.

"Auggie, I'll take care of your headache," Corinne rose from her seat. Once her hands touched my head, every thread of pain left. I blinked in surprise—why hadn't I asked her to do that before?

"Where—ah—will you be staying?" I asked. "In case I want to get in touch?"

"Just call me on that phone," Corinne nodded to the one she'd given me long ago. "I'll answer." She held an identical phone aloft as she took her seat again.

"James will want to see you."

"I know. Tell him we'll talk soon."

"My father says to remind you that you no longer have any control over Corinnelar," Valegar said. "He is monitoring our conversation at the moment."

"Really?" I reached for the ibuprofen again.

"He is also watching you through my eyes."

"No kidding." The few ibuprofen I had left rattled in the bottle as I worked to remove the lid.

"Auggie, no more," Corinne held out her hand and floated the ibuprofen away from me. The container dropped into her hand. It disappeared, then—to where, I had no idea. She'd sent it to the Larentii homeworld, for all I knew. Panic surged through me again.

"Cori—I just can't wrap my head around this," I said and stood abruptly, sending my chair rolling into the wall behind me.

"Auggie—I know what I am, and I realize that's hard for you to get," she said. "I really didn't want you to see—well, the taller, bluer me. It couldn't be helped."

"I've missed you," I blurted.

"I know. I've missed all of you, too. I want to cry for Nick and Maye. I haven't had any water in a year, so I can't make tears."

"What the hell?" I huffed. *Were they starving her?*

"Relax—we live on energy. Sunlight, Auggie. I can eat and digest, but sunlight is so much better and easier for me. I just can't cry if I don't take in fluids."

"That explains the sunlamps."

"Yeah. I burned the first one out, because I tried to pull more from it than it was capable of giving."

"My love, you weren't starving, were you?" Valegar turned to her, then.

"No, I managed," she shrugged.

"You're not drained now?" He reached out to touch her cheek.

"No, I'm fine."

"I will see you get enough light in a moment."

"Have you been to the top of Christ of the Andes?"

"Holy fuck," I whispered as both disappeared.

"What's the emergency?" Leo Shaw sat across from me at a restaurant he'd chosen. I wasn't sure I could eat after what I'd seen and heard earlier in the day.

"Rafe was almost killed by the creature who once was Merle Askins," I began.

"You're joking? He survived the drug?"

"Yes, but he's dead, now."

"Rafe killed him?"

"With some help, yes."

"Who helped?"

"Corinne—and the Larentii who thinks she's his."

Opal

"Corinne and Valegar showed up today," I informed Matt.

"Valegar?"

"He's the second son of Nefrigar."

"Oh. I haven't met him."

"Probably just as well; you have no idea how protective Larentii mates can be."

"What's she doing back here? Corinne?"

"I uh, contacted Bree."

"You contacted Bree." Matt went silent for a moment.

"Yeah. Told her what happened."

"What did she call me?"

"She didn't call you anything."

"That means nothing. She's probably pissed that I let things get out of hand."

"Stop being a schmuck."

"Did you see Corinne?"

"No—but Colonel Hunter did."

"Of course she'd go to him, first, since Rafe—well."

"She was disguised when she saved Rafe's fanny."

"So she did see him first."

"Yeah, I just don't know how that affected her."

"When you contacted Bree—did you put in a good word for Corinne?"

"I didn't have to—Bree already knew as much as I did. I think if the Larentii had decided not to accept Corinne, well, the blue fur would have flown."

Corinne

"I like this better," Valegar pulled me down to sit beside him.

"You're right—this is better," I sighed. He'd found a waterfall on the big island of Hawaii and settled there to soak in filtered sunlight.

"He meant a lot to you, didn't he?" Valegar's arms settled around me.

"He still does."

"I know. That upset you—to see him again."

"Yeah." My voice was a whisper.

His arms, as warm as a summer day, wrapped tighter around me, and he began to hum. It was the most restful sound I'd ever heard, sending me to sleep in seconds.

∼

Ilya

"Macallan, twenty-five year," I set my credit card on the bar before taking a seat. At least the bar had the Scotch on hand, even if it were one-fifty-five a shot. After today, I wanted three shots.

At least I was still alive to have three shots. If the Larentii hadn't shown up to save my ass—I decided not to wander too far down that road, or I'd end up asking myself why they'd bother to save any part of me.

That answer could be dangerous.

∼

Reth Alliance

Ildevar Wyyld, Founder

"Who did you send?"

Norian looked up from his comp-vid as I strode into his office to ask my question.

"I sent four—the Verain brothers, who somehow know at least three languages there, and Brade Deplan."

"The three Verain brothers?" I asked.

"All three, yes. They wanted to go."

"And you say they speak three languages from that planet?"

"Yes, let's see," Norian scrolled through his comp-vid to find the records, "Ah, Spanch, Franch, Ainglash."

"I believe you're pronouncing those wrong, but it matters little. Have they arrived?"

"No word as yet, Deonus."

"I wish to be kept informed. I am concerned that all three brothers wished to go."

"Look, I know you wanted to keep them separated when they joined the ASD, but for this particular assignment—they spoke the necessary languages, Deonus."

"What about Brade?"

"He spoke a separate language—Jerm?"

"Hmmph," I mumbled my displeasure. "I hope they speak better than you can pronounce," I said. "Have them record their meetings with the leaders they approach, and I want reliable translations on each meeting."

"Of course, Deonus."

"I wish we had a Larentii," I muttered as I turned to go. "They understand everything."

~

Ilya

I studied the photograph on the tablet Colonel Hunter had given me. Merle Askins, former Director of the CIA, had posed for that photograph, knowing we'd be drawn in. Was he acting on his own accord to kill me or another of Colonel Hunter's men, or was he following the orders of another?

I knew what those orders felt like—I'd lived with that illogical obsession for more than a year. Askins was dead, now, but that didn't mean he didn't have many more just like him—if they'd had the same blood type and had received his blood.

Once someone survived the drug, its effects could be spread like a virus, tainting any other with the same blood type. I suppose the same could be said for me—that someone else could be created just like me.

Forcing away the shudder that shook me for a moment, I turned back to the photograph. "How many?" I asked it. "How many more of you are out there, waiting to kill me?"

~

Notes—Colonel Hunter

It was late and I'd already called Laci to tell her I was coming home when Matt Michaels called.

"Director Michaels?" I said when I answered his call.

"I just wanted to put you on alert after Rafe was targeted in

Vancouver," he said. "If there are still survivors out there, they may want all of us who were involved taken down."

"That's not what I wanted to hear," I said, lifting my jacket from the hook beside the door. "Laci is just beginning to calm down and feel safe again."

"The thing is," Matt went on, ignoring my comment about Laci, "They don't have the full story—they likely have whatever the media has put in front of the public. That means that the aliens who killed all those people aren't included in that equation. They only see us as the perpetrators, and whoever they are, they want us to pay."

"I suppose it doesn't matter that Phillips had world domination on his agenda? That he'd planned his moves carefully to pull world leaders together so he could bend them to his will?"

"Somebody may want to step into his shoes," Matt responded. "Plus, we've never found those nuclear warheads he sent to the insurgents."

"You had to bring that up, didn't you? At least they've been quiet lately. Maybe they're still terrified that Corinne will make more of them dead."

"Or, if they learn she was taken away," Matt didn't finish.

"You know she's back, don't you?"

"I heard. I'm waiting for her to show up and slap me through a wall."

"You may have to explain that to me," I said.

"In time. Maybe. Look, I need to go. Just keep your eyes open. You may want to ask for additional security. It's times like these that I miss Nick and Maye the most."

"Yeah. Well, I'll consider the security part. Thanks for the heads up."

"No problem."

Corinne

"My love, what have you been doing?" Valegar woke me with soft words.

"Huh?"

"This—siphon—that you've attached to yourself to draw in sunlight?" If he hadn't been sitting beside me, and if he'd been human, he might have been tapping a toe, waiting for me to answer.

"Well, it's a way to get light at any time," I mumbled my excuse.

"That should only be used for emergencies," he scolded gently. "You should be filling yourself with sunlight whenever it is available, instead of a constant, crippled pull provided by a siphon. Besides, sunlamps made with Earth technology are very poor substitutes."

"Right." I sat up with his help, discovering that I lay naked on a bed inside a lavish hotel—one that bellied up to a beach in Oahu.

"Come, I will take you elsewhere, and I will assist you in pulling sunlight into your body."

"Can I have ice cream after that?"

"If you want it, yes."

"Do we have to be naked?"

"It helps if you are in your natural state, blue skin and all." The corners of his mouth twitched.

"Fine."

"I like this very much—all my studies of Earth will be put to the test," he smiled and folded space with me.

Ilya

At least nothing was broken when I woke on the floor in my hotel room. The mattress, sheets and pillows were strewn across the space, the chair and ottoman upside down against the window.

I appreciated the fact that I could straighten everything without having to pay for damages when I checked out. While I worked to put the room back to rights, I cursed the former President in as many languages as I knew.

"I'm leaving for the airport," I informed Colonel Hunter after buying coffee at a nearby shop and loading my bag into the rental.

"Good. Matt and I want a meeting with you when you get back."

"Tomorrow?"

"I have a ten o'clock with the Secretary of State, but Matt and I are available for lunch. We can eat and talk if you want."

"Of course."

"Any uh, unusual charges on your room, this time?"

"None, I'm pleased to say. Did Director Michaels say what his concerns are?"

"He may have intel on those warheads."

"I hope it's more reliable than last time."

"They were moved last time before we made it to the storage area. Finding something there is next to impossible without good information."

"Living informants are also an asset," I responded dryly.

"We do have a problem keeping them alive," he agreed. "I wish, well, we all know what I wish."

"I do." I stared at the wedding band I'd refused to remove from my hand. If I had my way, it would stay there as long as I lived.

"I'm hoping I can convince another person or two to join us—they may be working with us as liaisons of some sort—if I can convince them to do so."

"Who might that be?"

"The ones Opal said pulled your fat from the fire yesterday."

"Interesting choice of words, Colonel. I'll see you tomorrow."

Corinne

"Thank you for bringing me here." Val stood behind me as I paid my respects to Nick and Maye at Arlington National Cemetery. We'd gone to Australia first, to feed, and then he'd brought me here after I'd asked him to do so. That's when I got Auggie's call.

"Can you and uh—Valegar come to a lunch meeting tomorrow? Matt, Opal and I will be there. We'd like to talk to you."

"Go ahead and say Ilya will be there, too," I said.

"Rafe will be there," he confirmed. "Please call him that. I doubt he wants anyone else calling him—well, you should know what I mean."

"It's hard seeing him," I sighed.

"I know. Cori, we need information, and we may need it soon. That's why I'm asking you to meet with us."

"We'll be there," I said.

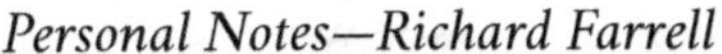

Personal Notes—Richard Farrell

"Hey, Doc." He was dying. Everyone else at Bethesda had considered it a blessing. Blinded in both eyes, all four limbs missing, paralyzed and experiencing renal failure after the IED explosion in Iraq, he had hours left at best. His voice was barely a whisper as he spoke—he'd heard me as I sat on the chair beside his bed.

"Do you remember when you told me how you loved to run?" I asked.

"Yeah. That'll only happen in my next life, now," he joked.

"Brett, just remember you said that," I told him before pulling the syringe from a pocket. I'd already used one; this was the second—and last—that I intended to use. I'd had a private meeting with Madam President—she'd given her blessing.

Two candidates I'd chosen personally had been moved to what Corinne had dubbed *the ugly building in Arlington.*

Inside, it was anything but. I'd had the top floor outfitted to my specifications, again with permission from the President. She intended to tell Colonel Hunter when—and if—my experiment was successful.

Yes, I'd kept my personal goals out of my proposal to the President, but the truth was this—I was empty without Maye.

I also had samples of her blood—and Nick's. This could fail, and I realized it.

If it failed, I intended to go down with my new charges.

~

Ilya

"Katya?" I answered her call when I walked through the door of my home in Silver Spring. Colonel Hunter had arranged for the house—I understood it had once belonged to her, for a short time.

Nevertheless, it was still owned by the Program, therefore I was using it.

"Papa," Katya's voice was thick with tears.

"What's wrong, little moth?" I asked.

"They caught Sergei—I don't know where he is," she wept.

"Hold on," I said and pulled a second phone from my pocket to dial Colonel Hunter.

~

Corinne

"Cori, I hate to bother you," Auggie said over the phone. I knew, just by the tone of his voice, that something was terribly wrong. Val followed in my wake as I folded space to Auggie's office.

I understood the problem the moment I saw his face.

Ilya's son-in-law was in trouble.

Val didn't bother to protest when I folded space the second time in mere seconds, where we found a naked Sergei Levinson tied to a chair, while his captors did their best to electrocute him with battery cables.

~

Katya stifled a scream when Val and I appeared in her hotel office, where she sat at her desk, crying.

"I need your chair," I said, allowing Valegar to settle the nearly lifeless body of Sergei on the chair she'd scrambled away from.

"Corinne?" she whispered as Val and I began to glow—it would take energy and talent to get Sergei back.

∽

"You can't tell your father I was here," I patted Katya's hand later, while she sat on the edge of her bed, stroking Sergei's hair back from his forehead. Val and I—we'd saved his life. Another few minutes and that may not have been possible.

Still, he had weeks of recovery ahead of him.

"Papa won't talk about you," she whispered. "Why?"

"A Sirenali's curse, young one," Val replied. "Once a Sirenali places an obsession, it can only be removed by that same Sirenali. If that Sirenali dies, as is the case, then the obsession tends to remain until the victim's death. Your father was instructed to kill Corinne. He cannot even hear her name without going into a terrible rage."

"How is that possible?" Katya breathed.

"This race we speak of was an abomination that should never have been created," Val snorted. "The same drug administered to your father also recreated a Sirenali."

"What happened to the ones who captured Sergei?" she asked. I could see that talk of Sirenali upset her, and the fact that her father was obsessed upset her more.

"Corinne blew them so hard against a wall, I believe they may not wake again," Valegar explained. "I'm sure many will appreciate that fact."

"Russian assholes," I muttered.

"What do I tell Papa?" Katya asked.

"Tell him the Larentii happened," I said. "He'll accept that. If he asks for names, say Rinnelar and Valegar."

"Do you still love him?"

"More than anything." I held up my left hand so she could see the ring on my finger.

"This is so sad. Thank you—for Sergei's life."

"You're welcome."

~

"Did you find him?" We found Auggie still in his office two hours later.

"Yeah. He's okay, now."

"Look—I didn't know about Rafe's daughter until he admitted she was part of the underground about six months ago," Auggie said.

"I know. We just wanted to check in; we need to find sunlight somewhere, to recharge."

"All right. Thank you. I know Rafe would be grateful, if he just," Auggie floundered.

"Yeah. I know."

"Come," Valegar took my hand and folded space.

~

Notes—Colonel Hunter

When they disappeared, I leaned back in my chair until it creaked. I sat there for several minutes, wondering how many times Cori would have to pull all our fat from the fire.

~

Ilya

I heard from Katya two hours after I received the frantic call from her. "Sergei's fine," she reported. "Now. After two Larentii showed up to save him. Those animals tried to electrocute him, Papa."

"You need to move—they know where you are," I stated flatly.

"I know. Three of our friends are here—we'll move Sergei in a few hours. If those people hadn't shown up, he'd be dead."

"I understand," I sighed. "I wish I were there with you—to help you find a new place." My other phone rang—I looked at the caller ID. "Katya, hold on," I said. Setting the first phone down, I answered the second.

"Get Colonel Hunter to bring them to the U.S.," the voice said. I understood it was Rinnelar—and I forced myself not to delve deeper than that.

"I will make the call," I agreed.

"Good."

The call was ended. Working to even my breathing, I lifted the first phone. "Little moth, let me call Colonel Hunter. I hope he will allow me to bring you and Sergei to the U.S."

CHAPTER 3

*N*otes—*Colonel Hunter*

I had no idea how this meeting would go; I'd already given permission to move Rafe's daughter and her husband to the U.S. Matt agreed readily when I called him. He'd already arranged transportation before we got off the phone.

They'd arrive in two days. For the moment, I'd allow them to stay with Rafe at the Silver Spring townhouse.

I waited for Rafe to put things together, though, and go after Corinne in her new guise. While she wouldn't harm him if he attempted to attack, I had no idea how Valegar would react. As much as Rafe had loved Corinne, I believe Valegar did the same.

"We're here," Matt walked in with Opal. He wore a grim expression —it appeared he wasn't looking forward to seeing Corinne again. I wanted him to explain that, but didn't expect the information to come my way. I hesitated to attach the word *subterfuge* to my curious observations, but I couldn't rule out the idea that something was going on.

Corinne

"How do I look?" Valegar asked.

"You look great," I said. He did—he wore his blond hair slightly longer than many Larentii, and it brushed his forehead nicely as he turned before me, showing off his black jeans, turtleneck, Loafers and bomber jacket.

It was winter in the U.S.; Val could warm himself with power, but he'd look strange to any human if he were dressed only in a short-sleeved shirt and jeans.

"Humans get cold easily," Val observed.

"Honey, you should talk to people in Alaska, Canada and other places that get really cold before making such a broad statement," I said.

"I merely wanted to see whether you'd point out the flaw in my observation," he smiled. "You did well."

"Are all our conversations going to be tests?" I asked.

"No, I merely wanted to distract you for a moment."

"Ah. That."

He was right—I needed a distraction. The closer the meeting time, the more worried I felt. I wanted to fling my arms around Ilya. Have him kiss my worries away. That wasn't possible and might never be.

"Val," I said, "Has there ever been a Larentii with an anxiety disorder or PTSD?"

"Are you feeling the effects of those, my love?" He came to me immediately.

"I just—this is so fucked up," I flung out a hand. I felt like crying and it wouldn't do to show up in Auggie's office sniffling.

"It is, as you say, fucked up," Val tucked my head beneath his chin and held me close. "We will get through this—I promise."

Twenty minutes later, we arrived in Auggie's office. Matt and Opal were already there. I wanted to glare at Matt; Val pulled me onto a chair before I could do so.

"Coffee? Water? Bourbon?" I could tell Auggie wasn't comfortable with whom—and what—he had in his office.

"We must change our bodies in order to feel the effects of alcohol," Val said. I watched as Opal attempted to hide a smile.

"Ah, my blue-skinned rescuers are here," Rafe arrived and nodded toward Val and me. Yes, we looked like Larentii; we'd only made ourselves smaller to fit on human furniture. "Thank you—for my life and that of my daughter's husband," Rafe added.

"You are welcome," Val nodded. "Rinnelar is quite adept at healing. She surprises me constantly."

"Awww," I turned to Val and offered him a smile.

"The—ah—President received an unusual message an hour ago," Auggie broke the uncomfortable silence that settled over us. "It is written in several languages, I assume to make sure we understand it."

"Which languages?" Opal asked.

"Spanish, French, English and German, along with another language we can't decipher."

"Do you have a copy of the message?" Val asked.

"Here," Auggie lifted a sheet of paper from his desk and handed it to Val. I looked at it while Val held it up for both of us to see.

"Alliance common," Val and I said together.

"Unfortunately, the English and German are poorly worded," Val added. "They should work harder on these language skills." He handed the paper message back to Auggie.

"Madam President wants to know what we think about this—among other things," Auggie said, setting the paper aside.

"What does it say?" Rafe asked.

"It is a greeting and an offer to relieve the planet of—and destroy—drug survivors and any remaining drug," Val interjected smoothly. "That includes you, Mr. Black."

"Is that why you're here?" Rafe sputtered. "To kill me?"

"Far from it," Val said. "We're here to—as Rinnelar would say—protect your ass. You have a choice, however. You can choose to have your blood neutralized, so no other may be made from it, or you take your chances with these new arrivals who work for the ASD."

"Neutralized?" Rafe immediately became suspicious.

"Just the drug in it," I attempted to smooth his ruffled neck hair. "You won't be changed in any other way. You'll still be the tough badass you always were."

"What?" Rafe's eyebrows lifted.

"No offense meant," Val said. "The choice is certainly yours, but I would consider the benefits carefully."

"How long and painful is the neutralization?"

"I can achieve it in seconds, and there will be no pain."

"Then do it."

I understood then that this was something he'd already considered—that someone, somewhere, could use his blood to create more like him, and exploit them for more nefarious purposes.

"The information that this has been done won't leave my office," Auggie declared as Val began to glow and reached a hand toward Rafe.

~

Personal notes—Richard Farrell

"Doc, I gotta tell you, I had a helluva dream," Brett said. His eyes were closed—he didn't realize he could see if he opened them.

"What was the dream?" I asked, sitting on the chair beside his bed.

"I dreamed I was running," he said. I watched a smile pass across his face. "Chasing rabbits. It was fun."

"Open your eyes, Captain," I said. "From here on, you can make that dream a reality if you want."

~

Jennifer Troutman, 1st Lt, US Army

The last thing I recalled was watching the armored vehicle in front of mine explode. Afterward, things get extremely hazy.

Until now.

My eyes were open; I stared at an unfamiliar ceiling over my head. Glancing to the side, I saw the familiar rails of a hospital bed. I'd been injured. Now I was in a hospital, somewhere—probably Germany. I couldn't say why I thought that, but it was the most sensible thing— the worst cases often ended up on a base in that country.

I didn't speak a word of German, although several words in that language bubbled to the surface of my brain.

"You're awake."

A scrub-wearing nurse smiled down at me and spoke in English. "Dr. Farrell will be happy to hear you're still with us."

"Am I—uh—whole?"

"As whole as I am," she smiled. "My name is Kathy. When Dr. Farrell says it's all right, I'll bring food and you can sit up to eat."

"Is she awake?" A hopeful voice sounded in the doorway.

"She is. Lieutenant, this is Dr. Farrell."

He was beside my bed quickly and taking my hand. I blinked at him in confusion. Part of me wanted to say I knew him. Another part of me knew that was impossible. "Hello, Dr. Farrell," I said.

I was stunned when he wiped tears away.

Captain Brett Walker

I felt some weakness, but Dr. Farrell said it would pass. He'd told me the drug was experimental and that I'd been chosen, since I was at death's door when it was administered.

I didn't know whether to laugh or consider that I really was dreaming.

"A change in your appearance is expected," Dr. Farrell said. I stared at my image in the mirror.

Before, my hair had been nearly red. Now it was dark, as were my eyes, which were blue, before.

I didn't mind the change and the Doctor was correct—I would run again. I was whole in the most miraculous, unexplainable way possible. At least I didn't have to worry about contacting family members—my mom was dead and my dad disappeared when I was little.

Nobody left, and contacting former friends or family was forbidden anyway, because of the secrecy surrounding the drug.

I didn't care—I was going to run again.

~

Notes—Colonel Hunter

According to Cori and Valegar, Rafe's blood was now neutralized. He could donate blood and it would be just as normal as anyone else's. We were discussing the tracking of other survivors when the call from Richard Farrell interrupted.

"Check your e-mail," Richard said before I could get an entire hello out of my mouth.

I tapped my keyboard and brought up the e-mail in question. Two photographs were included, without any text. I froze.

"Madam President gave permission," Richard quavered. "Colonel Hunter, it's wonderful, isn't it?"

"Holy fuck," I sighed. Maye and Nick's faces stared back at me from the e-mail. Across the room, I heard Corinne's muffled *holy shit*.

~

Corinne

Rafe drove the van; Auggie sat in the front with him. Matt and Opal took up the second set of seats; Val and I had to make ourselves even smaller to fit in the back. Our destination was the ugly building in Arlington, but on the inside, I'd made changes the last time I was there.

Richard Farrell, without informing Auggie, had gone over his head to get Maye back. I wasn't sure that doing this for personal reasons was the proper thing to do, but it was moot, now. It was done. At least the participants were military.

As of now, the Program was up and running again.

"I've forgotten how inelegant travel by Earth vehicle is," Val remarked as we bounced across a pothole in the ugly building's parking lot.

Auggie feels he needs an alternate form of escape, in case we left him here after folding space, I sent.

Understandable. I would feel the same, Val agreed. *Perhaps it is a good thing that our Karathian Warlock in the driver's seat never had his power awakened,* he added. *His shielding ability and the talent for invisibility is something he'd have had, anyway.*

Yeah. We were supposed to be reborn on Karathia, I heaved a mental sigh. *You see how that turned out.*

I'm pleased that you were reborn a second time as Larentii. Only the most deserving achieve that.

I held back from telling Ilya that he's almost immortal, I responded. I'd changed the subject to get Val away from talking about me—it embarrassed me, when most Larentii would merely acknowledge the truth in the statement.

He can still be killed; I'm sure he realizes that, Val responded. *Shall I transport us out of this infernal mechanism?*

Please.

Jennifer Troutman, her eyes and face identical to Maye's after she'd received the drug, smiled when Val and I walked through the door. She and Nick's clone, Captain Brett Walker, waited in a room on the top floor that was flooded with light.

Seats and plants were scattered about—it was decorated as a sanctuary for those recovering in Richard Farrell's personal hospital.

"This is Colonel August Hunter," Richard Farrell began introductions before I could accost him for what he'd done. "He's Secretary of Defense and the one in charge of the Program."

"I know who Colonel Hunter is," Brett Walker held out a hand. Auggie obliged.

"Thank you for your service," Auggie said. "I hear you were severely wounded in Afghanistan."

"Wounded would be putting it mildly, Colonel. I have to say, this miracle drug you've developed is, well, a miracle." It was hard to watch —Brett's words coming from Nick's mouth.

I coughed to clear my throat. Auggie shot me a frown before turning to First Lieutenant Jennifer Troutman. "I heard your convoy was attacked in Iraq," he said. "You're the only survivor."

"I haven't had time to deliver that news," Richard muttered.

Or a lot of other news, I pointed out in mindspeech.

Corinne, please don't, Richard begged. *You have no idea,* he cut his words short when I nodded toward Rafe.

After all, to everyone except Rafe, I looked like the old Corinne— before the taller, bluer Corinne. Only Rafe saw me as someone different.

For both our sakes.

This isn't Maye, this is Jennifer, I pointed out.

I know. Richard turned away for a moment.

He still doesn't realize what an abomination the drug is—especially to those who've been cloned. They have their set of memories, and another set that threatens to emerge. Some clones have an extreme amount of difficulty coming to terms with that, Valegar said.

So those who had Sirenali obsession were better off? I asked.

In some ways, he agreed. *But, as you realize, the orders to kill that were likely put in place are extremely unhealthy—to all involved.*

Auggie, I sent, *You'd better have Leo waiting to talk to both of them. Val says they'll have their old memories plus a new set trying to emerge. That could spell trouble.*

He threw a look in my direction that said he wanted words with Leo—plus the President and Richard Farrell—as soon as possible. One of Val's hands touched the back of my neck and his fingers began to massage it—if he hadn't, I may have spoken out of turn and rounded on Richard Farrell for doing what he'd done.

Jennifer and Brett didn't need to hear that. For now, they were grateful to be alive and free of pain. For that, I was happy. So many other problems could come of this, though, and I hoped they could overcome those obstacles and be their own person.

With the Program's resurrection looming over their heads, I doubted that was possible. They'd be expected to fill Nick and Maye's shoes, complete with their skill sets. Their own lives could drown in the choppy waters of those whose blood they'd been given.

～

Notes—Colonel Hunter

I wasn't given the opportunity to speak with Madam President before her meeting with the ones who'd identified themselves as ASD agents. I wanted Corinne with me, but I'd been instructed to come alone.

I was about to participate in the first formally arranged meeting with extraterrestrials, and I was terrified.

Relax, Auggie, Corinne's voice sounded in my head. *We're here, you just can't see us.*

～

Corinne

Val and I were shielded as we stood near the door in the Oval office. Four ASD agents were already there, with Auggie, the President and six Secret Service.

The ASD had figured out a way to get weapons past archaic detectors—all of them were armed with concealed laser pistols. Auggie and Madam President thought they were unarmed.

Remember, these are from current day, when Norian Keef was still in charge of the ASD, Valegar informed me. *You know that is not true in the future.*

Yes. I did some research. I understand Keef often played fast and loose with the rules in order to make things come out the way he wanted.

True.

"Wish to hunt survivors of Lyristolyi drug," one of the agents informed Madam President.

"It's polite to introduce yourselves first," Auggie pointed out.

"Apologize. I—Ralvus Verain. He, Dervus Verain. He, Invus Verain. He, Brade Deplan. We hunt drug survivors."

He'd pointed out each one as he named them, beginning with himself.

Half Elemaiya, Val's silent words conveyed his sarcasm. *They can no longer gate onto the planet, so they were transported by ship. In this time, they are still immortal. That will not be true in the future.*

This is going to be hard, isn't it? I asked.

Val massaged my neck again. *With Elemaiya involved and without Keef's understanding that this is what they are, many things can go wrong,* he said.

"Drug survivors dangerous," Ralvus repeated, as if he were attempting to convince a child.

He and his brothers are here to search for his King's crown, I turned to Val. *Brade is here to search for the Queen's.*

The crowns are no longer here, Val huffed.

They don't know that, I said.

We will allow them to discover that for themselves, Val cautioned. I understood that interfering with the idiocy of the expelled Elemaiya wasn't in our job description. We merely had to let them know that hunting drug survivors with ties to the U.S. was off limits. They could do whatever they wanted with those the Russians had made.

"I understand your concern," the President inserted smoothly. "I do not give permission for you to hunt any of those drug survivors employed by the United States. Your own laws say you must have my government's permission to hunt them. I do not give it."

"Where information come from?" Ralvus demanded.

"I have that information from one who calls herself Larentii."

"You lie," Brade Deplan rose from his seat and hissed. "There are no female Larentii."

I learned something, that day.

Never piss off a Larentii.

Valegar dropped the shield he had around us, folded space to place us before Brade Deplan and began to glow so bright a blue that Brade stepped back and fell onto his chair.

"You will never deny the existence of Rinnelar," he snarled. "Tell that to your deposed Queen."

~

"It was a moment of weakness, I think."

Valegar still wasn't speaking, Madam President's four guests had been ushered out of the White house, all four almost as pale as the building itself, and here I was, attempting to explain our uninvited presence in the Oval Office.

"At least they didn't call me a liar again," Madam President sighed. "I must say—this is—quite a shock." Val and I were still tall and blue—after all, you can't prove you're a Larentii unless you look like a Larentii.

"I think it's so much better, from an intrinsic standpoint, that is, than those foul Sirenali," Valegar finally spoke.

"But I'm only thinking about Corinne before," Madam President halted her words and considered the gaffe.

"To me, she is wondrously beautiful," Valegar stated. "You are very limited in your experience with other beings. We will go now. I will leave you with this word of warning—you should watch those Elemaiya—they are not to be trusted. The one who sent them has yet to learn that basic fact."

Val folded us out of the Oval Office.

~

Ilya

I waited for their arrival. If the Larentii hadn't healed Sergei, then Katya would have arrived—alone and widowed. She and I had much to be thankful for. A military plane was scheduled to arrive at a nearby base; I waited under an awning outside a small building to stay out of the falling rain.

"They're about to land," a pilot placed a cup of coffee in my hand. "I hope you take it black."

"This will be fine," I mumbled. "Thank you." The coffee steamed in the chill air while the pilot walked away. Rain continued to drip off the awning over my head, spattering onto the concrete surrounding the low building.

Ten minutes later, the transport pulled to a stop on the tarmac. I watched as the steps were lowered and someone walked out of the plane holding an umbrella. Katya and Sergei appeared moments later, and the woman carrying the umbrella held it over their heads as they descended the steps.

Without caring that I'd be soaked, I began walking toward them. Katya and I embraced on a cold, rainy day while Sergei looked on. I hoped at that moment that she would be welcomed as a U.S. citizen one day—and Sergei with her.

"Papa, this is nice," Katya took in the townhouse after we left the car in the garage.

"The kitchen could be bigger," I shrugged. "But it is okay for now. Sergei, please sit," I motioned him toward a barstool at the island. "I will fix something for lunch."

"Papa always cooked when he was home," Katya laughed.

"I love to cook," I corrected her. "You make it sound as if I did it only out of duty. Sergei, how are you feeling?"

"I feel good," he said. "A little tired, perhaps. Better than it could have been."

"I have a tentative meeting scheduled for you with Dr. Shaw," I said. "In case the kidnapping still troubles you."

"I will accept the meeting," he nodded.

"Papa, he has nightmares," Katya hung her head.

"Look, this is nothing to be ashamed of," I took her face in my hands. "Either of you. Take the help you need to feel better. Perhaps you both should go this first time."

"I'd prefer that," Sergei said.

I made a mental note to alert Dr. Shaw—my daughter was fragile after Sergei's abduction. It appeared I owed the Larentii for a great deal, and had no idea how to express that gratitude or repay the debt.

~

Notes—Colonel Hunter

James appeared in my doorway, his expression mixed. "What is it?" I asked.

"Cori hasn't come to see me, and we got this from the President." He held out a sheet of paper.

"I'll take a look, and Cori said she'd contact you soon."

"All right." He turned to walk away, but I could see in his sagging shoulders that he was disappointed.

The paper was a copy of a telephone conversation Madam President had with the new Russian Ambassador. The current Russian President had been contacted by the same four I'd seen in the Oval Office—asking for a meeting.

It made me wonder how that one would go. Lifting my cell, I punched in Matt's number and listened while it rang on the other end.

~

Corinne

"Where are you going?"

"To see James. He's depressed."

Val frowned. I could see he was still out of sorts with humans. "Honey, maybe you've never been human, so you don't realize that they often put their foot in their mouth when they're uncomfortable."

"That is one of the strangest idioms ever created," he pointed out.

"Is that Larentii logic?"

"There is nothing logical about it."

"All right—you got me there."

"If you weren't so adorable, I could possibly be miffed."

Notes—Colonel Hunter

"What are these?" I thumbed through photographs.

"Pictures of a street in Dublin. Guess who was seen there?" Matt asked.

"No idea." I kept looking through the photographs, hoping I'd see something—or someone—I recognized.

"It's the last photograph, taken earlier today."

Frowning at Matt, I set aside all photos except the last one. It was dusk in Dublin, five hours earlier and just before sunset. A scaled creature, mostly covered by a trench coat and hat, was following a woman into a narrow doorway on a Dublin street.

"That's a small hotel," Matt said. "He's identical to the one killed in Vancouver."

I reached for my phone and hoped my Larentii friends weren't still angry enough to stay away or refuse to answer.

Corinne

"James, it doesn't make me uncomfortable to be like this for days on end," I told him. We'd settled at a Starbucks table in Silver Spring. "If we were elsewhere and it would make you happy, I'd be my taller, bluer self."

"I'm just glad you're here. I was feeling left out."

"Honey, you never left my thoughts," I patted his hand. "I thought of you the whole time I was on the Larentii homeworld, more than four hundred years in the future."

James had trouble swallowing his coffee. "You can't tell anyone else," I waved a hand. "You won't be able to tell anyone else," I added. "Larentii are one of the few races that can bend time. No, I can't go back and change anything for you—that's considered interference and carries a very heavy penalty."

"I wasn't thinking of that, except for Nick and Maye."

I went still for a moment before squeezing his hand. "There's nothing I would love more than to go back and change that. I'd have to get permission and frankly, the person giving that permission isn't really my friend."

"Who?"

"You would probably think of him as King of the Larentii," I sighed. "That's how much power he holds." My cell phone rang at that moment. Auggie was calling.

"Auggie?" I answered the call.

"Cori, we've had a sighting of one of our scaly friends in Dublin, and he's with a Mary clone."

❧

Val wasn't happy to see Auggie and Matt so soon after Madam President's gaffe, but there wasn't anything else he could do. I'd sent a message to him while transporting James from Starbucks to Matt Michael's office.

I had no idea solving mysteries would be so aggravating, Val sent the moment he appeared. He didn't bother to disguise himself, either, so James was smiling as he studied Valegar from a corner of Matt's office.

I studied the photograph Auggie gave me shortly after my arrival before handing it to Val. Val enlarged it while everybody watched and then formed a 3-D image of it in a clear spot on Matt's floor.

"That's awesome," James breathed. We could walk in and out of the image while examining it from every angle.

That is *awesome,* I sent to Val. A corner of his mouth quirked at my compliment.

"Definitely a Mary clone," I nodded. "With a scaly clone version of Merle Askins wrapped up in a coat and hat. I still can't figure out why he's scaly instead of taking a humanoid appearance."

"They can do that?" Auggie asked. Matt didn't seem surprised. His lack of surprise didn't surprise me in turn. He had secrets. He'd either tell Auggie or not.

None of my business.

"Perhaps he hasn't discovered how to make the change, yet," Val surmised. "After all, they learn those things when they are younger—clones are reproduced as adults and do not spend a childhood in experimentation. I imagine this is all he knows at the moment."

"The clones will still look like the new Merle Askins, even if they learn how to change," I suggested. "That may hold them back, too—that once they're recognized as the altered Merle Askins, he'll be on everybody's radar again."

"Excellent point," Valegar agreed. "I understand there's still a warrant for Askin's arrest?"

"Yes, because the body has never been found—officially," Matt nodded. "We know the original was killed in Vancouver. What we don't know is how many of his clones are out there."

"The fact that they are successfully hiding from Larentii, in addition to others with power, indicates that there are remaining Sirenali," Val pointed out.

I'd been afraid to voice that opinion, but he was correct. Val and I—we'd have found them, otherwise, just by *Looking.*

"So," I said. "We have cloned Lyristolyi running around. Mary clones running around. Cloned Sirenali also running about and hiding the others. Then, we have Bright and Dark Elemaiya, employed by the ASD and supposedly looking for them, all while performing other, more self-serving duties. Everything is fucked up," I tossed out a hand.

"The Lyristolyi who arrived and made a debacle of the meeting over a year ago fucked things up most," Val said. I lifted an eyebrow in his direction at the use of foul language.

Well, he wanted to talk like humans. I think he was getting the hang of it rather quickly. "You're right," I said. "The Lyristolyi should have realized that a frontal assault would only force the criminals into any nook and cranny they could find. Now, after a year has passed, those cockroaches are venturing into the kitchen again."

"This means they had at least one alternate site to make clones and managed to hide it from everyone," Matt slapped the arm of his chair before standing. "And they likely still believe that we're behind the attack. Not good news for us," he added.

"Here's my question—now that Phillips is out of the way, who's calling the shots for them?" Auggie asked.

CHAPTER 4

*C*orinne

"Auggie, I think they're looking for Katya and Sergei."

Auggie gave me a startled look—one that said he hadn't considered that angle, yet. It made sense to me—they'd already caught Sergei once. Not only had he gotten away, but I'd pretty much damaged their goons beyond repair.

"It's my guess that the underground operating out of Dublin is putting a crimp in their plans, somehow. So they're going after them," I added.

"Katya and Sergei are here—currently living with Rafe," Auggie blew out a breath. "It probably won't be difficult to trace them to the U.S."

"Then we need to move them," I said. "Like yesterday."

"The house in Port Aransas is available," Matt said.

"Are you sure?" I began. After all, that's where Ilya and I were when he bought my ring.

"I think it will be fine," Matt said. "Besides, that one isn't on anybody's radar."

Somebody's put up a shield, haven't they? I sent mindspeech to him.

Somebody knows too much for her own good, Matt shot back.

Don't worry—your ass and your secrets are safe with me.

If you weren't who you are, and protected by who you are, I'd have my doubts, he returned.

Awesome. Pardon me while I have doubts about your judgment in times of crisis, I snapped back.

Look, somebody has already chewed my ass about that and the fact that it shouldn't have happened.

Who might that be? I asked sweetly. Honestly, I wanted to shake their hand for doing my job for me.

Hank Bell, he grumped. *If you know who he is, then I'll open a new bank account for you and put the first hundred thousand in there.*

You know I don't know who he is, so your funds are safe, I said. *Although now I want to meet him, just to say thanks.*

If he comes around again, I'll be sure to have him look you up.

He outranks you, doesn't he?

By a lot. Matt didn't sound happy about it. *You know who I was, don't you?*

Yeah, Jayson Rome, I do.

This is so fucked up, he rubbed his forehead. *Opal said you knew. I didn't know whether to believe her or not. You're not supposed to be able to see that in—well, you know.*

I wasn't supposed to get the drug twice, either.

You have a point. Has Valegar offered to study that phenomenon yet?

It hasn't come up.

Look, I hope we can be friends, he said. *Really. I know how badly I screwed up.*

I just want Nick and Maye back. Figure that one out, okay?

He lifted an eyebrow. *I'll ask,* he said and left it at that.

"When do we move Rafe and his family?" Auggie interrupted our silent conversation.

"How about now?" I asked. "I'll provide transport."

We startled Rafe by knocking on his door—I figured that was better than just showing up in the living room. He had a hand on the gun in his waistband anyway when he answered the door.

At least he suspected his daughter and son-in-law were still in danger.

"We have to move you," Auggie said when Rafe relaxed. "We have a sighting of unsavory characters in Dublin, and it's a good bet they're looking for Katya and Sergei."

"Do we have time to pack?" Rafe asked after standing aside to let us in.

"You do not need to waste that time, I shall transport everything," Val declared. In ten seconds, we were at the overly large beach house in Port Aransas, where it was raining.

"I'd feel better if you stayed here to guard them—if they decide to go out," Matt said. I gave Matt a look that said how painful that might be —for Rafe/Ilya to ignore me or treat me as an alien, when I was his wife.

There it was—the crux of everything. Yes, I was coming to care for Val, but Ilya would always be my husband.

"Otherwise, I'll be forced to place armed guards, and that could draw attention," Matt continued.

Auggie lifted a hopeful eyebrow when I looked his way.

"It makes sense, Lara'Kayan," Val said. "I will be here with you, should the situation overwhelm you."

"Opal is on her way to Dublin," Matt said. I'd made coffee for him, Auggie, James and me—Matt sipped from his cup after making the statement. "She'll be tracking clones Merle and Mary."

"I would like to go to Dublin." Rafe stood in the doorway, but he spoke with Ilya's accent. I drew a shaky breath.

"I won't let you go without a good disguise and powerful protection," Matt said. "At the moment, you have neither."

"You do not have to remind me of my heartache," he mumbled.

"Want coffee?" I asked brightly to break the gloomy mood. I admit, my hands shook as I made a cup of coffee for Rafe—as he liked it—and set it in front of him. He'd taken a chair at the island next to James—who sat opposite of Val. Val's hand rubbed my back and neck when I regained my seat; he knew what this was costing me.

"Papa?" Katya walked into the kitchen, followed closely by Sergei.

"Coffee?" I asked automatically. Rafe's eyes met mine across the island before turning to his daughter.

"I'll get it," he said, motioning for her and Sergei to sit.

"Rinnelar?" Sergei said in heavily accented English.

"Yes?"

"Thank you. For my life."

"I would prefer that you keep it," I said, giving him a weak smile.

"How do you do that—heal something?" Katya asked.

"We work at a cellular level, to put everything back the way it was," Valegar shrugged. He was getting his human gestures down quickly. "At times, if there is poison involved, we change the molecular makeup of the poison itself, in order to neutralize it."

"I've seen that first-hand," Rafe acknowledged. He placed Sergei's coffee in front of him and dropped his gaze as he reclaimed his seat. He wasn't looking at me deliberately. I understood why—he was doing his best to prevent his mind from making a connection between Rinnelar and Corinne.

I see it, Val informed me silently. *I will consider this. Perhaps there is a way to isolate the obsession and place a shield about it. Allow me to consult with my father and with Kalenegar, first.*

Thank you.

I would do anything for you, my love.

Yes, it was my human roots that made this difficult for me to understand—that someone who loved me would look for a way to overcome an obstacle, so I might fling myself into another man's arms and weep my heart out.

"I think I'll take my coffee outside," I said. "The sun is peeking through the clouds."

"I will join you," Valegar nodded. He transported us—I was rising to walk outside. We ended up on the beach instead of the deck.

"We cannot be seen, my love," Val said, taking my hand and lifting it to his lips. "I merely want you to love me as much as you love him."

"This is such a strange concept," I lowered my eyes. "When you're human—or seemingly so—you tend to shut others out when you make your vows to one."

"As you know," he lifted my chin with a finger, "you are no longer human. Were not human in your last incarnation, either. If helping you through this is my task, then I take it up gladly. Removing Ilya's jealousy is no problem—that can be done easily. You can do it yourself, if you so choose."

"I just hope segregating his obsession will be that simple."

"My love, we will find a way." I was pulled into arms that radiated the warmth of a summer day.

Soon—very soon—I would have to shove away my human feelings and admit that Valegar and I were meant to be. I would never give up Ilya, however, and the Larentii who held me understood that—even encouraged it.

~

Ilya

The Larentii were gone more than an hour. Suspicions formed, only to submerge and transform into other thoughts. Someone was keeping me from making a connection. I was grateful.

I hadn't had a destructive dream in several days, for which I was also grateful. Under normal circumstances, my suspicions would be examined until a conclusion was reached. In this case only, the suspicions slid away with barely a struggle.

Everything else received my usual, focused attention.

"Why would they keep making clones of those we recognize?" I asked. Director Michaels and Colonel Hunter now sat in the media room with me; Katya had accompanied Sergei to their suite so he could rest.

"Because their supply of the drug was either taken or destroyed," Val and Rinnelar appeared in the room. "They only had a few survivors left, in my opinion, so they are forced to make clones. They neither have the formula nor the ingredients to recreate the drug."

Val spoke; Rinnelar nodded her agreement. It made sense, too. Without a drug survivor to draw blood from, there would be no clones.

"What about," I began.

"They have to have blood from the original survivor," Val answered my question before I could voice it entirely. "They were foolish to allow the original Merle Askins to die in Vancouver. They should have sent a clone in his place."

"Then do they know that they can't make a clone from a clone?" Colonel Hunter asked.

"Unknown. It is also unknown how much blood was gathered from Askins before his death."

"If they started taking blood from him shortly after his survival, then they could have a thousand vials or more," Rinnelar pointed out. "It only takes a small amount to create a clone."

"Then we should search for their supply of blood," I said.

Corinne

Auggie, where's the rest of the drug from the U.S. stash? I asked.

Everybody in the media room knew I'd sent him mindspeech, because he shifted uncomfortably on his barstool.

"You don't know, do you?" I accused aloud.

"Not all of it—no," he shook his head. "You have to understand that some of it was sent to the Nevada facility, and we don't know what happened to it."

"Where are those people now—the ones who were there?" Rafe hissed. He'd understood immediately that our conversation concerned the drug.

"Most are dead." I said the words, my voice flat as I read the admission in Auggie's gaze.

"Murdered, most likely," Auggie massaged his forehead. "Although their deaths were meant to look like accidents, until they kept piling up."

"So the enemy may have the drug back in their hands," Rafe growled. "They may be misleading us for now by only making clones, until they unleash the next round of survivors to hunt us."

"That went downhill in a hurry," I turned to Val, who nodded in agreement.

"We know what Phillips looked like after his turn," Matt said. "A certain former Russian President comes to mind. I doubt that the current Russian President will be very accommodating if one of Phillips' clones shows up."

"You're assuming that one of Phillips' clones isn't pouring obsession into his ear already," I pointed out. "I think I hate the fucking Sirenali, already."

"Dearest, they're not all bad," Val corrected gently.

"The ones I've run into are," I defended my statement.

"You know that troubles often come from assigning the same traits to all within a race," he began.

"Yeah. You're right."

He smiled at me. *I love you,* he said silently.

Well, I love your blue ass, too.

What other color would it be?

I realized he was teasing.

I would like very much for your blue hands to be all over my blue ass, as you put it, he added. *But we must discuss some things first before physical sex can take place. Until then, I will be most happy with energy sex only.*

That doesn't sound ominous or anything, I replied.

It isn't—but there will be a risk if we engage in physical sex.

You just made it worse, I pointed out.

My love—I have not had my child, yet. If I have physical sex with you, I may not be able to hold back from implanting my embryo. I do not want you to be pregnant unless or until you wish it.

Until then, I hadn't even considered that option. Yes, I'd read about Larentii fathers forming the entire embryo in their bodies and placing it in stasis until a suitable mother could be found. Val had waited to place his child.

He'd waited for *me*.

I wanted to shiver and ask him to hold me at the same time.

Do not be concerned, my love. We will work this out between us, he soothed. *We will select our surrogate father together, too.*

Huh?

You may think of a surrogate as a godfather, only much more involved. He will help care for you and the child before and after he or she comes.

I need that much care?

You are Larentii, so that will likely be minimal. It is merely a precaution, Lara'Kayan. Non-Larentii mothers need constant attention. The child will need advanced instruction shortly after birth so he learns to control the power he has been given. It is a taxing job in many instances. Since many mothers are not Larentii, they are not equipped to handle those situations. Most mothers are returned to their races, without any memory of their pregnancy.

And that's why they're called found mothers, I grumped.

I see you have a problem with that concept.

I do.

Yes—Father said you would. You must understand that long ago, the mother was not compensated in any way. After Saa Thalarr became mothers of Larentii, that changed because of their influence.

I'm still not totally on board with grabbing unsuspecting women, I grumped.

Then perhaps you should use your influence with Kalenegar to effect changes there.

Influence with him? Riiiiight.

You may have more than you realize. You must present your case in logical and achievable terms, however, to command his attention.

You mean a smack on the shoulder won't work?

I wouldn't anger the Head of the Larentii Council without just cause, my Cori, Val cautioned.

Yeah.

"We probably should start looking for those responsible in the deaths of the employees from the Nevada facility," James said, breaking Val and me out of our private conversation. "Just to see who may now have possession of the drug."

"I shudder to think who may have it," Matt muttered. Well, he'd likely be able to imagine likely suspects, just as Val and I could. The drug in any hands could become a nightmare. This was the one ring—capable of corrupting whoever held it. In the wrong hands, it could spell doom for the entire planet.

"We should keep tabs on those idiots sent by the ASD, too," I pointed out. "I feel trouble may come from that direction, and in a way nobody will appreciate."

They cannot gate away from this world, now, Val advised me. *Those have been closed against them.*

Yeah, but they can cause too much havoc in other ways.

True.

I'd like to kick Norian Keef's snaky butt for sending them, I said. *Surely somebody better was available.*

I thought your Earth connections prevented you from speaking ill of the dead, Val hid a smile.

Norian's not dead in the here and now, I pointed out. *Besides, Hitler's dead. That doesn't stop me from saying what a colossal fuck he was.*

You're comparing Norian Keef to Hitler?

Only in the fact that they're both dead—one now, one in the future.

Ah. I so enjoy our conversations. They are so fresh and challenging, he grinned.

Well, conversation boy, what should we do about tracking the ass-hats who killed the folks from the Nevada facility? We need to sort that out and keep the folks here safe at the same time.

I may have a solution, Val's grinned widened.

What's that?

"I here," a new voice announced, startling everyone except Val.

I blinked in astonishment. I knew already that Norian Keef was a lion snake shapeshifter—this lion snake shapeshifter was a thousand times better than Norian would ever be in his best moments, and like Val, he was from the future and quite powerful.

Bekzi, the reptanoid, had arrived to help.

"Who is this?" Auggie stood, silently asking me for a more detailed explanation.

"This is Bekzi," I said. "And you should just hand over all the medals you can give to him right now—that's how good he is."

"You make embarrassed," Bekzi gave me a blinding smile.

Somebody really is looking after you, Matt informed me. He sounded grumpy, even in mindspeech.

"This is what you should do," Val said smoothly. "Bring Dr. Shaw here, to tend Katya and Sergei. At least one of us," he indicated himself, Bekzi and me, "will be here to protect them. The others can take Rafe wherever he needs to be and help him investigate the murders and drug disappearances. We will also look in on our ASD infiltrators from time to time, just to keep them out of trouble."

"I'd like to amend that and add Dr. Farrell and his new charges to the list of those staying here," Auggie breathed a sigh. "I think they'll need your protection as well as Leo's assistance."

"I agree," Rafe said. "Help from these three will be welcome," he nodded to me. "I would like to hear updates from the Dublin investigation, too."

"I can arrange that," Matt nodded.

"We want to be included in that loop," Sergei said. "We still have friends in Dublin, and they need a warning if we can get it to them."

"I'll ask Opal to look into it," Matt said. "I'll take any information you can give me in order to make that happen."

"We'll consider what information to give," Sergei said.

"Then give information to Rinnelar or Valegar," Matt said. "They can filter out anything I don't need to know."

"I will agree to that," Sergei said.

"I'd prefer that, too," Katya sided with her husband.

"Good. We're golden. Who's taking Colonel Hunter, James and me back to D.C.?" Matt didn't keep the annoyance out of his voice.

"I will do so," Val offered.

When will you let them know you can schlepp them around? I sent to Matt.

Maybe never—it'll blow my cover. You know—the one you promised not to reveal?

Oh. Right.

Your sarcasm is showing.

Really?

Now it's full-blown.

Then it's a good thing we're using mindspeech, isn't it?

You scare me, he said before Val interrupted the conversation by disappearing with him, Auggie and James.

"Not bother—he dig own holes," Bekzi walked over and patted my shoulder.

"Yeah."

~

Notes—Colonel Hunter

"Dr. Farrell, you're moving," I announced. Valegar had known to take us to the ugly building in Arlington. We found Farrell working (unsurprisingly) with Maye's clone.

"Where?" he asked, turning away from Jennifer. She looked identical to Maye, now, right down to the haircut. I wondered if Leo had made any inroads yet on Dr. Farrell's fixation and unwillingness to let Maye go.

"To the beach house in Port Aransas," I said. "Matt thought it a good idea, since we already have a team there to protect you and Rafe's family."

"Probably a good idea," he shrugged. "Although I'm hesitant to face —well, you know."

Farrell and I knew Corinne wanted to give him a tongue-lashing. Hell, I wanted to do the same. I wanted to yell at the President, too, but that would be disrespectful and hazardous to my position.

It was better to keep my mouth shut on that front. Perhaps Cori would do it for both of us. After all, we didn't own her, and I imagined that making enemies of the Larentii was something even Madam President would hesitate to do.

If the FBI, CIA or NSA wanted to make files on the Larentii race, Valegar would likely wipe them out the moment they were created. That made me smile.

You are correct, Valegar's voice sounded in my head. *It is our duty to protect our race and especially the few females we have. You have no idea how precious Corinnelar is to us—and to me.*

"She is precious to me and those around me," I declared aloud. "After saving my ass more than once, I can't say otherwise. She's saved your ass, too, Farrell, so I'd suggest you listen to her when she gives you hell."

I rounded on Richard Farrell when I said his name; he went pale and still at my words. What I didn't expect was what spewed from him immediately after.

"You kept her out of that meeting, when she should have been there," Farrell shouted. "You know as well as I what that could have prevented."

"We probably should hold this shouting match later, at a neutral site," Leo Shaw strode into the room. I could tell he was upset, too. Likely it was because Jennifer was listening and Brett walked in right behind him. They didn't need to know why they existed—or whom they resembled—all because Richard Farrell couldn't let Maye go.

"I think you should both listen when Corinne gives you hell," Leo lowered his voice. "Besides, I think I'd like to be in that meeting when she does."

Brett and Jennifer were only now noticing the tall, blue man standing nearby. Jennifer gasped; Brett looked ready to pounce. Valegar held up a hand. "There is no need to fear," he said. "Larentii are a peaceful race, although my mate will, as Colonel Hunter so baldly stated, give someone hell for fucking things up."

"You've met Corinne already," Richard sighed before nodding to Jennifer and Brett. "She'll help protect us where we're going. Just be prepared—you're about to be transported in a way you never dreamed possible."

～

Corinne

"Call her Rinnelar," Richard Farrell instructed when Valegar arrived with Jennifer, Leo and Brett at the beach house. "Trust me—it's for your own good."

"They will not forget," Valegar said. Only I saw the slight glow of power about him when he spoke the words—they wouldn't be able to forget, now.

"Want coffee or something to eat?" I asked Brett and Jennifer before giving Richard a look. He ducked his head—sometime soon, he and I would have a talk. He wasn't looking forward to it.

"I'd take a sandwich or something," Brett grinned. I had to remind myself that this wasn't Nick. Would never truly be Nick—even with Nick's face and talents. Richard's lecture grew longer in that moment.

"I think there's sliced ham and roast beef in the fridge," I said. "And a small grocery store in Port A if we don't have everything you need."

"I could eat," Leo declared before directing Richard toward the kitchen. Jennifer followed along, still confused by the fact that she'd gone sixteen hundred miles in less time than it took her to blink.

"Don't worry," I said, patting her shoulder. "We Larentii are powerful. You'll get used to it."

"I hope so," she mumbled. "I don't know whether to laugh or be sick right now."

"Then I'll hope for the laugh," I said. "Take a seat at the island. If you need your stomach settled, Val or I can take care of that for you."

"I can," Richard began.

"You—sit," I snapped, pointing a finger at him. He sat and kept his mouth shut.

Wise move.

"I'm really a nice person," I assured Jennifer, who was now looking as if I might bite her head off next. "Under normal circumstances."

"I think I had a drill sergeant like you once," Jennifer sighed.

"Well, I've never been military," I said. "Much to Auggie's disappointment."

"Auggie?"

"She means Colonel Hunter," Leo Shaw suppressed a smile. "Nobody else will get away with calling him that, so don't try."

"Who am I to interfere with an alien and a superior's affairs?" Jennifer shrugged.

"You know—I think I'll make you some cocoa," I told her. "Because you're awesome."

"I love cocoa," she said.

"I know," I nodded. "One cup, coming right out."

"What is this?" Rafe walked into the kitchen, followed by Katya and Sergei.

"Food and cocoa. Want some?" I asked.

"Food, yes. Cocoa—I would prefer coffee."

"All right, but only because it's you."

"I think Rinnelar likes you better than Dr. Farrell," Brett offered Rafe a grin.

"I would have thought it to be the other way around," Rafe said, taking a seat at the island.

"How little you know," I said and set a cup of coffee in front of him. "Here. Make yourself useful and hand this cocoa to Jennifer, down there." I turned away and allowed my shoulders to droop. Before the obsession, I would have rubbed his back or allowed him to put an arm around my waist.

All that—gone. I'm sure Val was right and there were good Sirenali out there somewhere. I silently cursed their race anyway while I made ham and roast-beef sandwiches.

Ilya

A part of me knew, I think. That part was blocked in some way. I didn't know whether to be angry or grateful that it had been done without my permission. It was something I couldn't dwell on, however—the notion always slipped away from my mental grasp.

"You not worry," Bekzi arrived and took the barstool beside mine. "Things happen. There reason. She need you."

"Well, since my brain can't exactly hold onto that thought," I began, "Tell me who you are. What you are."

"I lion snake shapeshifter. Some call reptanoid," he grinned. "Lion snake most dangerous poison. You not make mad."

"Are you a drug survivor?" I asked, realizing then that everyone at the island was now tuned to our conversation.

"No," he huffed, offended by my question. "Will explain sometime. Drug dangerous. Outlawed, most places. You know why."

"What's this?" Brett asked. Jennifer, who sat two chairs down from me, appeared stunned.

"You lucky," Bekzi leaned forward to look Brett in the eye. "Drug survivors on other worlds—they killed."

"What the fuck did you give us?" Brett rounded on Richard Farrell, who suddenly looked nervous.

CHAPTER 5

*C*orinne

Leo sat in a corner, arms crossed and listening while I handed Richard Farrell *the lecture*.

Val was still in the kitchen, keeping it soundproofed against the almost one-sided conversation Richard and I were having. "Look, death isn't always the worst thing," I said, flinging out a hand. "Sure—they're alive now—but this isn't their life. They were supposed to be reborn elsewhere, as someone else. Not this masquerade as somebody else. What you've done is cheated them of their next lives."

"The drug didn't cheat you or Rafe," Richard attempted to defend himself.

"Oh, yes it did," I snapped. "He and I—we were supposed to be reborn on Karathia. He and I would have met there. Not only did the drug cheat us of that, but as a result, it changed the history of Karathia itself."

"What the hell are you talking about?" Richard hissed.

"It's too complicated to go into now, but I will tell you this—sometime in the future, the throne of Karathia will be threatened. Rafe and I won't be there to protect it. Now are you getting my drift?"

"This is impossible," Richard wiped his face with a hand.

"Obviously not impossible—since you stuck your foot in it and did this," I hissed. "If you and Maye are meant to be, then you'll meet somewhere again—provided some other asshole doesn't come along with more of the drug to interfere in your future lives."

"What am I supposed to do then?" he said, tossing both hands in the air in a gesture of defeat.

"For now, you've done enough. Just don't do any more, okay? This is fucked up enough as it is."

"Is this why other worlds kill survivors and clones—to send them to their true next lives?" Leo asked quietly.

"I wish it were that altruistic," I sighed. "It's to protect the rest of their population from contamination—any drug survivor with the same blood type can make numerous copies of him or herself—effectively displacing souls and lives. Imagine if you were dying of a terrible disease. They can perform brain transferences, and a brain going into an identical body isn't going to quibble much. Granted the procedure is outlawed everywhere, but it won't stop the wealthy and determined."

"This is worse than I imagined," Leo leaned back in his chair, a thoughtful expression on his face. "Much worse."

"Just because Earth isn't as advanced as many other worlds, that doesn't mean we can't do our own damage with that fucked up stuff," I continued. "Whoever has the drug and uses it—or the blood of a drug survivor and uses it—is playing with a firestorm they can't control."

"Will it help if I say I'm sorry?" Richard pleaded.

"For now. I suggest you let Brett and Jennifer come into their own and pull your emotions out of it," I said. "They both deserve better than that."

"I concur," Leo nodded. "I'll help as much as I can, but dealing with a phantom set of memories in both of them will be difficult to handle."

"It was a weakness—a moment of weakness—when I went to the President," Richard admitted. "She was enthusiastic about the idea, when neither of us had sufficient information to make a qualified decision."

"Madam President needs some schooling too, but that will have to wait," I said. "Meanwhile, we have two displaced people out there who need our help."

"And a dozen mysteries to solve," Leo added.

"Yeah."

Were you listening? I asked Val when Leo, Richard and I walked into the kitchen. The others were still there, although they'd already finished their food.

Yes—you did well, although you were a bit more forceful than I may have been. I suspect it was necessary to get your point across.

I think it was necessary to get it out of my system, I replied. *I should feel ashamed, but I don't. Now, who wants to stay here while the others go to investigate the Nevada facility?*

I stay, Bekzi joined our silent conversation.

Looks like you, Rafe and me, honey, I informed Val.

"There's nothing here," Rafe shook his head.

He was right. He, Val and I studied the now-empty Nevada facility —it was merely a hollow shell, now. Every piece of equipment, every bit of trash, even, had been removed, leaving a squeaky-clean building behind.

Auggie, I sent, *were you aware that the Nevada facility had been wiped clean of evidence?*

My cell phone rang almost immediately. "When?" Auggie barked.

"In my estimation, according to the amount of dust that has settled upon surfaces," Val said, "approximately three months."

"Did you hear that?" I asked Auggie.

"I heard. Damn. Fuck and damn. Nobody was supposed to touch that place. By my orders."

"Somebody did," I sighed.

"I'll call Matt. See if he knows anything," Auggie said and hung up.

"I doubt Matt Michaels had anything to do with this," Val said.

"Why?" I turned to him.

"Look up."

I looked up, as directed. On the ceiling, scrawled in Alliance Common, were the words *fuck Earth*.

Ilya

"Who?" I asked, after Valegar translated the words for me.

"I imagine it may have been part of the same team of Lyristolyi that appeared to wreak havoc more than an Earth year ago," Val said. "I fear the reason Rinnelar and I can't get a better lock on the information is because that team has likely captured a Sirenali who survived the drug. That means all their doings will be hidden, even from the powerful."

"Are you saying that there may have been more of the fuckers than those at the meeting?" Rinnelar asked.

"I fear it may be true, Lara'Kayan."

"What does Lara'Kayan mean?" I asked.

"It means *forever love*, in the Neaborian language," Val replied.

For a moment, that troubled me before the thought slipped away.

Rinnelar appeared quite troubled that there could be more Lyristolyi than previously thought. *She is troubled by many things*, Val inserted into my mind. *Your obsession is one of them.*

I snorted my reply.

"The only thing left to do at this point," Rinnelar said, "is to question the asshole Rafe captured in Vancouver. Maybe we can get something from him that the humans couldn't."

"Ah—good choice," Val agreed. "Are you willing to travel with us?" he turned to me and asked.

"Most certainly."

"Good."

∾

Notes—Colonel Hunter

They came for me first—Cori, Val and Rafe, before going to the holding cell, which contained the only living captive from the Vancouver assassination crew. So far, nobody else had gotten anything from him, including a squeak when he was threatened with the death penalty.

Val and Cori could have gotten in without my help, but it was always wise to go through channels whenever possible. "Yes, they have permission to question the prisoner," I informed the Warden.

He nodded without questioning—I was grateful. I'd included myself in the visitation; I wished to hear first-hand what, if anything, Cori and Val might discover. Rafe—if he were left alone with our prisoner—might employ problematic methods to obtain information.

I wasn't willing to allow that to be recorded by prison cameras. Under normal circumstances, I would discourage such actions. Perhaps Cori and Val's concern had ramped up my own. They'd suggested that more Lyristolyi (yes, I'd had to ask how to spell it) had been here, perhaps all along, and we were only now learning of it. After the debacle at the meeting and the deaths of too many world leaders, I shuddered to think what more of the same creatures might do.

To add to that worry, I'd learned that they could appear human. That meant they could blend into the population and we'd have an impossible task before us—of identifying and capturing them. Especially if they'd captured a cloned Sirenali.

It made me wish for simpler days, when everyone imagined clear-cut foes from outer space—or at least one foe at a time. Soon, I wanted to speak privately with Cori and Val, just to ask them about all the aliens that could be on our world and what their ultimate goals might be.

The Warden stopped outside the holding cell and motioned for the door to be unlocked. In this case, rather than having him brought to us, we'd come to him.

~

Corinne

He sat in a corner, rather than on his bed, on cold concrete.

The temperature of the floor is forty-seven degrees Fahrenheit, Val informed me. *Much too cold for any normal human to withstand for long unless forced.*

"His internal body temperature is ninety-three degrees—and dropping," I informed Auggie. The man sitting in the corner blinked and focused on me immediately. "Something is worrying him," I added.

"I surmise it is the temperature-sensitive explosive planted in his abdomen, which the weapon detectors failed to locate," Val said. "Once activated remotely, I imagine it will detonate to destroy the victim and everything surrounding him, once it reaches his core temperature of ninety-eight-point-six Fahrenheit."

"What the fuck?" Auggie cursed.

"Do not fear—you are fortunate that Larentii are with you," Val said while holding out his hands.

The prisoner almost collapsed upon himself when Val reduced the explosive inside him to harmless sparks, which then flew from his startled, O-shaped mouth.

"I'll bet he weighs a lot less, now," I quipped.

~

"The explosive was not created by humans," Val explained later. "My hypothesis is that it was imported from elsewhere—built by those with less than lawful leanings."

"Do you think he'll talk, once the doctors are finished looking at him?" Auggie pointed his question at me.

"He doesn't know much," I said. "He was lured in with the promise of big money if he made Rafe dead. They grabbed him, drugged him and planted the explosive, telling him that if things went wrong, he'd go boom," I said. "Things obviously went wrong. At least he was smart enough to lower his body temp after those who booby-trapped him found out."

"Can he describe his captors?" Rafe asked.

"He doesn't have to," I said. "I saw all that in him. He was commanded by a Mary clone and the real Merle Askins."

"Why didn't you see this before? When you arrived in Vancouver?" Rafe asked.

"That's a great question," I turned to Rafe. "Where are the bodies of the others who died—besides good old Merle?"

"If there was Sirenali interference at the moment, it may have obstructed her abilities to see such things," Val observed.

"Then how did she know to help me?" Rafe demanded.

"I knew you were in danger," I blurted. I almost said it was because he was mated to a Larentii, but I didn't. Still, it was a close thing. "I only recognized Merle, because, well," I hung my head.

"What she hasn't admitted is that she tagged Mr. Askins before," Val said, his voice dry and humor shining in his eyes. "So she would recognize him in the future, no matter what he looked like or what obsession was placed upon him."

I had tagged him—in his office when I'd accosted him there. I wanted to make sure I'd know the asshole the next time—if there were a next time. It was a trick devised by Karathians, not by Larentii. My current race would consider it interference and didn't do it as a rule.

It had helped me greatly in this instance, however. Merle was tagged—his clones wouldn't be.

"I'll hear this story later," Auggie held up a hand. "I'll call to see if we can take a look at bodies—they're at a CIA-run facility."

"Fitting," Rafe gritted, "That Askins would end up there without anyone the wiser."

❧

In death, bodies are so empty. Without the life force that filled them, they are merely a shell. I studied Merle Askins—the fine, dark scales covering his face and hands—larger scales covering his limbs and torso. All I could see in him now was the fog of obsession.

"He probably saw himself as a monster after surviving the drug," Val said. He, Auggie and Rafe stood beside me as we studied the remains on the table.

"Because he had limited knowledge of other races?" I asked, looking up at Val's set expression.

"Very limited knowledge."

I realized then that Madam President's unfortunate remark still rankled with him. "Honey, they just don't know any better," I threaded my fingers with his.

"Larentii were made first of all races," Val said.

"How can you know that?" Auggie turned sharply to stare at Val.

"If you had met the ones responsible for creating all races, you'd know it, too," Val pointed out.

"Surely not," Auggie began.

"Do not question what you cannot comprehend," Val said.

"I've seen enough of Merle," I said, breaking the tension. "Let's look at the others."

Drawers were pulled out for the next two; one had been shot by Rafe, the other showed no physical signs as to why he died. "How did you do this?" I asked Val. I'd have separated his particles. Somehow, Val had avoided doing that, leaving our intended attacker just as dead.

"He was threatening you," Val said. "A Larentii is always allowed to protect his mate. I merely separated his life force from his body, so your esteemed Colonel and our compatriot, here, could examine the body at their leisure." He'd nodded toward Rafe when he'd said compatriot. He'd almost said co-mate—I understood that quickly.

Val was already considering Rafe/Ilya a member of our family.

Wow.

"Can you see anything in either of these?" Rafe asked me. I stopped still for a moment. It was a question he'd have asked—well—Corinne.

"Not a clone," I said of the first one—the one Rafe had killed. "Had an obsession," I sighed. "No idea what it was, as usual. No ID from fingerprints?" I turned to Auggie.

"Nothing in the database."

"Could be a drug survivor—in fact, that is most likely," Val agreed. "Since Rinnelar cannot find his identity any other way."

"What about the other one, then?"

I turned to the other one—the man Val had killed to protect me. Now I could see much in him.

Unfortunately.

"Denton Kemp," I sighed. "Former Black Ops. More recently of the CIA. He and Merle were like this," I held up two crossed fingers. "Also, recent visitor to Ireland. Need I go on?"

"I'll get Matt on the phone," Auggie said and hauled his cell from a pocket.

Cori, Matt greeted me in mindspeech when we walked into his office.

Matt, I nodded in return.

"Please sit," Matt said aloud. "So, Denton Kemp, eh. He's been undercover—according to the CIA—for a very long time."

"He's under a sheet in the morgue, now," I pointed out. "He and Merle, both."

"I imagine Askins led him astray," Matt blew out a breath. "He was a decorated officer in the military."

I felt the same way and offered Matt a slight nod of agreement. Askins had too much blood on his hands, and a rather large percentage of it was innocent blood, or nearly so.

"I'm glad you wanted to come by," Matt sighed. "I heard from Opal about an hour ago. Those in the Dublin photographs, according to latest reports, are headed this way and bringing some of their less than sympathetic goons with them."

"Why?" Auggie asked.

"Because Matt and Opal just emptied Dublin of the underground, and now the hounds are on the scent," I said.

"Better to fight them on familiar terrain—to us, anyway," Matt said. "I'm hoping that if we capture the right ones, we may be able to get to those behind this new movement and bring it down before it has a chance to develop into a new world-domination scheme."

"Fucking hell, Michaels," Auggie snapped. "You could have warned us ahead of time."

~

"Where do you suppose they are?" Rafe asked. He, Val and I were back at the beach house in Port Aransas. I felt weary after Matt's bombshell. We sat on the back deck of the house, in full sunlight; Val was nearly naked while I wore a tank top and shorts in order to soak up as much sunlight as possible.

Rafe wore Ray-Bans, jeans, boots and a light jacket—the temps were in the high fifties on the south Texas beach. Val had chosen to cover up his sweet spot with a Speedo. Yes, some people can wear Speedos. *All* Larentii can wear them.

"You wanted to see us?" Sergei and Katya joined us on the deck.

"Yes," Rafe nodded. "It seems that Director Michaels has arranged for your friends from Dublin to come to the U.S." he began.

"That's wonderful," Katya said.

"He's using them as bait, to draw the enemy in," Rafe concluded.

"And that's not so wonderful," I said.

"I beg you to protect them—as you did me," Sergei pleaded.

"Honey, I'll do my best, but with Sirenali involvement, that may be too little too late," I said.

"Do they know when and where they will arrive?" Katya asked. She pulled Sergei toward the love seat so they could sit together.

"He only gave them a time and place to show up at the Canadian border—plus enough cash to get there," I said. I anticipated having another conversation with Matt Michaels—when I was calm enough not to call him a half-meddling cactus molester.

"That is quite humorous, my love," Val said aloud.

"What?" Rafe turned toward Val.

"She called Director Michaels a half-meddling cactus molester."

"Not out loud," I defended myself. "I just thought it. I can't help if Val reads my thoughts."

"I love your thoughts," Val chuckled.

"Sure. Good thing I don't have to use the bathroom, then. You'd back away quick. What can we do to help Katya and Sergei's friends?"

"I go get them," Bekzi offered.

"I'll go with you," Rafe nodded.

"Daddy, they don't know you," Katya began.

"Would it be better to take Katya or Sergei with us?" I asked.

"You're going?" Val lifted a blond eyebrow.

"I think we're all going," I said.

"What's this? Where are you going?" Leo walked onto the deck, a cup of coffee in his hands. "We have a session planned for the afternoon," he reminded Katya and Sergei.

"We need to grab their friends before the bad guys do," I said. "Then you can talk all you want."

"Then I'm not staying here by myself," Leo grated.

"Fine."

"I believe they are currently caught in a snowstorm," Val announced. He'd gone *Looking* for them, evidently.

"What?" Katya turned concerned eyes to Val.

"I understand that it was their plan to pose as hikers. A heavy snowstorm is falling where they are and they only have tents to protect them from the elements."

"How does he know that?" Leo whispered.

"I'll explain later," I offered. "For now, we really ought to get them out of there. Val, are they armed?"

"Yes," he nodded.

"Damn," Rafe muttered.

"I'll make sure nobody freezes if you'll disarm them," I suggested to Val.

"Done," he agreed. "We will return shortly," he said, and leaving a shouting crowd behind us, transported just the two of us to a forest in Quebec.

Snow fell heavily about us and in the distance, I could see the top halves of two, bright-blue tents. Winds whipped and moaned about them; if they hadn't been half-buried by snow, they'd have toppled over with the force of the storm.

"Honey, what's that sound?" I turned to Val when the mechanical growl reached my ears.

"My love, the vision of those in the tents has just been cut off," Val said.

"Sirenali," we said at the same moment.

"Well, well, fancy meeting you two here," Opal landed in the snow beside us. She was capable of folding space, just as Val, Matt and I could.

"There is a Sirenali nearby," Val said. "My vision of those inside the tents has been negated."

"Mine, too," Opal agreed. "I figure whoever is driving that Snowcat has a Sirenali with them."

"They believe there will be no opposition when they take those inside the tents?" Val asked.

"Yes," Opal confirmed.

"Then I suggest we remove those inside the tents and send them to Katya and Sergei," Val offered.

"Want to replace them with us?" Opal wagged a finger between herself and Val.

"You want a full, frontal assault?" I asked.

"Suits me." Opal pulled a pistol from a jacket pocket and checked the charge. She still carried the weapon I'd given her last time. A ranos pistol would make short work of any attackers—and destroy their Snowcat, too.

"So you can't bring one in, but if somebody gives you one," I grinned at her.

"Yep. You don't know how many times I've thanked you for this." She held the pistol up.

"We have movement," Val whispered.

We did. Someone was using a camp shovel to dig his way out of a tent. He'd heard the Snowcat, just as we had. Once he had enough room to move his head and shoulders out of the entrance, someone in the tent handed a rifle through.

Brave man, Opal sent.

Yeah. Val, I'll move them, I began.

The ground exploded in a half-mile radius around us.

CHAPTER 6

*C*orinne

I wanted to curse. Val and Opal remained grimly silent nearby, so I kept my mouth closed. Leo was busy in the media room, checking Sergei and Katya's friends for injuries and hearing damage.

At least they'd settled down and stopped shouting when they landed at the beach house next to Katya and Sergei. I imagined Leo was swamped with questions, not least among them how they'd arrived in Texas before getting blown up in Canada.

"Matt's got people searching for those responsible," Opal grumbled before searching for a chair. "It's obvious we can't get a handle on them because of Sirenali involvement."

"I figure the Canadian government will have something to say if they find out who sent these folks in their direction," I pointed out.

"He's doing damage control," Opal said. "Neither of us imagined they'd get attacked like that. I went anyway, just to make sure they were safe in the snowstorm."

"Anything left of the Snowcat?" I asked.

"I can check on that," Opal nodded. "Be back in a few."

"I love her," I said after she disappeared.

77

"She is most competent," Val agreed. "She added her shields to mine to protect the tents and their inhabitants," he added.

~

Notes—Colonel Hunter

"These are the satellite photographs," James said, handing his tablet to me so I could look at the huge crater in Quebec, where pristine wilderness used to be. The dark pit was made more prominent by the heavy layer of snow that surrounded it.

"Matt says they barely had time to get those people out of there before everything exploded," I shook my head at the damage. "If the Canucks hear of our involvement," I blew out a breath.

"So everybody's all right? Cori, too?" James asked.

"They appear to be fine," I said. "I just heard from Leo—he says no hearing damage, even, so Cori and Val had some serious protection going on."

"I miss seeing her every day," James said. "I haven't had good cookies in more than a year."

"I never thought I'd consider the days at the mansion as the good old days," I said. "But you're right. I miss seeing her all the time, too."

"Nathan wants to move up our wedding date—just in case," James shifted uncomfortably.

"So Corinne can come?" I asked.

"Yeah. We want her to stand with us, as a member of the family," he said.

"You know she will—if it's at all possible."

"Do you know where she'll be—where she'll go—when this is over?"

"I have no idea where the Larentii homeworld is," I said. "Ask her. She'll be more likely to tell you than me, I think."

"Why?"

"Corinne has always considered you the son she wanted," I sighed. "Rafe, too. They'd protect you with their lives, unless I'm much mistaken."

"I wish there wasn't a problem with Rafe," James dropped his gaze. "You know he'll go nuts if he figures out who she is, now."

"You want both of them there at the wedding, don't you?" I was beginning to understand James' dilemma.

"Yes. Nathan's family will be there—I want Cori and Rafe there as mine."

"Let me talk to Shaw—perhaps he can present this to Corinne and Val. They may be able to come up with a viable solution."

"I just worry about the wedding turning into a disaster if Rafe goes nuts," James admitted.

"I see your point," I said. "Meanwhile, ask Director Michaels for a meeting. We probably should inform the President of our involvement with a newly-formed crater in Quebec. We should also investigate the types of explosives used. Get Captain Finch on the line —I want to speak with him."

"Yes, sir."

∾

Corinne

"Nothing left of the Snowcat except burned, twisted wreckage," Opal reported when she reappeared. "It looks as if it were controlled remotely—at least there at the end. The driver and his pet Sirenali may have made a run for it before the explosives detonated. "

"So, they wanted everybody to pile out of the tents and then boom," I mimed an explosion with my fingers.

"Looks that way. The Snowcat was armed with remotely controlled guns, too, if my hunch is correct."

"So if the explosion didn't work?" I guessed.

"That's my guess, too," Opal agreed.

"I find this fascinating—the lengths some humanoids will go to just to kill others of their kind," Val said.

"It's frightening," I said. "We lost Nick and Maye and I still miss them," I added. "Besides, are Lyristolyi and Sirenali considered humanoids?"

"If they spend more than half their time in a humanoid guise, the Larentii consider them humanoid," Val said. "Although in the Archival Index, they have a coded description that any Larentii can decipher easily. It indicates that they have at least one alternate shape. The Saa Thalarr are also listed as such."

"I ran across some of those," I nodded. "Thanks for clearing that up."

"I regret that I was not there to meet you upon your arrival. I would have enjoyed showing you the Archives and answering your questions."

"They're all fine," Rafe strode out of the house and chose a chair nearby. "Thank you for saving their lives," he nodded to Val and me. "Sergei and Katya didn't need that blow."

"I'm glad we could do something about it," I said. I was also glad Val and I had gone without the others, but I didn't say it aloud. The explosion as it happened around us was terrifying enough, and we'd been shielded throughout.

"Honey," I turned to Val, "I need sunlight."

"I, too," he agreed. "Come, I will transport us."

~

Ilya

"How are you feeling?" Opal asked. "Any bad dreams or unexpected rages, lately?"

"They disappear almost before they can form—on both counts," I replied. "Do you have an explanation for that?"

"None at the moment," she shrugged.

"That's—Rinnelar. She's," I couldn't get the words past my lips.

"I believe Val has devised a way to keep the obsession from manifesting," Opal said. "If I were you, I'd be glad about that."

"I am glad. I feel jealous," I admitted.

"Don't. Or, if you just can't help it, ask him to remove it. It's fairly simple for a Larentii to do; it doesn't harm you in any way and doesn't interfere with anything else except your jealousy."

"That's a fascinating concept," I mumbled, unsure whether I should ask the Larentii for any favors. I felt I owed him enough as it was.

"You'll be surprised at what Val might do for you—if you ask," Opal said. "He won't interfere past what he's already done, but that, in essence, was to protect Rinnelar first."

Opal's admission ramped up the jealousy I already felt. "Don't let it get too far or I'll call him back here myself," she cautioned.

She was right—we didn't need dissension among our ranks. We needed to stand firmly together or we could end up losing this war. The explosion in Quebec was a grim reminder of that reality.

There were so many questions I wanted to ask—not just of Opal or Val, but of Rinnelar. That's not all I wanted from her, but was terrified to even entertain such thoughts.

"I know this is hard for you," Opal said. "We'll sort it out, just have faith and bear with us."

"Before, I'd be ripping this deck apart while having this conversation."

"I prefer the more peaceful version," she deadpanned.

"As do I. I finalized the deal on the Italian villa. Should I inform Rinnelar?"

"I'd wait—we haven't tested Val's solution to its fullest extent," she replied. "It's difficult to gauge the strength of any obsession placed by a Sirenali."

"Ah. Probably wise."

"Probably."

❦

Corinne

I hadn't meant to fall asleep while soaking up sunlight. I woke in Val's arms, both of us naked, of course. "Are you rested?" Val breathed against my cheek. "If not, I will sing you back to sleep."

"We should get back," I yawned.

"Then I will see that you sleep again when we arrive."

"Okay."

~

Captain Brett Walker

We'd been talking with Dr. Shaw much of the morning, then working out under Dr. Farrell's supervision most of the day. Therefore, Jennifer and I knew little about the events of the day or why there were now five new people at the beach house.

When we walked into the kitchen, searching for something that might pass for dinner, we found Rafe and Rinnelar working together to cook dinner while Val and Opal, another new arrival, sat at the island to watch.

"Is that chicken and dumplings?" I sniffed the air. My stomach growled, informing me that chicken and dumplings was exactly what was on the menu. I loved chicken and dumplings.

"Correct," Rafe turned and nodded at me. "A drink is in order, perhaps? We have Scotch, wine, rum—the liquor cabinet is fully stocked."

"How about an old-fashioned?" Opal asked, rising from her chair. "I make a pretty good one."

"I'll take it," I nodded. "Jen—what about you?"

"Wine?"

"We have pinot noir, Riesling, cabernet sauvignon, shiraz, several others," Rinnelar said. "Your choice."

"Pinot noir," Jen said immediately.

We watched as Rinnelar popped the cork from a bottle with barely a look, caught it neatly and set it in front of Jen while the bottle turned itself and poured into a wineglass.

"How do you do that?" Jen breathed as the wineglass floated toward her and set down gently by her hand.

"Power, young one," Val said. "Her hands are covered in flour, else she'd have done it in a more conventional way."

"That's amazing," Jen said before lifting the glass and tentatively tasting the wine. "Good," she nodded.

"It's my favorite red," Rinnelar smiled and went back to cutting dumpling dough into squares before dropping them into boiling broth. Rolled and cut dumplings—my favorite.

"Our werewolf is hungry," Val announced. I went still.

"Huh?" Jen's head swiveled toward Val.

"It is time Dr. Farrell told both of you what you are," he said.

"I was waiting," Richard Farrell snapped as he walked into the kitchen.

"What were you waiting for?" Val demanded. "Perhaps for the time when the full moon comes and he begins to feel its pull? Perhaps for that time? Things were different for Nicholas, because he'd grown up seeing it in others. This—you have three days, Doctor. I suggest you get to it. If you have limited experience with this, then I expect you to allow someone better versed in the change to tell him."

"I suppose you think you're going to?" Farrell wasn't happy, and I could scent the anger and embarrassment flowing off him. Yes, it shocked and worried me, but not nearly as much as the rest of the conversation had.

"No, I suggest that Opal make contact with one nearby. William Winkler is in residence down the beach—he is the Dallas Packmaster and will do this for us, I think."

"What the bloody hell?" Dr. Farrell exploded.

"You should have considered this before the drug was administered," Val said, his voice soft. "If you cannot calm yourself, I shall do it for you."

Dr. Farrell took a step toward Val, his face dark with anger. Val rose from his seat before becoming nearly nine feet tall and blue-skinned. Farrell stopped in his tracks. Not because he wanted to, but because Val used his power to prevent Farrell's approach. A long, blue finger snaked out and tapped Farrell lightly on the forehead. Farrell's body dropped gently to the floor as he lost consciousness.

"I'll call Winkler," Opal said and pulled out her cell phone.

Corinne

William Winkler, werewolf and Dallas Packmaster, arrived in an hour, accompanied by his son, Wayne. "If anybody except Opal had called, I'd be calling them delusional," Winkler said shortly after his arrival. "Now, what's this about a drug and replication?"

"Tied up with national security," Matt Michaels wandered in. I gave him a look—one that said he'd never fool me for a minute. He pointedly ignored my look and paid attention to Winkler instead.

"Want chicken and dumplings?" I went right over Matt's head and employed what would interest any werewolf—the promise of food.

"I smelled it the minute I got here," Wayne declared.

"Then come have some," I invited. "The others are already eating."

That's how Val and I came to know the Dallas Packmaster and his son, who acted as his Second. Richard Farrell, who was now awake again, functioned in a better, more civilized manner as he ate. I suppose he realized that nobody should ever pick a fight with a Larentii.

"Larentii," I pointed to Val and myself when Winkler asked.

"I've only had dealings with one Larentii before," Winkler said.

"Pheligar," Val said.

"How did you know?" Winkler's interest was piqued.

"He is my uncle, as well as the Liaison for the Saa Thalarr, who in turn had dealings with Lissa."

Honey, you're treading shaky ground, I warned.

"You know about Lissa." Winkler's words were flat, his depression immediate.

"We didn't intend to open old wounds," I apologized to Winkler.

"It's all right," he held up a hand. I knew he was lying; I just didn't want to make things worse for him. And it would be interfering to tell him that in the future, Lissa was just fine, thanks. The thing was, someone had already alluded to that fact; Winkler just didn't know what to make of it.

We all had many paths to walk before the future arrived. I wanted to sigh. I forced myself not to do so.

⌇

"Will I turn into something?" Jennifer now stood beside me as I stared out the plate-glass windows at the gulf, lit only by a waxing moon. Somewhere out there, Winkler and his son were attempting to teach Brett what it meant to be werewolf.

"No, hon," I draped an arm about her shoulders. "You weren't meant to turn. What you'll do eventually is tap into others' thoughts. You'll know who has murder on their minds, or sometimes, who's committed it, if they're thinking about it."

"That's frightening," she shivered.

"I know." I hugged her tighter. When Maye was turned, she'd been a volunteer, fully advised on the potential effects of the drug. Jennifer hadn't had a choice. I understood what that felt like, although I'd gotten the drug directly, instead of a survivor's blood after the fact.

Maye hadn't fought PTSD, either. Jen struggled with it, just as she struggled with emerging memories that weren't her own. I wasn't sure Richard would have a chance with her—she was beginning to realize how detrimental the drug actually was.

"Rinnelar," Rafe's voice interrupted my thoughts. Jen and I turned at the same time to see what he wanted.

"There's something on the news I think you should see," he said. Jen and I followed him toward the media room.

The devastation in Star Cove, Texas, not far from where we were, looked as if someone had set off a bomb, there.

"Twenty-eight years ago, Star Cove was destroyed. Since then it has been rebuilt, only to suffer nearly the same fate," the journalist declared. "While some homes still stand, most along the main canal have been obliterated. Authorities are attempting to search through debris for survivors and bodies, but in places, it is still too hot to make the attempt. A cause for this explosion and fire is still under investigation."

"Those fucking Elemaiya," I snapped. "I knew they were trouble the minute I saw them."

~

"How did they get here?" Winkler was exhausted when dawn arrived; still, he wanted to hear about Star Cove. He'd built the small town initially, before its first destruction, then rebuilt it afterward and sold the property. "I thought Ashe got rid of the fuckers."

"He did, and prevented them from gating in again," Val explained. He, Winkler and I were having a private meeting on the beach house's deck while the others stayed inside the house. As a precaution, Val placed a soundproof shield about us, so nobody else would hear our conversation.

"Then how?" Winkler buried his face in his hands.

"They arrived by more conventional means, courtesy of the ASD," I said. "That's Alliance Security Detail, in case you haven't heard of it before. They arrived by ship, then by anti-grav transport to the planet. They were sent to hunt the remnants of drug survivors, clones and any remaining drug. You see how quickly they became distracted."

"What distracted them?" Winkler dropped his hands and turned dark eyes on me.

"What they were sent here for in the beginning," I shrugged. "The Dark King and Bright Queen have sent them to find their crowns."

"They're not here," Winkler growled.

"We know that; they do not," Val interjected. "Rinnelar and I know where the crowns are in the future; the current King and Queen will never see or touch them again."

"What are we supposed to do about these four, now?" Winkler asked. "It took Ashe to defeat them before."

"Ashe was only coming into his power at the time," Val pointed out. "Perhaps Rinnelar and I can do something about them, now."

"It looks as if your hands are full already, if what Matt says is accurate."

"Matt is still in the dog house, in my opinion," I said. "Meanwhile, those Elemaiyan murderers think they'll get away with this."

"I can have the Corpus Christi Pack hunt them in two days, at the full moon," Winkler offered.

"At least one of them can level power blasts," Val said. "Your wolves will die if they attempt to take that one."

"This sucks," Winkler muttered.

"Perhaps I will ask my father to notify Ildevar Wyyld of their betrayal," Val said. "It will require careful maneuvering, but it can be arranged."

"Do it," I said. "Somebody needs to reel these fuckers in before more people die. Families died in those blasts, Val," I flung out a hand.

"Then I will contact Father now," he said and disappeared.

"I'd give anything to be able to do that," Winkler sighed.

"Come on, I'll make coffee for you," I offered. "He'll be back in a few, but you look like you haven't slept for a week."

"I feel like it, too," he said and followed me into the house.

∾

Wyyld II

Ildevar Wyyld, Founder

Reth Alliance (future)

"I barely remember that," I said. Nefrigar and Valegar, his second son, stood in my study. They'd brought news of an event that had happened more than four centuries earlier.

"In my estimation, at least twenty-two humans died in those blasts," Valegar said.

"In the past, I don't recall hearing of this," I countered.

"Humans attributed it to other causes, because they didn't have evidence or reason to believe otherwise," Nefrigar said.

Nefrigar, Chief Archivist for the Larentii Archives, was a depository of information in his own right. Most of what he housed in the Archives also resided in his head.

"How will this affect the timeline?" I asked.

"It will not affect it, if you or your past self asks for help from the powerful to intervene."

"Whom should I contact, then?" I asked.

"I suggest someone familiar with that world," Valegar said.

"Who?"

"Belen."

"He outranks me, you know."

"We're aware," Nefrigar admitted. "Nevertheless, he could prove himself invaluable in this case. It is my suspicion that Belen is one of the few who can transcend the timelines in any guise and at any point."

"Fascinating theory. I'd like to discuss that with you, sometime."

"As you wish it," Nefrigar smiled. "I think of him as a recurring comet, who travels at will through the universes. I believe he was created for that purpose."

"Now, my curiosity is certainly aroused," I said. "Perhaps I will discuss this with Breanne when I see her again."

"I would very much like to hear what she has to say," Nefrigar offered a slight nod. His eyes were alight with speculation, however, which was wondrous to see. I think even the higher gods would pause before engaging in debate with the Larentii Archivist.

"Very well, I shall contact Belen immediately," I agreed. "I will present your request most persuasively."

"We thank you," Nefrigar said. He and Valegar disappeared, leaving me to ponder his words.

～

Unofficial communication from:

Geethe Cheriss, Prime Potentate of Lyristolys

To: Outland Commander Fisk Boralus

Subject: Drug Survivors, Clones and Contraband Drug Supplies

Communication received on multiple survivors and clones. It is the decision of the Hidden Council and myself that planet Earth be eliminated. Ensure that it appears to be the work of dissident members of the population. Standard protocol is engaged. Accomplish destruction at earliest opportunity. All evidence of this communication must be destroyed upon receipt.

Fisk looked up from the comp-vid to study his team. It included a mute Sirenali, who'd had his tongue removed at birth. Keeping the

Sirenali with the team ensured that the powerful would have no knowledge of his presence—as long as they remained within the Sirenali's protective range. The Sirenali had been appropriated by the Lyristolyi government after dismantling a criminal organization. He'd been subjugated by the Hidden Council ever since.

Fisk smiled grimly. He had a job to do—and a planet to destroy. "Standard protocol is engaged," he announced and erased the message on his comp-vid.

~

Corinne

Val, Rafe and I accompanied Winkler to Star Cove—at least the remnants of it. News crews were milling about—streets into the small community were tied off with crime scene tape.

More than one journalist recognized Winkler when he stepped out of his SUV; microphones appeared in hands immediately and all of them crowded about him.

"Was it a gas explosion?" One of them demanded.

"Everything in the community is electric," Winkler waved off the speculation with one hand. "A gas grill certainly couldn't cause that sort of devastation," he added. "I think this was done deliberately."

"By whom? One of your enemies?" Someone else asked.

"I haven't owned any property here or had any dealings with this community in more than twenty-five years," Winkler replied. "If they're after me, they're a bit slow on the uptake."

"Please, allow Mr. Winkler to pass," Rafe stepped in to act as Winkler's temporary bodyguard. The county sheriff, who'd been talking with local police and two FBI agents, began walking toward the yellow tape which flipped and bounced in the breeze off the gulf.

He recognized Winkler, too, as did the FBI. This meant we'd be let through, while the carrion-crow-minded-media would have to remain behind.

An FBI agent held the tape up so Winkler and his entourage could slip through. I could hear journalists shouting more questions at our backs. I considered a swift, heavy downpour over them—but that would require a bit of cloud manipulation over our heads. I decided against it.

Val chuckled beside me.

"We're pretty sure this was planned—the investigation has turned up evidence that a rocket launcher or some other weapon may have been used," the sheriff said as we walked toward the remnants of burned and blasted houses.

"We just can't determine the reason this community was targeted," one of the FBI agents added. "Nobody living here should have been on anyone's hit list."

"We need Matt Michaels here," Winkler said. "I have a theory—which has nothing to do with me, by the way—but I'd feel more comfortable explaining everything to him, first."

"He's on the way—flew out of D.C. an hour ago," the other agent said. "Probably be here in three hours, depending on the speed of the military jet he took. Scheduled to land at the Naval Air Station in Corpus."

Human methods of travel are so slow and mundane, Val sent.

I hear that, I agreed. Ever since I'd been able to fold space, it was my preferred means of travel.

At least the burned bodies of adults and children had already been removed—if that hadn't happened, I'd have been even more furious than I was as we studied the destruction caused by four Elemaiya.

I want to kill them, I sent to Val.

Dearest, can you find them—by Looking? *I fear you cannot*, he replied. *I have already attempted it. They are hiding behind a Sirenali, now, I think. No idea how they managed to capture one, nevertheless, it is done. Perhaps one of the gods will assist us in our search*, Val's words were enigmatic.

Then I hope he gets here soon, I grumped.

The gods appear in their own time, and not by any plan or desire of others, Val quoted.

I suppose that's in a Larentii book somewhere, I said.

Dearest, you have not had time to read all of them, yet. I'd just made him smile.

So a god is coming to save our asses? I went back to our original conversation.

Our asses, as you put it, do not need saving. Human asses, on the other hand, do.

Right. What about those ass-hats from Lyristolys? The other ones we can't find? My mental voice sounded petulant. *That doesn't even include the clones and any drug survivors with less than stellar intentions.*

We are assisting with those searches, and doing what we can to keep those about us alive and well. Far more than most Larentii are allowed or willing to do.

Hmmph.

Dearest, when we get back to the beach house, I hope you will allow me to take your mind off all this.

How do you propose to do that?

I shouldn't have asked, especially in that tone of mental disbelief. The wave of sexual desire that washed over me almost sent me to my knees. Val took my elbow to prevent that. Unfortunately, his touch only made the desire more acute. If I'd known what sort of sexual mojo a male Larentii possessed, I'd have kept my mental mouth shut.

Something wrong? Rafe's voice sounded in my head.

Nothing to see here, I grumped as Val sent another wave of desire in my direction.

What the hell was that? Rafe demanded.

You were mentally connected to Rinnelar when we ah, were being frisky, Val replied. *I suspect you have an erection at this point.*

None of your business, Rafe snapped.

That remains to be seen, Val snapped back.

You'll not be seeing, Rafe began before another wave of desire hit both of us. Rafe stopped still, looking as if someone had sucker-punched him in the gut.

Honey, please stop. I don't want to have a climax next to the FBI, I wheezed in mindspeech.

Very well. The moment I have you and Rafe to myself, Val said.

Rafe lifted an eyebrow but didn't comment. Perhaps he was feeling the effects of intense sexual arousal after more than a year without, just as I was.

"I'm sending images to Matt," Opal said, breaking up our mental foreplay. It was just as well, I tended to be noisy while having an orgasm.

"What did I miss?" Matt Michaels walked up. Well, somebody didn't take the time to finish his flight.

It's Mr. Foldy-Space Pants, I silently accused.

I really wish you'd give me a break, he whined back.

Come on, you know that's funny, Opal intervened.

All of us stopped still as Val sent another wave of pleasure, silencing even Matt.

CHAPTER 7

orinne

All of us returned to the beach house feeling depressed. After Val's last bit of tomfoolery, we'd witnessed first-hand where people had died. Thoughts of the children, some of them sleeping at the time of the assault, enraged me.

It shocked me, too, that Val held one hand while Rafe gripped the other when I was ready to become tall, blue and violent.

I wasn't ready to ask how Val had accomplished that feat with Rafe, because I didn't want to know. Not now, anyway. I still felt angry and depressed over the attack on Star Cove. Those Elemaiya were going to die if I ever found them again.

"Papa," Katya came to Rafe, "Opal says we can't go anywhere without Val or Rinnelar," she leaned her head on Rafe's shoulder.

"What is it, little moth?" he asked, rubbing her back.

"Cabin fever?" I offered.

"I think so. Sergei is feeling restless. I think we both need to get out for a while."

"Is there something in particular you want to do or somewhere you want to go?" I asked.

"I now own a villa in Italy," Rafe said. "Would you like to see that? Provided Rinnelar doesn't mind taking us?"

"I wouldn't mind," I breathed, once the shock wore off. He'd bought it, because that's where we'd spent our short honeymoon.

"I will provide transportation," Val said immediately.

"Where?" Matt said. "Just asking," he held up a hand before I could say anything.

"I was going to answer your question," I replied. "Not jump all over you."

"Truce?" he asked, holding out his hand.

"I guess," I sighed and clasped his hand to shake on it.

"Good. Opal and I would like to come with you, then. Bekzi will stay here to protect the others."

"I want to have dinner at Gino's while we're there," Rafe said. "That means we spend the night tonight and perhaps tomorrow night as well."

"Is that the restaurant you always talked about?" Katya turned a hopeful gaze on Rafe.

"It is," he smiled at her. "The food is wonderful."

"I'll be coming with you," Leo announced, cutting his eyes toward Sergei. I wanted to sigh. I didn't. Leo wouldn't include himself unless it was important to Sergei's health, mental and physical.

"All right," I shrugged. "Pack your duds. We're going to Italy."

"Duds?" Sergei blinked at me.

"Clothing," Rafe explained. "An American idiom that defies explanation."

"It derives from Middle English," Val began.

"Honey, they don't care about that," I patted his arm. "They just want to go somewhere."

I understood that he wanted to comment on short attention spans, but didn't say it. I rubbed his back to console him. Matt, the cheeky bastard, snickered.

"Don't be a jerk," Opal swatted at Matt. I snickered, that time.

They want to have energy sex, Val informed me.

I thought so, I replied. *I just didn't want to embarrass anybody by saying it aloud.*

You, my love, have never experienced energy sex. They have. They know to anticipate it greatly.

While I feel like an awkward virgin, I snapped. *Sorry, didn't mean it to come out quite like that.*

I will make sure you are cared for afterward, he observed.

I need care afterward? Now I was starting to worry.

The ecstasy is so great, the participants generally lose consciousness. If we are not on the Larentii homeworld, then other Larentii must be present to ensure the safety of all participants.

What. The. Hell. Are. You. Talking. About?

You'll see. Val smiled gently.

And so will they, I huffed. *I don't want a bunch of strangers watching me while I'm making whoopee.*

Dearest, it's not like that. They know to be discreet if anyone involved feels uncomfortable.

Right. Who's coming? Anybody I know?

I just sent the call—there have been several replies. I expect them to work it out among themselves.

Right.

Dearest, you're repeating yourself.

On purpose.

Ah. I assure you, I understood the first time.

I'm not questioning your understanding. I'm beginning to question my involvement in energy sex.

Please, dearest—I have been looking forward to this since the moment we met.

All men are alike, no matter what planet they're from, I grumped.

I call your attention to the fact that I am Larentii. Men are, by definition, human.

Fine. Didn't mean to ruffle your tail feathers.

I do not have, he held up a hand.

I know, I know. I should have said males. My bad. As for Larentii having tail feathers, it's only an expression. Wait, you're just yanking my chain, aren't you?

Dearest, you make me laugh, he said.

"I think this is the most interesting conversation I've never heard," Katya interrupted.

"Young one, we didn't mean to converse at such length and exclude you," Val smiled. "We are—as you might say—merely poking at one another."

"Corinne had such a look on her face," Katya grinned.

Rafe went crazy, trying to get to me. If Val hadn't been there to intervene on my behalf, he could have done me harm. I was too stunned at first to recall that I could place a shield about myself when he came after me with murder in his eyes.

That meant I was forced to watch as he destroyed everything surrounding my hastily erected shield in an attempt to kill me. When the tears came, that's when Val put a stop to it and rendered Rafe unconscious.

"There was no harm done, young one," Val attempted to soothe Katya. "I merely placed your father in a healing sleep. He will wake shortly with his obsession in check."

"I didn't mean to say her name," Katya brushed tears away.

"Honey, don't cry—this really isn't your fault. A Sirenali did this to us," I said. My voice shook, but I was determined to keep Katya from having a breakdown.

Val and I hadn't yet cleared away the destruction Rafe had caused with only his fists and strength. It made me glad he didn't have his warlock abilities wakened—the damage could have been much more severe—to the house and to me.

He and I—we should be together on Karathia. As it was, that had been stolen away from us. My sigh was shaky and I was close to tears.

"Are we still going to Italy?" Katya quavered.

"I'll see to it," Val said gently. "We'll bring your father around.

Please, someone take over for me—Rinnelar needs my attention," Val announced.

"I will." Opal sat next to Katya on what remained of a sofa.

"Come, dearest," Val said, gripping my hand and folding space.

"I wish I could say there is no cause for tears, but that would be an untruth," Val wrapped large, blue arms about me. Without a word, he'd convinced me to remove my human disguise once we arrived at a secluded spot next to a waterfall on one of the Hawaiian Islands.

Before I could wipe away the next tear that fell, he did it for me. "Hush, dearest. He loves you very much. That is why the obsession is so violent. If he could, he would turn that destruction upon himself, instead."

"I don't want him to do that," I quavered. "He doesn't deserve this."

"And neither do you. Wicked Sirenali have been a curse since their creation. If your Ilya had his way, you would be in his arms while he soothed your hurts and fears." A hand stroked and massaged the back of my neck—exactly where the tension was. I buried my face against Val's chest and sobbed.

Ilya

The room was dim when I woke. I had no idea that Val or any Larentii could leave a mental or physical message waiting, like anyone might leave on a phone, a card or any other communication device.

She is most upset, the message came. *I have repaired the bones in your hands. Do not make me regret that act by destroying your bedroom and harming yourself a second time.*

I cursed myself instead. Val was correct—there was no sense in allowing my anger to surface a second time, just so I could destroy more of a house that did not belong to me. And the harm I'd brought to *her*, well, I feared that would never be repaired or forgiven.

All it had taken was the mention of her true name. The obsession had surfaced after that, destroying all of Val's good work at keeping it submerged in my consciousness. Yes, I realized he'd been secretly working to hold it back. I wanted to thank him and curse myself again in the same breath.

"Papa?" Katya's voice came from a corner of the room. I'd failed to see her sitting there, waiting for me to wake.

"Little moth, I am better now," I reassured her. "I hope I didn't frighten you when the obsession manifested."

"They told me that's what it was. I didn't understand until now." I could hear the closeness of tears in her voice.

"Come," I sat up on the edge of my bed and beckoned to her. "Sit with me. We will talk about this."

"But," she began.

"No, my precious girl," I said. "I will never harm you. The obsession only makes me violent toward—you know." I gritted my teeth as I said the words.

"You love her," Katya said and rose from her chair.

"I do." I studied my hands in the dim light. Val had repaired most of the damage, just as he'd said. All the cuts and abrasions were healed; only a few small bruises remained of the wreck I'd made of my fists.

"This makes me afraid," she took one of my hands in both of hers while shaking her head. "If this obsession thing can make the strongest person I know do things he would never do," she didn't finish.

"I know, my little moth," I sighed, grasping her fingers with mine. "And I would never do that. Never."

"Papa, I was hoping she wasn't dead. That you would be together, and you would be happy. I know you weren't for a long time—not after Alexi's death. I worried about you going to the Americans. I worried that they'd only use you and then toss you away. She made sure that didn't happen, didn't she?"

"I think she had much to do with that," I agreed. I almost smiled when she said it, too. After all, if I hadn't been treated well and if I hadn't fallen in love with *her*, I would have found a way to escape.

Colonel Hunter had turned out to be an honest man. Those were rare, in my experience.

"What do you think it would have been like—if you'd been reborn on the world meant for you both?" Katya asked.

"I don't know," I said. "I can only hope that it would be as beautiful as I have imagined it. Now, who told you these things?"

"Opal. I like her, Papa. She answered most of my questions, and some I didn't know to ask."

"I get the idea that Opal—and Director Michaels—are much more than most think," I said. "I've heard *her* referring to it often."

"I hope a day will come when you can say her name again, Papa."

"As do I."

Corinne

I understood that I wasn't wholly awake. I heard the voice anyway. The one that told me all wasn't lost. The words were spoken by a male but softly, while a kiss brushed across my forehead. At first I panicked, worried that Val had left my side.

No, dearest, he soothed. *I am here. Someone else who loves you has come. Do not be afraid.*

The hum that came was that of another Larentii—Val's song was different yet no less soothing. I fell asleep again quickly.

Valegar, Second Assistant
Larentii Archives
Secured Personal Notes

I hadn't expected Kalenegar to arrive. He'd ordered the other volunteers to stay on the Larentii homeworld and he'd come himself at my request for someone to guard us during energy sex.

Instead, there'd been no pleasure, only pain at a carelessly dropped name and the obsession that activated as a result. I'd assumed Kalenegar had muted his M'Fiyah with Corinnelar.

It became obvious that he'd unmuted it. I was surprised by the concern in his eyes as he soothed Corinne. Before he was done, Breanne, his first mate, arrived to help. I could see that both were worried about Corinne. I held her tighter against me as a result.

"She is weary," Breanne shook her head. "I'm considering calling for Kay to come, but I have no idea whether she can work through two sets of Ilya's aura lines to get to the proper ones."

"Remember he has to deserve the help," Kalenegar chided.

Breanne frowned at him, which made him hold back further comments. She was the Mighty Heart, after all, and her primary concern now appeared to be Corinne instead of Ilya, and whether he deserved a place among immortals.

"I will think on this," Breanne said after several moments of silence. "Will you stay or come with me?" she asked Kalenegar.

"I will come," he nodded. Both disappeared. I breathed a heavy sigh. My poor Corinne. Her suffering would continue while those far above me made a decision.

Corinne

The rain falls on the just and the unjust alike. I frowned as I stared out a window at Rafe's newly-acquired Italian villa. Outside, the rain poured down in sheets, spattering in waves against the outside wall, as if it were fiercely determined to make its way inside.

"Not the way I imagined a homecoming would be," Rafe walked up. Not close enough to touch or even nearly so—he stayed far enough away to give me space in case he frightened me.

He'd never frightened me before. He did, now. I'd seen firsthand how quickly the obsession could activate and how violent his rage could be—*against me*.

Yes, a part of me knew he didn't mean it. Not the real Ilya/Rafe. He couldn't control it, however, and it terrified me. Somehow, I'd fooled myself into thinking that his love would ultimately protect me against his rages.

It hadn't been Ilya's love that saved me and I mourned that loss. Yes, I was Larentii and should be able to protect myself easily from him. My heart wept that protection was necessary.

Without a word, I folded space to the outside garden. It wasn't until I was soaked through and shivering did Val pull me back inside. Rafe had disappeared into the master suite and didn't appear again until the following morning.

~

Larentii don't get colds. Only one of that race can be depressed for extended periods. That one was me. Opal made breakfast for the others; I was barely able to get myself out of bed. The moment I shuffled out of the bedroom, Matt handed a cell phone to me.

"Corinne," Auggie barked. "You need to pull out of this."

"Auggie, you're not my boss anymore," I pointed out. I sounded tired, even to my own ears.

"I'm still your friend," he said. "This is scaring me. Stop scaring me, Cori. I mean it."

"Yeah."

"Come, you need sunlight," Val took the phone from my hand. "We will contact you later," he informed Auggie and ended the call.

~

Notes—Colonel Hunter

"Shaw, what the hell is going on there?" I barked into the phone.

"To me, it looks as if her PTSD symptoms may be waking again. Evidently, this started when Rafe attempted to attack her."

"Fuck," I muttered.

"What's wrong?" Shaw asked. Somehow, he knew something was up—probably from my level of upset and the decibels in my voice.

"Those fuckers who burned that town in Texas just fried two

Corpus Christi Police officers. That's what. We need Cori's help. Fuck," I repeated while wiping a hand down my face in frustration.

"When did that happen?"

"Ten minutes ago."

"Fuck." Shaw echoed my profanity. "Val took Corinne away. I have no idea where. I can only assume he'll bring her back, although I couldn't blame him if he didn't. Rafe appeared to be doing so well, yet one mention of her name brought on a violent outburst. The family room at the beach house was destroyed—until Valegar repaired everything. I wish I possessed such power and talent."

"I think there's a reason we don't have it," I muttered dryly.

"Probably true. I'll let you know if Corinne and Val return."

"Thanks." After ending the call, I dropped my face into both hands and muttered *fuck* a third time.

~

Twenty-five Miles Northeast of Kuujjuaq
Near Rivière-Koksoak
Norde-du-Quebec Region
Canada

"Repeat after me—I am Reginald Phillips, former President of the United States."

"Who are you? You keep telling me who I am, but you never say who you are, Doctor," the patient complained.

"Ah, already you display your intelligence," the doctor beamed. "I am Merle Askins, formerly of the CIA, and now in charge of your convalescence. You have undergone surgery to restore your face—you were injured severely in an attack in Washington, D.C."

"Is this how you've always looked?" the patient asked.

"I was also injured. You must excuse my appearance," Askins replied. "I had to undergo a similar recovery, but alas, there was no surgery to restore my features."

"Why do you have a Russian accent?"

"It is nothing, merely a by-product of my injuries. My voice was also affected."

"I don't believe you."

"Ah, my dear Mr. President, why shouldn't you? Who wouldn't want to be the former President of a great nation? Why would I tell you differently if it were not true?"

"For one thing, I believe I'd have a better view out my window," the patient grumbled.

"Ah—but there are those who may still wish you harm. We must protect you any way we can, you know."

"From what?"

"From those currently posing as the government of the United States. You must save the country, Mr. President. I and my colleagues are counting on it."

"Who is that one over there—the one chained to his bed?"

"He is of no concern—he assists us when necessary, but that is all. You will direct his actions soon—when you have regained your health."

"What sort of assistance?"

"Mr. President, he is capable—when ordered, of course—of amazing things. Some might call him a wizard, in fact. Do not worry; he will obey your orders. We keep him well-fed and as happy as we can, except for the chains, of course. Those we dare not unlock, lest he find a way to escape."

"I fail to understand what keeping him will do for us."

"But you will, Mr. President. I assure you of that."

Notes—Colonel Hunter

I hoped Matt Michaels was calling to let me know Corinne had come back to the villa. That wasn't the reason for his call.

"I just got word from my team in Dublin," he said. "We have images of a man who looks enough like Zoran to be his twin brother."

"Where?" I sat straighter in my seat, as if that would better prepare me for the bad news coming.

"They lost him," Matt grumbled. "Followed him into a pub and then poof, he was gone."

"You think it's just a coincidence?"

"No."

Most people would have said perhaps, or that there might be a chance, however small. Matt blew right past those possibilities, landing a verbal punch to my already sour stomach.

"Fuck. What are they doing?" I snapped.

"No idea, but it's a cinch the ASD assholes who were sent here to track drug survivors aren't worried about the clones running the Russian Program now."

"No, they have their own brand of shit to spread," I responded. "If I could get my hands on the ones responsible for sending them here in the first place," I slapped a hand on my desk.

"Finch and his team are searching the site in Canada, but so far, there aren't any clues or trails to follow," Matt informed me. "I was planning to ask Corinne to help, but after the incident at the beach house, we may not have assistance from that quarter."

"I hope you're wrong," I said. "Without her, we're faced with two sets of enemies we can't handle."

"Understood. Look, I'll call if I hear anything new." The line went dead.

"James," I called out. "Come here." He arrived quickly. "Here," I handed my cell phone to him. "She'll know it's you calling. If she'll answer anybody's call, she'll answer yours."

Cloud Chief, Oklahoma

"There's nothing here except abandoned buildings," Brade complained.

"They were here once; our King demanded we search here if nothing was found in Star Cove," Ralvus hissed. A truce between Light and Dark Elemaiya had never occurred before, and he greatly disliked the fact that he and his brothers were the forerunners to what could become a regular alliance.

Everything hinged on the stolen crowns—and their return to the rightful owners. The one who'd taken them—the one calling himself Ir'Indicti? Nothing but an upstart, in Ralvus' opinion. He'd surely had help from some quarter, else he'd never have withstood the power of the Bright Queen and the Dark King.

"There's nothing here—see, the ring is still dull," Brade held up his hand. There, resting on his smallest finger, was a ring his Queen had lent him. In some way, the ring was connected to her crown and would shine when it was near. They'd discovered that it reacted to the echo of power, too, when they'd searched Star Cove. *Stupid humans, to deny them the right to search their homes.* Brade snorted at the memory.

The ring had not shone for years, otherwise. Brade was determined to undo that great mischief. His Queen had charged him with this task and he was determined not to fail her.

"Where's our dog?" Invus, youngest of the Verain brothers, asked.

"Over there," Dervus pointed toward a bare patch of grass. "Probably sniffing for a place to piss." Invus laughed at his brother's words.

Somehow, the Dark King had acquired this living tool for them. As long as it kept quiet and did its job, they held back from taunting and delivering blows.

Mostly.

Not far away, Gerrett, the mute Sirenali, had his back turned to them. Did they think him deaf as well as mute? It was better if he ignored the insults, as any rebelliousness on his part would be met with blows and curses, at the very least.

The last burns he'd gotten from Ralvus still hadn't healed completely. *Better not to react,* he told himself. *Much, much better.*

"I say we drive to the nearest town and ask questions," Invus suggested.

"Good enough," Ralvus agreed. "There's nothing here."

Corinne

"Honey, what's wrong?" I asked. The call came from Auggie's phone, but it was James placing the call.

"We, uh, have problems," James muttered.

I wanted to say *you and me both, honey,* but I didn't. James was upset enough as it was. I still felt shaky, but not as bad as I was before Val had gotten me away from Rafe. "Do you want me to come?" I offered instead.

"I wish you would," James sounded lost. Something else was going on beside murder and chaos.

"We will arrive shortly," Val took the phone away and spoke to James before ending the call with a thought.

Auggie's office was our destination in a blink.

The minute we arrived, I understood James' dilemma. Nathan had been called away to work with Captain Finch in Quebec. James was worried about Nathan's safety, after the massive explosion there. He didn't want Nathan anywhere near that.

"Honey, we don't always get to pick and choose where we're sent," I pulled him into a hug.

"I'm sorry, Cori," he mumbled. "I just can't help it. I'm afraid for him."

"I know."

Nearby, Auggie cleared his throat. James stepped away, looking ashamed. I leaned in to kiss his cheek. "Don't worry," I said. "Until we actually have something to worry about."

James jerked his head in a nod. "Auggie, what's going on?" I asked.

"We have two dead police officers in Corpus Christi and no idea where those ASD assholes responsible for the deaths are. Plus, we've had a sighting of Zoran's double in Dublin."

"They're making clones of him?" I went still. Val's hands dropped onto my shoulders, attempting to keep me calm. We didn't need more Zorans. After all, Auggie and I knew Zoran was merely Reginald Phillips in disguise.

"Auggie—what was the word on Phillips—after the attack in D.C.?"

"Madam President thought it best to report that he was in seclusion," Auggie mumbled before turning away.

"Great. So everybody still thinks he's alive. This is the worst possible news, you know. They can haul a clone out and present him as Phillips and we're in deep shit again."

"I realize that now," Auggie blew out a breath. "Madam President thought we could announce his death after a while, from a long, ravaging illness. She didn't want the people to mourn again so soon after so many others died."

I didn't want to get into the mistakes made by Madam President before and during that meeting; if I'd been allowed to attend, so many things could be different, now.

"So we have at least one clone of Zoran. Possibly more. Many more," I pointed out instead.

"Yes. I have a request from Matt, too. He wants you to work with Finch in Quebec."

"For how long? Finch is an insufferable prick, if I remember correctly."

"Dearest, I will be with you," Val spoke quietly behind me as his fingers massaged my shoulders. "He will be respectful or I will teach him manners."

"Manners and Captain Finch are polar opposites," I said. Val dropped his hands as I turned to face him. I didn't add that it wasn't fair that ass-hat Finch was still alive while Nick and Maye weren't.

"Matt, uh, asked Dr. Farrell to take Jennifer and Brett to Quebec— Shaw said they were getting restless and wanted something constructive to do. Both have training in explosives," Auggie said.

"Are they there, yet?"

"They're still in Port Aransas, but they're getting ready to board a plane."

"Tell them Val and I will take them," I said. "I think they need our presence more than anything else, right now. What about Leo?"

"He's flying to Quebec now to meet Finch's team."

"Good."

"Cori, what about you? What happened in Italy?" Auggie began.

"Auggie, I don't want to talk about that. It's upsetting."

"You know Leo won't leave it alone."

"Tell Leo we'll talk. Someday."

"Dr. Shaw may not understand the Larentii mind," Val supplied. "While Corinnelar has many human traits and habits remaining, she is still Larentii. I may ask my father to help her compartmentalize her grief and terror, in order to function at her best when needed."

"Be sure to explain that to Shaw," Auggie gruffed. "To me, Cori will always be one of us. I'm sorry if that offends you."

"It does not, although please understand that she belongs to the Larentii just as much or more than she ever belonged to any humans."

"Val, let's go get Jen and Brett," I said. "I wish I could make Farrell fly the conventional way, but I guess we'll haul him to Quebec, too."

CHAPTER 8

*C*orinne

"Rinnelar?" Jennifer looked up from her packing. She had a new, military-issue duffle, in which she was placing carefully folded and rolled clothing.

"Hey, Jen," I said. "Call me Cori. I can come out of the closet now that Rafe's not here."

"I'm sort of excited to go on assignment," she grinned. "Why is it safe to call you a different name, now that Rafe isn't here?"

"Long story," I said. I didn't say what else I was thinking—that from now on, I should probably stay away from Rafe. Every cell in my body wanted to ache and protest at the same time. I shoved down the pain of seeing and not seeing him—either way I'd come out the loser.

"Will we be briefed on the assignment?" she asked.

"I think you'll understand when you see that big hole in the ground," I replied. "Captain Finch has probably been all over the robotic delivery vehicle. Not sure if he's found anything, yet."

"Finch is sort of a legend," Jen said. "Everybody hears about him. Nobody sees him," she added.

"I've seen him and let me tell you, his reputation is put to shame by the magnitude of his insolence."

"Aww, you're spoiling the dream of my future ex-boyfriend," she laughed.

"It's good to hear you laugh," I said.

"I'm happy to be alive to laugh," she agreed. "I have weird dreams and strange thoughts now and then, but I guess that's a small price to pay for my life."

"You ready?" Brett walked in, looking as if he'd lost some sleep. Considering that he'd gone out with William and Wayne Winkler on a werewolf run during the full moon the night before, it was understandable.

"She's almost ready," I turned to Brett. "Any problems last night?"

"A few. Nothing I couldn't deal with. I don't feel uncomfortable now—like I did for the past few days."

"You have to let the wolf out," I shrugged. Yeah, I'd read plenty about werewolves in the Larentii Archives.

"I can't believe—well almost can't believe—that werewolves are real," Jen shook her head and stuffed folded socks into her duffle.

"Vampires are also real, young one," Val folded into the room. "I will arrange for accommodations while we are in Canada—the weather is unforgiving at the moment."

"What he means is there's a blizzard going on," I reassured Jen, whose eyes had widened at Val's words. "Don't worry, if Val says he's taking care of us, then we'll be taken care of."

"Thank you for your support, dearest," he flashed a grin at me. "I believe that Captain Finch is—as a human might say—freezing his ass off right now."

"Probably holed up in a tent," Brett said.

"He is. I will provide much better housing when we arrive. He may stay in a tent if he wishes after that."

"Doubt it," I muttered. Val laughed.

"From inside a warm house, the snow is incredible," Jen said. Outside, the snow was falling and blowing so hard you couldn't see more than two feet in front of you. Inside Val's Lodge, as we'd dubbed it, we were comfortable.

Even Captain Finch held his questions back after seeing all nine blue feet of Val when he transported him and his team inside.

After all, their tents had all but blown away in the blizzard. Nathan grinned and flung his arms about me when he arrived and that, I believe, also helped keep Finch at bay.

His questions would come, though, when he imagined he wouldn't be killed outright by what was surely an alien working for the government.

"We should go get Leo," I said. "He's stuck at the airport in Montreal."

"Master wolf, do you think you might keep all here in line and refraining from harming one another?" Val lifted an eyebrow in Brett's direction.

"Sure thing," Brett lifted his coffee cup in a salute.

"Very well. We will return with Dr. Shaw shortly." Val took my hand and folded space.

~

Jennifer Troutman, 1st Lt, US Army

"Master wolf, huh?" I wrinkled my nose at Brett.

"It's my commanding presence," he teased. "Besides, Finch doesn't outrank me." Brett sipped more of his coffee.

"Corinne says he's a jerk," I sighed. "I was hoping for something different."

"Heroes are seldom what we build them up to be," Brett agreed. "The real heroes, though, are the ones who are even better in person."

"I can't figure out who—or what Corinne is. Yes, I know they're Larentii, but there's something else there and you know it."

"I was thinking that she's one of those heroes who are better in person, and we hadn't even heard of her, before."

"You think she was part of the original Program—the one Dr. Shaw talks about?"

"Possibly. Shaw is slowly giving us information—trying not to scare us, I guess. I think he's waiting to tell us what happened to the original members."

"They have to be dead, or we'd have met them by now. Don't you think?" I couldn't keep the worry out of my voice.

"Jen, don't worry about that, all right?" Brett rubbed my shoulders. I had to admit to myself that his touch felt really good.

"What's going on?" Dr. Farrell interrupted our conversation.

"Just need more coffee," Brett held up his cup and walked out of the room. Dr. Farrell wore a frown as he watched Brett leave. Somehow, I always got the feeling that Dr. Farrell was waiting for something—expecting something, in fact—from me. I had yet to determine what it was.

She is mine filtered into my thoughts, causing me to gasp.

Corinne

We found Leo standing at a window, gazing out at the occasional snowflake that blew past the Montreal airport. Miles to the north, that same storm system was dumping snow on the ground at an alarming rate.

"Leo?" I said softly. After all, Val had shielded us from everyone else's sight—only Leo could see us and I didn't want his reaction at our arrival to draw attention.

"Corinne?" He beamed at me when I stepped up beside him.

"Val and I are here to take you to the location," I said.

"I hope there's more than a tent waiting—I got the official weather report a few minutes ago," he held up his cell phone.

"There is, thanks to Val. And we have coffee and food there, too," I said. "Uh, how's Rafe?"

"Depressed."

"That's not what I wanted to hear," I sighed.

"I know. I wish there were a way to fix this," Leo nodded. "Come on, let's get out of here before I'm hauled in for a psych eval for talking to myself."

～

"So. Not dead after all," Finch groused as he took a seat at the kitchen island. Val had designed this one after what was at the beach house, so there was plenty of room for everyone.

"Not dead," I poured a mug of coffee for myself. "Want some?" I held up the pot.

"Sure. That blue guy—what's he to you?"

"He's my Larentii mate," I said, turning tall and blue to drive my point home.

"Christ," Finch lowered his eyes and shook his head. "Were you this —before?"

"Yep."

"How can you—just change like that?"

"Larentii can command atoms," I shrugged. "Hell, we can command the smaller particles, too."

"That must be handy," Finch raised his eyes and looked around the kitchen. "I guess that explains our new quarters, then."

"That explains it," I nodded.

"That guy you were with last time—he still alive?"

"Yes."

"Where?"

"I'm not at liberty to say."

"Ah. Do you know whether I could beat him in a fight?"

"You would be pulped and on your way to paper if you threw a punch in his direction," I snapped. "You have no idea who you were rude to the last time we saw one another."

"Yeah. I'm beginning to see that. What about the two who came in with you? They don't recognize me for some reason."

"Long story," I said for the second time that day. "Try to be nice, okay? Jen idolizes you—as a hero. Try to hold onto that image, all right?"

113

"Wow," Finch whispered. I set his coffee on the island in front of him.

"How is this place powered?" Leo walked into the kitchen. Automatically, I poured coffee for him.

"Solar power, sent from sensor to sensor from above the atmosphere to the ground," Val appeared.

"Somebody is way, way more efficient than Earth," I smiled at Val.

"It is common in both the Reth and Campiaan Alliances," he shrugged. "Worlds that failed to harness wind, solar and water power often drained and destroyed themselves," he added. "We Larentii developed this practice before anyone else."

"The original hippies," Finch said before sipping his coffee.

"You just can't help yourself, can you?" I snapped at him.

Val didn't do anything to Finch. He did do something to Finch's coffee cup—the one he still held aloft.

Its particles separated in a flash of sparks and disappeared while Finch stared at his now-empty hand in shock.

"He can do that with your body, too," I said. "Sometimes, it doesn't take stripes on a uniform to understand who's in charge."

"Show some respect," Leo barked at Finch. Well, Leo did outrank him. I wanted to laugh. Leo seldom got his underwear in a twist, but Finch had tied it in several knots, by the look on Leo's face.

"In trouble, are we?" Brett stood in the doorway. He'd heard the conversation from a hallway away, just as any werewolf could.

"Shut it," Finch snarled and stalked out of the kitchen.

"I see why he hasn't been promoted recently," Brett shook his head. "Poor attitude."

"I think the term *poor* is understating it," I said. Brett laughed.

"Those ass-wipes have struck again," Auggie huffed into his cell.

"Where this time?" I asked.

"Cordell, Oklahoma," he said. "Walked into a shop and ended up burning it to the ground. Three dead, this time—the owner and two customers."

"Dearest, they are hitting places where Ashe employed power," Val said softly beside me. We were lying together in bed after a long and exhausting day. Auggie's call interrupted our rest.

"How are they reading that?" I asked, turning to Val.

Auggie, who hadn't heard Val's comment, demanded to know what I meant.

"Auggie, hold on," I said. "I have to ask Val something."

"They may have a spelled artifact of some sort," Val said. "One that perceives spent power and works in a way similar to that of a radiation detection device. When Ashe was young, he hadn't learned to deactivate a site or shield its detection after employing his power."

"What about us?" I was worried immediately.

"Larentii power is natural and cannot be detected by any spell or artifact," he replied. "The gods and other powerful beings must shield or disguise their signature. Most already know this. The Mighty Hand was forced into his power much too soon, before he gained adulthood. Pockets of power residue are only to be expected. It should not matter, as the gates the Elemaiya use on Earth have been closed against them. These four, as you know, used conventional means to facilitate their arrival."

I blinked at Val for several seconds, wondering how to explain all that to Colonel August Hunter. "Auggie, we have problems," I said.

West Wing—Residence

He studied her. In all their time together, she'd never suspected a thing. He missed Hal's advice, but then that hadn't been Hal. He'd only known him as Hal.

"Dear, does this dress look appropriate for the OPEC meeting?" she asked.

Yes, he was Graye Sanders, the President's husband and First Gentleman—to everyone else. He knew the truth. She certainly didn't.

It had taken careful maneuvering on his part, and on Hal's part while he still lived, to keep him away from that stupid bitch Corinne.

He'd shied away from the camera from the beginning, even telling journalists that he didn't want to distract anyone's attention away from his wife and her position at the White House. That had inadvertently been the best decision he and Hal had made.

It meant he was still operating in the shadows—there were goals to accomplish, after all. Now that Corinne was dead or at least gone—his wife hadn't indicated otherwise for more than a year—he felt it safe to come out of the shadows and implement the *Backup Plan*.

Corinne

I wished for Rafe while Val, Leo and I studied the burned ruin of a small business in Cordell, Oklahoma.

Sunset had come and gone, so emergency lights were employed as local authorities and the OSBI rummaged through the wreckage for clues. Val held a shield about us, preventing our detection while we watched.

"I'll get Auggie," I said. "He should see this."

"Shield yourself," Val instructed.

"On it, honey," I said and folded space.

Auggie didn't seem surprised to see me. Matt sat in his office, as if he were waiting for me, too. I gave him half a frown before transporting both to Cordell.

Auggie cursed when he saw the rubble. Matt's brows knitted together but he didn't say anything. "Where's Opal?" I asked.

"I sent her back to Dublin," Matt said, refusing to take his eyes off the scene. "She's attempting to track the Zoran clone, but isn't having much luck. Bekzi is guarding those left at the beach house. How's the weather in your part of Canada?"

"Not so hot," I replied.

"Hmmph." Matt refused to laugh.

"You know, maybe Brett or Mr. Winkler could help us out, here," I said. "What we need is someone who can scent where those fuckers went, unless they skipped or relocated or whatever the hell they do. I understand doing it more than once or twice a day may be too much for some of them."

"Good point," Val turned in my direction. "If they relocated here, they may be saving energy before relocating to their next target."

"I'll call Winkler," Matt pulled out his cell phone. "Want to pick him up?" he turned to me and asked.

"I'll pick him up," I agreed. After all, a Sirenali couldn't hide mundane scents. They could only conceal themselves and those about them from detection by the powerful. Unless the Elemaiya thought to shield the ground they walked on, and it was my guess they didn't have the talent, then a good tracker could follow their trail.

"I'll be back," I said and disappeared.

I almost gasped when I saw Winkler. No, he looked exactly as he had when I'd seen him before. This time, what I read in his face wasn't pretty.

Yes, I researched his background when I read the history of Le-Ath Veronis. There was a gaping hole in that history, however, according to the Larentii account of things.

Somehow, Winkler had been saved from his own suicidal plan of handing his son the Dallas Pack by forcing him to make a challenge against his own father. Sadly, there was no record of who'd actually done the saving.

It had to be someone powerful enough to pull him back from the point of death, because his son had obeyed Winkler's wishes and torn out his throat.

I'd never wanted to give someone a lecture so badly in my life as I contemplated the aging werewolf. Gray was showing at his temples and there were lines in his face that wouldn't be seen in the future.

Winkler was tired. Tired of the everyday problems that demanded his attention. Tired of seeing his contemporaries fall. Tired of living without the woman he loved. Tired of waiting for another wolf to challenge him for the Dallas Pack.

Therefore, he intended to do what his father had done before him—demand that his son take his place in the tradition of any Pack—by killing the Packmaster in a challenge.

Come the full moon in two months, Winkler intended to die.

"Does your nose still work?" I asked, ignoring the vision of a large wolf with his throat ripped apart.

"It works fine. If Lissa were here, she'd be better, but she's not here." He tossed out a hand.

Lissa. *Queen* Lissa—of Le-Ath Veronis. He had no idea. I was still working on the conundrum of who'd been there to bring Winkler back, leave a doppelgänger in his place and haul him into the future before handing him over to the Saa Thalarr.

Damn.

"Well, I'll buy the chicken-fried steak if you'll do some tracking for us," I said.

"At Don's Restaurant in Del City?"

"If that's what you want."

"I'm ready," he said, shoving his chair back and standing. Dressed in black jeans, boots and a polo, he was still handsome enough for the cover of a men's magazine. I didn't tell him that. Instead, I transported him to Cordell, where the others waited.

"Here's where the trail ends," Winkler sighed as we stood outside a local restaurant, which was now closed for the evening. Even the sign that spelled out Betsy's in green neon was dark in the window.

"You think they relocated from inside?" Matt asked.

"I can get us inside to check," I offered.

"Do it," Matt jerked his head toward the door.

It was—and wasn't—a mistake.

Captain Brett Walker

I'd learned plenty about scents in my brief association with the Dallas Packmaster. He'd told me to follow my gut, which in wolf terms meant instinct. Something about Dr. Farrell smelled off to me. I realized it when he took a barstool two down from mine—and next to Jen's.

What I didn't know how to do was confront him about it—or whether that was even wise. After all, how do you tell the man who saved your life that something doesn't feel right with him?

No, it wasn't a physical illness—as far as I could tell, he was in good health. Something whispered that it was mental or emotional, but I couldn't fathom the truth or the reason behind that notion.

Whatever it was, it made my gut churn. I didn't like it.

My wolf liked it even less. I realized I was growling softly when Dr. Farrell patted Jen's shoulder. They were human and didn't hear. For that, I was glad. I was determined to watch closely, however.

From now on.

Corinne

Dead customers were piled in a corner, with the wait staff and cooks piled atop them. If Val hadn't shielded us, we'd have been hit by the first blast leveled by one of the Dark Elemaiya.

Winkler was already wolf by the time the second blast came, which knocked out the window behind us and rattled chunks of tempered glass onto the sidewalk outside.

I cannot get a location on them—there must be a Sirenali here, Val informed me.

Matt was realizing the same thing—somewhere, at the back of this small restaurant, four Elemaiya and at least one Sirenali hid themselves from us while one leveled power blasts in our direction.

I'm getting behind them, I told Val, then folded space before he could protest. I found them in the kitchen, all facing the front where the others were—except one.

The Sirenali.

Before any of them realized I was there, I extended power and *Pulled* the Sirenali away, then folded space to the beach house in Port Aransas.

It was then, after I put my hands on him, that I realized the damage that had been done to him at a very young age.

~

Matt Michaels, Director

Joint NSA-Homeland Security Department

Something changed. Valegar and I knew it the moment it happened. Suddenly, all four Elemaiya were visible to our power searches.

Did Corinne destroy the Sirenali? I asked Val mentally as I leveled a blast of my own toward the kitchen area where the four were hiding.

Winkler, in wolf form and released from Val's shield, leapt toward the kitchen. I barely had time to throw a shield around him before he had one Elemaiya by the throat, neatly biting his head off with one vicious jerk.

Val took a more direct approach, by eliminating the wall between the kitchen and dining area, revealing the other three to us. Winkler savaged a second one while Val separated the particles of the other two.

"Where's Corinne and the Sirenali?" I asked as Winkler regained his human form. He was naked and bloody, didn't give a damn that he was and spit on the bodies of the two he'd killed.

"She's at the beach house," Val turned bright blue eyes on me. "With the Sirenali. She says if we want to kill him, we have to, in her words, go through her, first."

"Damn," I grumbled before turning to the pile of bodies in a front corner of the restaurant. There had to be at least fifteen people in that pile.

"Ah. I see I have arrived too late," Belen said as he appeared nearby.

Val held up a hand to prevent Winkler from growling at the new arrival.

~

Corinne

His name was Gerrett. He told me so in mindspeech. His own mother had cut out his tongue at age five before selling him for a very high price.

There are others like me, he said as I tended the burns that festered upon his body. Those four Elemaiyan assholes had tortured him; that was obvious.

That's not good news, I'm sorry to say, I informed him silently. He snorted his agreement.

Who are they? I thought to ask.

I have two older brothers—our mother sold all of us into slavery. She will likely do the same to any other children she births. We are a source of income for her.

Honey, I've heard of some fucked-up childhoods, but yours may be the worst, I replied. "There, all healed," I said aloud as the last of his burns disappeared, leaving pink, healthy skin behind.

I wish I could thank you in my own voice, but as you see, I can only do it this way.

That's all I need, I said.

I have heard Larentii never involved themselves in the troubles of others, he ventured.

"That's because you never met me before," I smiled at him. "When this is over, I'll try to find a safe place for you."

In my experience, there is no safe place for a mute Sirenali.

"Let me work on that, all right?"

~

Matt Michaels

"What the hell happened here?" The county sheriff walked into the restaurant, where it now looked as if someone had set off a bomb following a tornado. Paper napkins littered the floors and crushed tables; ketchup, salt and pepper was strewn in loops and strings throughout.

He hadn't even seen the pile of bodies, yet.

"Matt Michaels, Director of the Joint NSA and Homeland Security Department," I whipped out my ID.

"What the hell are you doin' here?" he gritted.

"The two in the kitchen killed those people in the corner," I jerked my head toward the pile of bodies. "We took out the two in the kitchen. Unfortunately, the owner is at the bottom of the civilian pile. The two in the kitchen are responsible for the massacre in Star Cove and for the deaths of two Corpus Christi Police Officers. My team and I were tracking them. We got here too late to save anybody—the owner, his wait staff and the customers were already dead."

"What the fuck were they doing here, then?"

"Who knows? My experts still can't figure out why they attacked Star Cove." My experts didn't know, but I did. I carefully stepped around that fact.

"They're dead, though? Dead-dead?"

"As doornails. FBI has been called to remove the bodies and hand them over to forensics." I wasn't about to tell him that there were originally four offenders, and that two had disintegrated, courtesy of an angry Larentii.

"You need anything, you let me know," the sheriff jerked his head in an abrupt nod.

"Sure thing. I appreciate the offer."

Director Keef will investigate the deaths of his agents, Valegar informed me in mindspeech.

Director Keef can kiss my ass—after he explains why he sent the four worst candidates in his employ to kill locals, I replied, my mental voice stiff with displeasure. If Keef wanted to mix it up with me, I was ready.

"Be careful not to tamper too much with the timeline," Belen warned. For a moment, I'd forgotten he was there.

"What?" I began.

"These four—they were supposed to survive," Belen informed me. "I suspect that the rift was caused by the one known as Corinnelar, as she was created and inserted into the timeline—by those meddling with souls by using the drug."

"Is there a problem with her existence?" Valegar's words sounded deadly.

"No," Belen held up a hand. "The Mighty Heart has already approved of her; therefore, my judgment is moot in the matter. I haven't met her. I wish to rectify that."

"I have to stay and clean up this mess," I said.

"I should get back," Winkler interjected. I noticed that Valegar had managed to clothe the naked werewolf and clean the blood away before the sheriff arrived.

"I will transport you," Val offered. "I wish to check on Corinne."

"I'll go with you," Belen nodded.

"Is anybody staying here to help clean up?" I complained.

"I will," Colonel Hunter offered. Leo Shaw nodded mutely in agreement.

"Great. Go out and haul those forensics people in here. Those bodies are distracting."

Both stepped over broken glass, blood and ketchup to get to the door.

Corinne

"Oh, you're back," I said the moment Val arrived with Winkler. Someone else appeared behind them. Someone I didn't recognize.

He was tall. His features swam in my gaze, he shone so brightly. I blinked to clear my vision. A smile broke across his face, like the sun on a glorious morning. When I fell, I fell slowly, buoyed by the love that washed through me.

CHAPTER 9

$\mathcal{C}$*orinne*

"I don't believe this." I rubbed my forehead.

"He doesn't wish to crowd you—or upset you," Valegar took my hand and kissed my fingers. "He says when you are ready, to call for him. He will most certainly answer."

"Where is Gerrett?"

"Entertaining himself in the kitchen. Apparently, he enjoys cooking—and eating. I believe he has devoured two large omelets and a ham steak. He is currently cooking a meal for the others, some of which he may also eat."

"They were starving him," I muttered, closing my eyes. "I could tell when I healed him."

"I believe he is more than grateful that you were his rescuer." Val was smiling when I opened my eyes again.

"How can a mother sell her children?" I asked.

"I have seen many terrible things in my time," Val sighed. "Father helped me compartmentalize them, so they did not interfere with my well-being."

"A blessing and a curse, then," I breathed.

"To some, perhaps. To an immortal, it is self-preservation."

"I see your point."

"I knew you would." He leaned in to kiss me.

"Did Winkler get home all right?" I asked when Val pulled away.

"He did."

"Awesome. Val, I need to talk to you about that."

"I do not have the ability to *Change What Was*," he said.

"You already knew what I was going to say?"

"I had a good guess," he shrugged.

"I'm supposed to have it," I grumped, turning my head away. "I don't even know where to begin."

"All in good time, my love," he said, turning my face toward him again with a gentle finger on my chin.

"But it's already too late for Nick and Maye," I said, my voice trembling. "I don't want it to be too late for Winkler, too."

"Dearest, are you sure this responsibility is yours?"

"Honey, I couldn't find the records of who was there in the Archives. That spells me—to me. I couldn't find any records of me anywhere else in the Archives, either. So I've popped into the timeline unexpectedly. Unless you have another explanation for it."

I watched as he lowered his eyes, then listened to the deep rumble of his sigh. "I cannot explain it better than that," he admitted after a moment. "Father says the same—that the timeline was changed through use of the drug—another reason to destroy that abomination."

"How soon before Norian Keef comes hunting for those responsible for the deaths of his murderous agents?" I asked.

"Not long, if Belen is correct. I do not doubt his calculations for a moment."

"Honey, I get the idea that those Lyristolyi aren't done with us yet, and the schmucks making clones? They're making it worse. All we need is a pissed-off Norian Keef lion snake to arrive and throw another wrench into the works. Who knows who will come with him? My guess is that whoever it is, they'll only make matters worse."

"The roots of this disaster are spreading, most certainly," Val agreed. "Like those of a poisonous weed."

"And that doesn't even touch on the problem with Rafe. We need him and his talents, but I'm afraid to be near him, now. It's dangerous for both of us."

"I can attempt a stronger compartmentalization, or ask Father to place it, this time."

"Honey, I don't know," I rubbed my forehead. "Besides, we should get back to Canada—Finch is probably driving everybody nuts by now."

"Do you wish to take Gerrett with us when we go?"

"Yeah. I want to make sure he's okay. Will you make sure he understands English? I've only spoken in Alliance common to him—he understands that."

"Of course. I will warn Captain Finch to steer clear of him—unless he wishes to draw your ire."

"Good plan."

"I will transport Rafe, Katya and Sergei to Canada, too, after I call Father for help."

"Great." Just the thought of seeing Rafe again made me feel nauseated and depressed.

"Dearest, do not discount the role he will play in this. He has a part, just as you do."

"I know." I felt like crying.

"Come now—go spend time with Gerrett and the others in the kitchen while I ask Father to help me with Rafe. I will send mindspeech when it is safe to join me in Canada."

"All right."

Ilya

I was used to Valegar and—her. What I wasn't prepared for was the scrutiny of Valegar's father, Nefrigar, when he arrived.

Somehow, I understood that he played an important and vital role for the Larentii, but he merely described himself as Chief Archivist for his race.

Perhaps I would learn more about what that meant, someday. For now, he studied me with bright blue eyes that held eons of knowledge and experience in their depths. "I will attempt to compartmentalize the obsession," he said. "Valegar's attempt was made in an effort to only rein in the urge it created. The obsession overwhelmed it, as you know. Therefore, I will make the containment much stronger, this time. Don't worry, you will feel no discomfort."

"I deserve discomfort," I muttered, still feeling angry with myself.

"This is not your fault—never forget that," he said, placing large, blue hands on either side of my head.

"Not her fault, either," I mumbled as Nefrigar applied more pressure.

~

Corinne

When I arrived in the kitchen, I found Bekzi acting as interpreter for Gerrett's mindspeech. They were having a lively conversation, mostly spoken in Russian, with Katya and Sergei's friends.

I could see that Bekzi had made friends with them already, and was paving the way for Gerrett to do the same.

"When we go to Canada?" Bekzi offered a grin as he switched from Russian to English.

"Uh, when Valegar announces the all-clear," I said. It became obvious that Bekzi and the others were planning to come with Gerrett and me.

"Good. He bring Rafe. That very good," Bekzi nodded. "We eat, first. You want something? Coffee? Food?"

"Coffee," I sighed. "I'm really not hungry, and I had sunlight not long ago."

"You pale," Bekzi shook his head. "Not worry. Everything work out."

You didn't see the pile of bodies in that Cordell restaurant, I sent mindspeech.

I know this. Please, not worry. Some things—can't help, he shrugged.

The others seem to think Norian Keef may come himself, since we killed his murderous, Elemaiyan agents.

Hmmph. He Grz-gitch. He try harm, he get more back. I could tell there was no love between Norian Keef and Bekzi the reptanoid. From what I knew of Norian, I didn't care much for him, either.

How soon, you think? Bekzi thought to ask.

No idea. Whenever it is, it'll be too soon.

Agree.

Ilya

"This will be the test," Nefrigar announced. Whatever he'd done, other than squeezing my head between his hands, I hadn't felt.

I froze. What would the test be?

"This," Nefrigar smiled and transformed. Before me now stood her—Corinne—as she'd been when I first met her. I blinked in astonishment at her dark hair and blue eyes.

I felt a churning in my gut, but that's all.

"Now, this." Another transformation came. This time, Corinne as she'd been after receiving the drug a second time. Blonde hair, brighter blue eyes. A smile that lit the room.

I heaved. Valegar's hands went to my head and stomach to ward off the nausea.

"Now, this." Nefrigar became Corinne the Larentii. With Valegar's hands on me, I didn't even feel ill. Whatever Nefrigar had done, it appeared to be working. If it had truly been my cabbage standing before me, I'd have thrown my arms about her and wept with joy.

Instead, I wiped moisture from my eyes with a shaking hand and nodded my gratitude to Nefrigar.

"Good," he said. "Very good. If the compartmentalization appears to weaken, let Valegar know immediately. We will perform repairs quickly."

"Will I be able to touch?" I asked. I didn't realize how shaky I was until I heard my voice tremble when I spoke.

"Under observation," Nefrigar nodded after a moment of thought. "She will be wary, now. Approach with caution."

"I know." I had to defeat the trauma in her past as well as work to eliminate her current vision of me. That could prove quite difficult. At least I could think her name, now, without going into a rage.

"I warn you now, never bring harm to her. She will be the mother of my grandchild, someday," Nefrigar said.

Yes, I'll admit that I hadn't considered that. Jealousy enveloped my mind.

"Ah. That we can remedy easily," Nefrigar said while light poured out of him. When my vision focused again, the jealousy was gone. Instead, I felt nothing.

I couldn't decide whether I should be angry or not.

"Not would be the best option," Nefrigar interpreted my expression. "If you wish to see our Corinnelar again."

"I see your point," I rubbed the back of my neck with a still-shaky hand.

"Ah. Wise man," Nefrigar smiled. "I shall go. Valegar will be available should you have need or further questions."

"Thank you," I nodded respectfully. I'd met so few in my lifetime who were deserving of respect. Nefrigar was so far outside my realm of experience, that I almost felt I should bow in his presence.

"Not necessary," he grinned and disappeared.

"Are you ready to be transported to Canada?" Valegar asked.

"As ready as I'll ever be," I said.

"Very well. I shall notify Corinne so she can meet us there."

Corinne

Your Ilya appears fine, Val sent. *Come to Canada and bring the others.*

You know they're all prepared to come, don't you?

I received mindspeech from Bekzi. He says Sergei and Katya's friends feel uncomfortable without their presence. Therefore, this is the best solution.

All right. I'm bringing everybody.

Very good. I look forward to seeing you, dearest.
Honey, I just want your arms around me, I said.
I will ensure that this happens.

Reth Alliance

Ildevar Wyyld, Founder

"They're dead. All four of them," Norian hissed.

"Have you considered that these deaths could be justified?" I asked.

"They killed my agents, after inviting them in and meeting with them." Norian was furious and only attempting to hold back his anger because he stood before me. Anyone else would feel his full wrath.

"How can you be sure that one of Earth's governments did this?"

"It was the government that refused to cooperate, and I have images of two of their top officials involved in this massacre, recorded by Invus before the vid was destroyed.

"Were there other images? Before or after?" I remained skeptical, while Norian insisted that his four were blameless in the event.

"No. Invus feared for his life, therefore the recording was made. It was a justified recording, as you now know."

"What do you want to do about this?" I asked. I didn't keep the weariness from my voice.

"I wish to send an elite team to destroy," he began.

"No," I held up a hand. "You will go yourself, and take one or two others with you that I deem trustworthy. I expect a full investigation and not a trail of revenge, you understand?"

"Yes, Deonus." His half bow was performed out of habit and not respect.

"I wish to be kept informed," I called after him as he walked away.

"Caches of nuclear weapons are located here and here," Fisk informed his team, pointing to two mountain ranges in the Middle East. Even

Morrett, the mute Sirenali, craned his neck to see the map on the table. He backed away quickly at Fisk's angry head jerk.

Morrett knew the planet was marked for destruction; Fisk merely had to find a way to do it that looked as if it were done by the inhabitants instead of a hidden Lyristolyi drug tracking team.

He wished he could warn someone, but he couldn't. With no voice and no mundane way to communicate, he couldn't inform the population of Fisk's plans.

Twice before, he'd witnessed the destruction of planets at the hands of Fisk's team. It sickened him. You didn't kill all for the sins of a few.

"Here," Fisk tossed a comp-vid in Morrett's direction. "Go read something and stay out of our way."

Morrett caught the comp-vid neatly and turned away.

Reading. It was his only escape. It made him wish he could read Earth's languages—perhaps he could read some of their paper books. There were still plenty of those. He'd found many during his travels across the planet with Fisk. Fisk refused to allow him to take any, although he had one hidden in his clothing.

It contained mostly pictures, hand-drawn and whimsical. With the images, the story almost told itself.

Morrett already loved the book.

With a sigh, he opened the internal library on the comp-vid and searched for a title he hadn't read, yet.

Corinne

Bekzi transported us to Canada—he offered and I felt too shaky to do it. A part of me wanted to see Rafe. Another part was terrified to see him.

Val waited for me in our bedroom, his arms going around me quickly. I buried my head against his shoulder while he hummed his soothing song.

It is called trilling, dearest, he said as he tucked hair behind my ear. *Come, lie down with me—you are still shaking.*

❧

Personal Record

    Lendill Schaff

"Child," my father, Kaldill Schaff, said. He seldom contacted me by mundane methods. His face appeared on my comp-vid the moment I sat up after waking.

"Father," I acknowledged, my voice stiff.

"Here." A cup of tea appeared on my bedside table. Mentally, I cursed the fact that I was half-humanoid and born without any of the gifts my father and brothers had in abundance.

It didn't help that my father was also King of the Elves—it only widened the gap between us and left me open for the insults my brothers often leveled in my direction.

"Thank you," I gritted. One should never show ingratitude toward my father. He was generous and never pointed out my flaws—at least in my presence.

"Drink—it will make what I'm about to say go down easier," he said.

I drank. The tea was hot but not too hot, just as my father commanded. I emptied half the cup before he spoke again.

Patience—it was a virtue with my father. My humanoid side dictated that I have very little of that precious commodity. "What is it, Father?" I muttered.

"Ah—Norian Keef will come to you shortly, to ask you to accompany him to the planet known as Earth. He wishes to avenge the deaths of four wayward agents. You will go with him, but you will advise caution. In all things, do not anger the Larentii."

"What the hell do the Larentii have to do with this?" I demanded.

"You will see," he said and ended the communication.

The moment the comp-vid screen went dark, it lit again. Norian was calling. I cursed softly before accepting the transmission.

~

Ilya

I expected Finch to start growling, his frown was so intense. It was obvious he didn't appreciate my presence—or Sergei's. If I thought it wouldn't start a fight, I'd ask him what the problem was.

I hadn't even seen Corinne—she'd been taken straight to the suite she shared with Valegar. Instead, I attempted to run interference between Sergei, Finch and myself. If he wanted a fight, however, I didn't intend to hold back.

Captain Walker's eyes also followed Finch wherever he went, but he watched Dr. Farrell just as intently.

Farrell's actions appeared strange to me, too, and I was at a loss to explain it. The normally calm doctor was short-tempered and restless. His eyes followed Lieutenant Troutman, much like a drowning man might follow water.

Jennifer, on the other hand, appeared uncomfortable under his gaze. Whenever Farrell came too close, she automatically moved toward Captain Walker. It didn't take much to determine why, I think. There were the beginnings of a relationship, not fully realized, and she looked to Captain Walker for protection—at least in her unconscious mind.

It made me wish for Corinne's presence so we could discuss these problems, but she was absent. I worried that she was now too afraid to be near me. Depression threatened again at the thought but I fought it down, determined not to fall into that chasm again.

Katya was pleased to be reunited with her friends, and I hoped she —and they—could reel Sergei in if Finch threatened in any way.

I considered contacting Colonel Hunter to describe the potentially volatile situation, but held off. The weather promised to clear the following day, so an outing to investigate the circumstances surrounding the explosion could serve to calm Finch down.

"Papa?" Katya placed a cup of hot coffee in my hands.

"Thank you," I gave her a smile.

"I didn't know it would feel so uncomfortable here," she whispered as she leaned her head on my shoulder.

"When Corinne comes back to us, things will be better," I soothed.

"I hope that's true," she agreed. "And I hope it happens soon."

Corinne

"Dearest, Father has sent information while you slept," Val woke me with his words and a kiss.

"What?" I mumbled, still half asleep.

"He says that present day, which is his past as you know, Norian Keef, Lendill Schaff and one other have embarked for Earth. They will arrive in three days."

"Perfect news to wake to," I sighed.

"Sarcasm?"

"You know it."

"Are you ready to face the others?"

"I suppose."

"They feel your absence," he kissed my forehead.

"I hope that's all they feel. I don't need or want murderous attacks."

"Come, I believe there is coffee if you want it."

"My hair's a mess," I complained. I'm sure Val recognized my words for what they were—a stalling tactic.

"I will take care of your appearance if you wish," he said. "Rise with me, my darling, and we will go out to the others."

I went, but I wasn't happy about it. The impending visit by Norian Keef didn't sit well, either. For me, that was the icing, which would land on the snow-covered cake in our part of Canada.

I swear I felt cold, even with Val providing a constant balloon of warm air around me. When I walked into the kitchen with Val, I could see and feel the tension gathering.

Leo was still with Auggie and Matt, so he couldn't help calm the emotional waves emanating from everybody. Poor Bekzi and Gerrett were making sandwiches and coffee for everyone while both shook their head at the state of things.

Well, fuck.

"Everybody, listen up," I announced our presence, which until then had gone unremarked. "If you can't get along, then go sit in the corner. If you can't get along and don't go to a corner, then I'll put you in one. We have bigger fish to fry than dealing with pettiness and jealousy, right now. The Director of the ASD will be here in three days, looking to avenge those ass-hats we offed in Oklahoma. We have to stand together and make sure nobody dies, okay? It's important for the future."

"What the hell would you know," Finch snarled.

I didn't have to put him in a corner—Val did it for me. He was forced to sit there, his nose in a small circle and unable to move it, for half an hour. I hoped he was a good boy after that, because Val had lost patience with him.

~

Notes—Colonel Hunter

"I have a ride back to D.C. arranged for you and Dr. Shaw," James informed me over the phone. "Matt, too, if he wants it. A jet is waiting at Tinker AFB for you."

Tinker was located in Midwest City, a suburb of Oklahoma City. It would take roughly an hour to get there from Cordell, with smooth traffic. I considered calling Corinne, then thought better of it.

The bodies of the two beheaded ASD agents had been taken away at Matt's orders; they'd be examined at a facility located south of Atlanta. The others—all locals—had already been sent to a facility in Oklahoma City. Most of them bore burns on their bodies. I wanted to curse for the hundredth time at the dead Elemaiya who'd killed innocents. Those four may as well have declared war on us the moment they arrived in the Oval Office.

I blew out a breath—Madam President was waiting to be briefed on the incident, and I wasn't looking forward to giving the information to her. The locals were already gossiping that this was a terrorist act and frankly, I couldn't say they were wrong.

"Meeting tomorrow with the President," Matt said when he ended the call on his cell phone. "You got us a ride?"

"Yeah. We just have to get to Oklahoma City, first."

"No problem; Winkler sent a car and driver," he said. "Grab Shaw and let's get on the road. Oklahoma gives me the fidgets."

~

Corinne

"You think they'll sneak out of bed and cause trouble?" I asked Val. It was late and the others had gone to bed.

"I say they will," Rafe walked in, a bottle of imported beer in his hand.

I went still. I hadn't expected him to still be up.

"Cabbage, it's all right," he held up a hand. "Keep a shield about yourself if you want—I can sense it from here. I believe Nefrigar has done more for me than I may have imagined—I only wish to touch you, now."

To tell you how much I love you. And how I've missed you, he added in mindspeech.

"I think I'll have to get used to that," I held up a hand. I could see how much my words and gesture upset him. I was upset, too, but I didn't say it.

"Shall we sit and talk," Valegar suggested.

"Yes. Please," I heaved a sigh. My legs already felt like rubber and my hands trembled. I was afraid to trust this change in Rafe. I could recall with perfect clarity the rage in his eyes when he'd come after me both times—the first immediately after the obsession was placed, and then at the villa in Italy.

I was terrified to trust Rafe again, even though a powerful Larentii thought him to be safe. We sat on sofas divided by a large table, facing one another. Val sat beside me and took my hand.

"You must understand that she loves you—it is merely difficult for her to disassociate the obsession-afflicted man from the one she trusted before," Val told Rafe.

"I can see how that could happen," Rafe lowered his eyes and stared at the beer bottle in his hand for a moment. "I also understand how her past plays a part in this—although I was hoping for a permanent cure for her PTSD."

"We are learning, just as you are," Val said. "We have never had a Larentii join our ranks after surviving the drug. Every day brings something new, including the fact that her past lives are bleeding into her current one."

"Yes. At times, I experience the same." Rafe dropped his American-sounding accent for his native one. Ilya was now present. He sounded bitter.

I understood that perfectly. It made me want to cry.

He'd lost a wife and a son.

I'd lost a husband and a son.

He now bore an obsession to kill me if he could. I didn't trust what had been done to hold the obsession at bay. I couldn't trust him, either.

Not anymore. This wasn't the Ilya I'd known. This one was afflicted with a disease no Larentii could cure. They could only provide a temporary fix that could weaken or disintegrate with no notice.

Yes, my PTSD was in the driver's seat and I couldn't muster enough logic to defeat it. I felt horrible for the pain Ilya was experiencing.

I felt horrible from the pain in me, too.

I had no ready answer for either of those things.

"I don't know what to do," I wept.

"Shhh, Ilya's here," he crooned. I had no idea how he'd reached my side so quickly.

"Breathe slowly, dearest," Val soothed. "I will allow no harm to come to you."

I felt as if I were drowning—in both fear and desire. The desire came from Val—I recognized it from before. Perhaps he was attempting to forge better memories between Ilya and me. Perhaps I would be angry with him about that.

Later.

Ilya kissed me. A kiss I remembered. One that told me I was more important than anything else to him. Valegar transported us to the bed in our suite.

I will never forget my first experience with energy sex. It was achieved during normal coitus, giving Ilya and me a pleasure we'd never experienced before while I wept with joy at the loving touch of his hands and body.

Opal

I poured more Scotch in my glass and swallowed half of it before turning my gaze on Matt. We were in his office and it was late at night.

Something was up—we both felt it.

"Look, I know you disagree with the way I'm handling things," he said, waving his empty glass at me.

"You're not handling much at all," I pointed out. "You're standing back and letting Corinne do it, for the most part."

"We have limitations on interference," Matt reminded me.

"But this—what's happening now—wasn't exactly in the game plan. You know we can interfere all we want if rogue gods are involved."

"I don't think a rogue would come within a hundred light-years of this place," he replied. "We have absolutely no proof of that. Besides, I have to keep my job, and if I go too far off the reservation—sorry, that was the wrong word to use—anyway, I have to keep my job, at least for a while longer, even if it involves disguising myself and taking on another name."

"I disagree—you need to involve yourself now, before everything goes to hell," I retorted. "Cori doesn't need to carry this load by herself."

"Well, you're not in charge, here," he hissed. "So back off. I'll let you know if we need to up our game."

"Right," I said, just as his cell phone rang.

Notes—Colonel Hunter

I was asleep when the call came. Laci lay beside me, her breathing soft and even. The vibration of my cell phone didn't disturb her sleep as it did mine.

Rolling off the bed, I stalked into the bathroom and shut the door before answering. Only an emergency would interrupt my sleep like this.

"What is it?" I barked without looking to see which White House staffer generated the call.

"Madam President is dead," the voice informed me. "Of an apparent heart attack."

CHAPTER 10

*C*orinne

I wasn't aware of anything until I woke. I understood then why Larentii always had others stand guard during and after energy sex, whenever they were away from their homeworld. It took the term mind-blowing and lifted it to the fiftieth power, at the very least.

If Ilya had been human, it would have torn him apart, the force was so great. Most Larentii arranged to have humanoids shielded if they were included in the backwash of pleasure.

Ilya got the full force of it and managed to survive.

I imagine his shield kicked in at an appropriate moment.

"Dearest, wake, there is news," Val whispered against my ear.

I only wanted to sleep longer, or be transported into sunlight and sleep longer.

"Whuh?" I asked.

"The President is dead," he informed me. "I fear it is not from natural causes, as others are currently reporting."

"Fuck." I was awake and standing beside the bed in a blink while Ilya disentangled himself from the sheets.

"What is it?" he asked.

"Madam President is dead. I need sunlight, coffee and a trip to the White House, because I intend to get to the bottom of this."

                          ~

We ended up in Auggie's office with James while we waited for Auggie and Matt to arrive after their meeting at the White House. The Vice President had already been sworn in; I was grateful for that bit of news, at least.

As the former Secretary of State, I knew he was a decent, fair-minded human being—as long as the enemy wasn't planning to pay him a visit. He suffered from an undiagnosed case of PTSD, and wasn't getting treatment for it. I worried that something small could set him off and then we'd all be in trouble.

As for Madam President's death, it smelled of betrayal and assassination to me, and I wanted to see everybody who'd had contact with her in the past two days.

I'd read in their faces what they weren't willing to tell anyone—whether they were involved in this debacle.

"Cabbage, you look as if you're a pressure cooker turned too high," Ilya cautioned as he patted my hand.

"I know," I mumbled. "I can't help it. I'm so mad I could blow something apart."

"Dearest," Val warned.

"Yeah."

"Thank God you're here." Auggie looked gray as he stalked into his office, James and Matt right behind him. "Look, I need your talents, Cori, and I need them fast. I also need to keep you disguised, if possible. We don't want to alert any enemies to your presence, unless I miss my guess."

"I can handle that," I began.

"No, I need you to look like a regular staffer," he said. "James, show her the photograph."

James handed a tablet to me, where a young woman in a

photograph smiled at me—it was the picture used for her White House Staff identification.

"Your name will be Laura Quimby, assistant to the current Chief of Staff," Auggie said. "You'll say you were called back from vacation by your boss, who's already been informed and sworn to secrecy," he added.

"But what about," I pointed at Val and Ilya.

"Oh, they'll come too—as bodyguards for Matt and me. James has more photographs for them. You'll have a better excuse for getting in and out of sensitive areas."

"I see. I really want to take a look at anybody who had dealings with Madam President in the past two days," I said.

"We'll do our best to accommodate that request," Matt said. "Most are scheduled for questioning by the Secret Service, at President Granville's request. You'll help herd them to and from their appointments. It's disguised as a debriefing, sort of, to record and compile Madam President's final hours in office."

"Do you know how sad and fucked up that sounds?" I rounded on Matt.

"Yeah. I do. Not my fault," he held up his hands.

"All right," I offered a curt nod in apology.

"Come on—get your disguises together. Cori, will you help with Rafe's?"

"I will see to it," Val offered.

"Good. Cori, James will drop you off at the employee entrance. Make sure your badge has the proper barcode and chip. The Chief of Staff will be waiting for you in his office. I assume you recall where that is?" Auggie asked.

"I do."

"Perfect. Let's get on this, people. I want to know what happened, who's behind it and what we should be doing about it. Now."

~

"How's Nathan?" James asked as we drove through crowded D.C. streets.

"He's fine. Finch is being an asshole as usual, but he should be minding his manners unless he wants Val to put him in a corner again."

"What?" James jerked his eyes off the road for half a second before turning back to his driving.

"Just what I said. I'm sure he's still pissed about it, too, but if he knows what's good for him," I shrugged.

"I don't believe this," James muttered before a chuckle escaped. "I hope Nathan got pictures."

"Val can probably pull up an image for you, if he didn't," I said.

"What do you think happened? To the President?" James turned to a more serious topic.

"I don't know, but I doubt poor health played into it. Last time I saw her in the Oval Office, she was in very good health. If I don't find anything at the White House today, I may ask Auggie to let me see her body."

"This whole thing is so frustrating," James said. "I voted for her, you know. Sure, she did some things I disagreed with, but that happens no matter who it is."

"All that time Zoran was trying to kill her and take over, and this happens now," I said.

"At least he's dead," James gripped the steering wheel tighter.

"Yeah, but we have no idea whether he has clones running around or not. We've had a Zoran sighting in Dublin—don't forget that. Plus, the American people still think Phillips is alive. Madam President never announced his death to the public."

"You had to scare me worse than I was already," he grumped.

"We'll get through this," I patted his shoulder. "At least I hope we will."

"Right."

"You think this outfit is all right?" I asked.

"You look perky," he grinned.

"Great. Perky. Not one of my usual attributes."

"No, it fits her character. She's the youngest of three girls. I looked through a lot of photographs of her, and that's exactly how she is."

"I hate doing bubbly," I sighed. "I'm the sarcastic, older sister type."

"I disagree," he said. "And, I haven't had my reading fix in a long time," he complained.

"Honey, I don't know when or if I'll ever get back to writing again."

"Dang."

"Did you say dang? I haven't heard that in a possum's age."

"Stop with the hillbilly," he grinned.

"You started it."

"Okay, you're right. Here we are," he drove up to the employee entrance. "Have your badge ready—that's Secret Service there at the door, waiting to check everybody."

"Will do, boss," I quipped.

"I get you all to myself for a talk, and it had to be on the day the President died," he said as I opened the door.

"Honey, we'll get to the bottom of this," I promised.

"I sure hope so. I'll be here to pick you up later; just let me know when."

I nodded, straightened my perky outfit, shut the car door and walked toward the frowning Secret Service agent at the employee entrance.

That morning, I saw twenty faces in detail before lunchtime. None of them had anything to do with Madam President's death.

"Laura, we have a lunch appointment with the President," the Chief of Staff, Kyle Lakin, informed me when the line of interviewees dissipated.

I found myself scrambling to get used to the name and title assigned to me.

"Yes, sir," I nodded and rose to follow him to the Oval Office.

"Anything?" the former Vice President asked when Kyle and I stood before his desk.

"No sir. Nothing yet," I reported.

"Damn." He cursed and stood to pace behind the President's desk. "I trust you'd let someone know if I or anyone you come across has been compromised?" He turned back to ask.

"Yes, sir."

"Good. Make sure it stays that way."

"Sir, I'd like to meet everyone assigned to guard you, and everyone you're scheduled to have contact with in the days to come," I said.

"You're that good?" The Chief of Staff asked.

"She's that good," President Jonathan Granville stated. "She's the reason the PM of Great Britain and I survived the attempt on our lives in London."

"Thank you, sir. One more thing, if I may," I said.

"Of course," he inclined his head and sat down again.

"I'd like to review your choices for Vice President. Just as a precaution," I said.

"I think I'll allow that," he agreed.

"How was your day?" James asked when he picked me up at eight that evening.

"Long. I need sunlight," I said. Auggie, Rafe, Matt and Val were in meetings with the President all afternoon, but I didn't see them. I only heard from Val in mindspeech. He probably needed sunlight, too.

"I'm taking you to the ugly building in Arlington," James said. "Colonel Hunter says President Granville wants you at the White House every day until further notice. The real Laura Quimby's vacation has been extended in Scotland."

"She's on board with all this?"

"I believe Matt told her it's a matter of National Security. She's been to the American Embassy there, where a new passport with an alias has been provided for her, and all her vacation expenses have been comped. All she has to do is keep quiet that she's really someone else."

"Poor girl," I sighed. "Can't even use her real name because a Larentii borrowed it. And, on top of everything else, Mr. Snaky Pants Norian Keef will be here in two days."

"Snaky Pants?"

"He keeps his alter ego hidden, but he's a lion snake shapeshifter. He's sort of an asshole, too, but don't tell him I said that. I'll tell him myself."

"You think I'll end up meeting this guy?" James sounded worried as he turned a corner.

"Nothing would surprise me at this point. What we have to do is get to him before he can cause trouble and show him exactly what his shiny agents did while they were here. All of which resulted in their deaths."

"Do Larentii do this sort of thing all the time?"

"No, honey. Larentii have a four-word standard they all live by. *Stay. Out. Of. It.* They don't interfere as a rule unless they are threatened in some way, or their mate is threatened. Somehow, I've been given special permission to be here, and Val was allowed to come with me."

"Wow. What's the Larentii homeworld like, then?"

"Imagine an Earth with no industry, no shopping, no streets or roads—just wild, with tree-covered mountains and wide, open meadows where falaca graze. The houses they build, well, think of the marble buildings in Rome, with most of the roof open to the sky. They don't need kitchens or bathrooms, so anything in their home is purely for other comforts."

"Television?"

"None. Their version of television is folding space to another world and watching real people. Most of the time, those people don't even know they're there. I wish you could read some of their histories in the Archives—they're written from a neutral standpoint, because there's nothing for the Larentii to gain by slanting the story in one direction or another."

"That's incredible," James breathed. "Wow." He shook his head at the thought of it.

"Val's father is Chief Archivist there. It's scary what he knows and has seen. Val is one of his four sons, all of whom are Assistant Archivists."

"Where do you think you'll go for sunlight?" James asked as we pulled up to a stoplight.

"I don't know. Val likes Hawaii."

"Can I go?" he asked wistfully.

"You know, Nathan probably needs a break, too," I said. "Why don't we take both of you?"

"We just decided—we want our wedding here," James floated by in the pool fed by Val's favorite waterfall. He and Nathan were both naked and swimming—or in James' case, floating, while Val and I soaked up sunlight. At Val's insistence, we were both naked and our full, blue selves.

"Hawaii is beautiful," Val agreed. "Of course you should marry where you feel happy and at peace."

"That's as good an excuse as anything we could come up with," Nathan stopped swimming for a moment to tread water and talk.

"I'll make sure it's paid for," I said.

"I still have money in that account you opened for me," James said. "We decided to use that for the wedding."

"Then we're good." I leaned against Val's chest and closed my eyes with a sigh.

"Holy shit," James breathed.

I opened my eyes to see what had happened.

In this case, it was what had arrived.

"I am a who," Kalenegar, Head of the Larentii Council, declared. Ridding himself of his clothing with a thought, he sat beside Val and me. "Continue frolicking," he waved a hand at James and Nathan. "Have sex if you want. Larentii are surprised by nothing."

I clapped a hand over my mouth—it wasn't polite to guffaw. At least I didn't think it was.

"Lean back, close your eyes and rest," Valegar said, pulling me closer. "Kalenegar is here to feed with us."

I opened my eyes again. "You know there are some politicians," I said to Kalenegar, "who think that sharing our sunbeam here will deplete the amount of sunlight available for all of us."

Kal studied me for a moment before his eyes lit with humor and he smiled. "Tell that to the plants," he chuckled and turned his face toward the light.

"His cock is huge," I heard Nathan whisper to James.

I collapsed against Val, laughing.

Ilya

"Cabbage?" I found her sitting in the kitchen at the ugly building in Arlington. It was obvious that wherever she'd gone with Valegar, she'd taken James and Nathan with her. Both sat beside her at the island while eating soup and sandwiches from a nearby deli.

"We have some for you, too," she turned and gave me a smile.

"We went to Hawaii," James explained. "I feel so relaxed, now."

"Roast-beef?" I asked, heading for the white paper bags stacked on one end of the island.

"I got two for you," she said. "Plus au jus if you want to dip."

"That sounds wonderful." I opened bags to find dinner. "Do we have anything to drink?"

"Depends on what you want," she said.

"I'll take whatever you have."

"I'll have some, too," Leo Shaw walked into the kitchen. "Everybody here, now?"

"We're all here. I should take Nathan back to Canada later, but that can wait," Corinne said. "You need something?"

"I'll go back to Canada with Nathan, then," Leo said. "I hear things may be a bit strained, there."

"If Finch would stop being an ass," James said.

"Leo, you need to watch Dr. Farrell," Corinne suggested. "I think he's having issues, since he's only now learning that Jen isn't Maye."

"That concerns me," he said. "In fact, it was a call from him that turned my attention back to Canada."

"I'll take you. Call if you need me afterward, too," she offered. "I don't want him stalking Jen or giving anyone she's interested in a hard time."

"Understood. Did you learn anything at the White House, today?"

"Nothing significant," she shrugged.

Taking my sandwich and au jus from a bag, I took the barstool next to Corinne. "Did you decide what you wanted to drink?" she asked while Dr. Shaw rummaged through the bags for a sandwich.

"How about Macallan?" I asked.

"Thirty year," she held out a hand and a bottle appeared there. "Glass with ice," she said as those items appeared in her other hand.

"I love you," I said while opening the bottle.

"Just as long as it's you," she sighed. I understood exactly what she meant. The other me—the obsessed me—terrified her. I sipped excellent Scotch before turning back to her. "Here," I turned her head toward me with a finger and leaned in for a kiss.

"Mmm, Macallan," she whispered as she tasted it on my lips. "My favorite."

Corinne

My second day as a White House staffer was much like the first. Nobody I saw knew anything. Yes, Val and I had already employed our *Looking* skills, with no results. Whatever had happened was successfully blocked by Sirenali involvement.

Some employees, these closer to Madam President than those the day before, wept as they answered interviewers' questions. I heard through rumors and by reading it in some employees' gazes that Graye Sanders was packing to move out of the residence.

His personal staff would be leaving with him. I made a mental note to ask President Granville for a moment with them before they left.

Meanwhile, Norian Keef's scheduled arrival the following day weighed on my mind. I worried that he'd walk in with guns blazing, or slither in with fangs dripping and things would go south in a hurry.

In addition to that, I had an unnamed worry that aggravated my senses and wasn't identifiable in any sense. Forcing my thoughts away from that sense of dread, I focused on the line of people waiting to be interviewed.

∽

"Did you know about this?" The Chief of Staff and I were having another lunch meeting with President Granville. We watched the noon news program while they had sandwiches.

There, on the screen, was the last thing I expected to see.

The perfect image of former President Phillips spoke with a well-known and respected news anchor. "Yes, I've issued the invitation to Graye Sanders to stay at my home in Virginia," the Phillips clone announced. "I spoke to him this morning, and he's considering my invitation—for after the funeral, you understand."

"Have you spoken with President Granville?"

"I've left messages for him, but I'm sure he's rather busy at the moment. Taking the reins of the finest country in the world is a heavy burden, especially when it lands on your shoulders so abruptly."

"He hasn't left me a goddamn thing," Granville growled.

"He was always good at spouting fiction," I said. "And this is his clone, in case you hadn't guessed already."

"I know the original is dead," Granville nodded. "What I can't figure out is how they got him to look like his former self."

"Surgery can be an amazing thing," I sighed. "Because that's exactly what has happened, here. You need to warn Graye Sanders that he needs to reject the invitation."

"I'll do that tonight," the President said. "I have a full schedule this afternoon. Kyle, make sure to send word to Graye."

"I'll see to it," the Chief of Staff agreed.

"Cori," the President turned to me. "What do you think they're doing?"

"Trying to get back in the White House, if my guess is correct," I said. "And then he may set his sights on world domination again."

"I hate this," Granville shook his head at the screen.

~

As it turned out, Graye Sanders didn't wait for a visit from President Granville. He and two staffers left in a limo that afternoon, with packed bags.

Word came to Granville through others that Graye would be staying at Phillips' estate in Virginia until after Amelia Sanders' funeral, scheduled for the following week.

Auggie, Matt, Rafe, Val and I fit ourselves into the meeting time Granville originally scheduled with Graye Sanders.

"The media is fascinated by the fact that the opposing party is now extending its hand to Amelia Sanders' husband," the President huffed.

"Sir," Kyle Lakin poured two fingers of bourbon in a glass and handed it to Granville while we sat in the Oval Office. Granville nodded his thanks and drank it in two swallows.

"What do you think?" He turned to the rest of us, then.

"The law states that Phillips can't run for the White House again," Matt began.

"But it doesn't keep him from bucking for the VP position," Auggie pointed out. "I'm waiting for somebody to suggest just that."

"That means they'll need my cooperation," Granville countered.

"Which will be easy if they get one of their schmucks to place an obsession," I said.

"You know what will happen if we attempt to call them out on this —in public or private," Matt agreed. "It'll sound like bad blood and sour grapes between parties, at a time when everybody is harping that we need to stand together."

"I'm sorry Amelia didn't announce his death when he actually died," Granville said. "We're stuck in the middle of a mess we made for ourselves."

"It would have taken some creative explaining," Matt nodded. "He wasn't slated to be here. The Secret Service records indicate he was abroad at the time."

"Where are those Secret Service agents now?" I asked. "I'm sure they're either dead or obsessed, wherever they are."

"They're with the new and unimproved Phillips," the Chief of Staff said. "I checked on that earlier."

"So they've likely been programmed to report that all is well in Phillipsland?" Auggie asked.

"Yep. The Director confirmed that this afternoon."

"No," I said, holding up a hand. "Has anyone laid eyes on them? Since the real Phillips and the real Hal Prentice died?"

"No," Kyle breathed.

"Fuck." I rose and pinched the bridge of my nose. "They may look like the original agents, now, but there's a really good chance they're replacements and all on board with the new agenda."

Dearest? Val sent.

Cabbage? Ilya's sending was right behind Val's.

"Wherever and whoever they are, they're obsessed—I can almost guarantee it," I said as Val rose to stand with me. "Phillips—and his clone—are Sirenali. Why wouldn't he obsess his employees?"

"Dear God, we're stuck in the middle of a bad sci-fi movie," President Granville moaned.

"Honey, we've been there for a while," I turned toward him and shook my head. While it may not have been proper to address POTUS as honey, he didn't seem offended. What I did see in him was this—he was terrified now to meet with anyone or go anywhere without me. While I couldn't blame him, it would put a crimp in my plans.

We have Norian scheduled to show up tomorrow, I sent to Val, Auggie and Matt. *The President wants to add me to his staff,* I added. *Like immediately.*

It would be better if you provided protective services, rather than clerical, Val offered. *I may have a solution too, for additional security.*

I blinked at him—he knew something I didn't. *I have to get permission, first,* he said. *I am contacting Father now. Perhaps you should contact Belen—he will have a say in this, too.*

Why? I began before it hit me.

Belen was the ultimate supervisor for the Saa Thalarr. Whatever he said went, as far as they were concerned. If the future Belen contacted the future Saa Thalarr, that would make it even better.

After all, some of them were currently making their homes on Earth, in the here and now.

Val wasn't wrong—we probably needed help wrangling Norian and his team, as well as keeping President Granville safe—if we wanted to preserve the timeline as much as we could.

"We will have more security solutions for you shortly," Val announced. "I can arrange to have both you and your Chief of Staff shielded from harm, and provide some talented bodyguards."

"Are these bodyguards to be trusted?" Kyle Lakin asked.

"You will never be guarded by better or more trustworthy," Valegar replied. "Father is arranging it now."

"We're here," someone announced. I blinked as I studied the ones who'd come.

Justin Griffin, Mack Walters, Drake and Drew Tatsuya, Gavin Montegue and Anthony Hancock crowded into the Oval Office.

"What the hell?" Granville recognized Hancock.

"I graduated," Tony grinned. "From Earth."

"I want to add one more," I said.

"I know the one you want," Val nodded. William Winkler—the one from the future—also appeared.

I had a plan, now, as far as the current Winkler was concerned. I just needed some time to put it together and make it come out right. "We can only do guard duty," Tony Hancock explained. "We're not allowed to do more than that. We can only stay as long as we're needed, or if we're ordered to leave by you, Mr. President," Tony nodded to Granville.

"Good enough—for now," Granville agreed.

～

It took some doing—and several hours, to manipulate the Secret Service records and the minds of other agents to accept the new arrivals.

Val showed me how to accomplish all those things. None of those who'd arrived would be susceptible to any obsession. *Who are these people?* Rafe silently begged for an answer.

"Saa Thalarr," Winkler answered Rafe's unspoken question. "Don't worry, you are in the best hands possible."

"Saa Thalarr?" Rafe asked.

"Ah. I'll let Corinnelar explain that to you—or Val. You must understand that our very existence protects itself—you will be unable to speak of me or any of the others without permission."

"That's not frightening," Rafe mumbled.

"Very true," Tony Hancock smiled.

CHAPTER 11

*C*orinne

"Mack, Winkler and Justin took the first shift," I told Auggie. He, Matt, Val, Rafe and I sat in the kitchen at the ugly building in Arlington. It was late and we were still working out the protection plan.

"I'm still trying to figure out how Mr. Winkler is from the future and in Texas at the same time," Auggie yawned.

"Auggie, stop worrying about that. The President is having enough trouble coming to terms with the fact that Tony Hancock isn't dead. He, Gavin and the Falchani Twins will work the day shift tomorrow," I added.

"Maybe we should leave you in your current disguise, then," Matt suggested.

"Perhaps," Val nodded reluctantly. "It will allow her access to most meetings and such."

"And there I thought I could give up the perky outfits," I grumped.

"We have shields added to Valegar's on the building," the Falchani twins walked into the kitchen. "Any chance of a late dinner?"

"What would you like?" I asked.

"Fish?"

"Be right back," I said and folded space.

"This is very good," Ilya said. I'd gone to Paris to get something everybody would like, bringing back turbot aux beurre blanc, salad and cheeses. I added a good white wine to the mix and all humanoids were enjoying their dinner.

"Norian Keef just landed on the planet," Drew looked up from his fish to announce.

"Great. I was thinking daytime," I grumbled. "Not ten minutes after midnight."

"My love, would you like to accompany me?" Val asked. "We will greet Mr. Keef as our true selves."

"Awesome," I said. Val took my hand and we folded space.

Personal Record

Lendill Schaff

Norian looked annoyed when the two Larentii appeared in front of us. I, on the other hand, was outright terrified.

Father had warned me. Norian probably didn't realize how much trouble he could be in if he didn't mind his manners.

"Mr. Keef," the female Larentii began.

I blinked first because she was female. I blinked again when she frowned at Norian. "I see everything you have planned, you stupid, snake-assed excuse for an ASD Director," she snapped. "I warn you now, either listen to what I have to say or I send you right back where you came from—without the ability to bite anybody."

Ilya

One of Corinne's captives looked as if he were about to explode. The other had a confused expression on his face.

"I have ensured that they can speak and understand English," Val said, following behind as if he were herding both men.

"Well, what do we have here?" Colonel Hunter asked. "Want coffee or something stronger? I warn you, you won't get away from Cori. Not when she's like this."

"Who are you?" the second man asked. The first was turning purple with anger.

"I'm commonly known as Colonel August Hunter, Secretary of Defense," he introduced himself. "I have other titles, but those aren't as widely known."

"I'm Lendill Schaff, Vice Director of the Alliance Security Detail," he said. "I understand it is proper to extend a hand to you?"

"As long as you're not armed," Colonel Hunter held out a hand and clasped the one the Vice Director extended.

"I am not—the Larentii, here, made sure of that," he said.

"Please, sit," Colonel Hunter invited. "If you're hungry or thirsty, we will provide something. We must talk about those four agents who were sent, and how many murders they committed while engaging in a secret agenda I assume was never sanctioned by your agency."

"They committed murders?" Schaff asked while taking a seat at the island.

"They murdered twenty-two, including children, in a small town in the state of Texas, then two police officers in a nearby city before traveling to the state of Oklahoma and murdering everyone they found in a restaurant, there. Val and Cori will have to give you the particulars on their secret agenda; I'm still attempting to understand it myself."

"They had no secret agenda," the first man exploded.

"Shut up and sit down," Corinne snapped at him. When he refused to move, he found himself floating through the air before being dumped onto a barstool. When he attempted to slide off the stool, he was held there with power.

"Now," Corinne shook herself, as if dealing with the first man gave her the shivers, "Have either of you heard of the Elemaiya, and what happened to them?"

"My father said the race as a whole was beginning their descent, but I didn't know what he meant," Schaff said.

"Then you are the one we wish to speak with," Val nodded. "I know who your father is. He is most wise, I assure you. Those four sent by Director Keef, here," he jerked his head toward the other man, "were all half Elemaiya. They were sent on an alternative mission. Did you ever ask yourself how they came to know some of Earth's languages? It's because they were here before, when the gates were still open to them. More than three decades ago, the Bright Queen and the Dark King chose this world as their final battlefield. The one who prevented them from destroying Earth took their crowns so they couldn't do the same thing to any other worlds. The four agents sent by Director Keef were searching for those crowns, in an effort to get them back. They traced pockets of power left behind by the one who took the crowns and banished the Elemaiya from this world. Wherever they found the traces of power, they killed innocent inhabitants in an effort to obtain information those inhabitants did not possess. Is any of this getting through to you?" Val asked.

"You mean to tell me that they didn't search for drug survivors or remaining drug dust?" Director Keef hissed.

"They did not," Val stated flatly. "I hope you know that a Larentii does not lie—there is no reason for us to do so. I can recreate images of the carnage your four agents left behind if you wish to see it, or bend time and fold space to allow you to witness actual events, although I warn you that the images of dead children upsets Corinne a great deal."

"At least one of your agents had the talent for power blasts," Corinne leveled her gaze on Director Keef. "He burned that small town in Texas. Some of those babies were sleeping when they died. Maybe next time, you'll be more careful when you hire somebody."

"What do you expect me to do about it?" Director Keef hissed.

"Unless you can bring back the dead, maybe you ought to climb back on your spaceship and get the hell away from here," Corinne snapped.

"We should give a full report to the Founder," Schaff suggested. "That means examining the sites, recording images and gathering evidence before we go. We should also collect the bodies of our agents, to return them to the Alliance."

"You'll only get two of them," Colonel Hunter said. "Valegar separated the particles of two. Those bodies no longer exist."

"A Larentii felt it necessary to separate particles?" Schaff asked, his voice expressing wonder. "Norian, they must have attacked a Larentii."

"They were leveling power blasts at my Corinnelar," Val agreed stiffly. "I am allowed to protect my mate."

"May the stars never fail us," Schaff muttered. "I'll pass that along to my father."

"So the Larentii are responsible for the deaths of two of my agents?" Norian huffed.

"Yes," Val nodded. "If your Founder, Ildevar Wyyld, wishes to question a Larentii," he began.

"Norian," Schaff warned, placing a hand on Keef's arm.

"Who killed the other two?" Keef demanded.

"A werewolf, whom I refuse to identify," Corinne said. "Without his help, those fuck-ups you called agents would have killed more people, looking for crowns that are no longer on this planet."

"Then where are they?" Keef asked.

"With the Mighty Hand," Valegar replied. Keef snorted his disbelief. Schaff went completely still.

"You know what he's saying, don't you?" I spoke for the first time. Schaff had gone pale at Valegar's words.

"The Three are waking?" he shuddered.

"Hmmph," Valegar snorted.

"What in the name of the eternal light is he talking about?" Keef turned to his second-in-command.

"The god wars," Lendill muttered and dropped his gaze. "I can't say more than that. All I can say is that I need to have a long talk with my father when I get back."

"I thought you didn't get along with your father."

"I don't get along with my brothers."

"I see." Keef clearly didn't.

"Who the fuck are you?" Keef rounded on me, now, since I'd spoken to Schaff.

"That is a Karathian warlock, whose power hasn't been wakened," another man arrived in the same manner that Val and Corinne could travel.

"Father, we're handling things," Schaff muttered.

"And fucking them up quite well, I might add," the new arrival announced.

~

Corinne

Lendill Schaff had no clue.

None.

His father from the future had arrived to defuse the situation. Lendill thought it his father from the present. Kaldill Schaff tossed a glance in my direction. I understood much from that swift contact.

None of this was supposed to happen, yet here we were, having a discussion that should never have taken place.

I knew the drug was to blame for every bit of it. I began to understand better why it was death on other worlds to have or use it.

I understood something else from Kaldill Schaff, too.

Sometime in the future, the drug would be found again. I shivered at the thought.

I'm here now, because we may need you in the future, Kaldill sent mindspeech. *In all the history of the drug, you are the only bright spot in it.*

~

That night turned out to be a very long one. Val and I—or mostly Val —bent time and folded space with Norian Keef, Lendill Schaff and Lendill's father, Kaldill. We were silent, invisible witnesses to the destruction caused by four half-Elemaiyan ASD agents who had a secret agenda.

Norian recorded every murder they committed on his handheld, while Lendill looked away in disgust and Kaldill silently blessed the spirits of the dead. When we ended up at the small restaurant in Cordell where the four Elemaiya died, Norian asked the question I knew was coming.

"He's with me," I said, meaning Gerrett. "If you think to take him, then you should think again."

"You will leave him where he is," Kaldill decreed. I watched as a blank look washed over Norian's features before he nodded.

The King of the Elves had spoken.

~

"Child, I think you should stay to help," Kaldill said to Lendill when we arrived at the ugly building in Arlington. Val had bent time again to bring us back just after we'd left.

"What about me?" Norian sniffed.

"You may do whatever you like, although your expertise would be useful," Kaldill leveled his gaze upon Norian. "Much is happening here. It will serve as good training for what you may face in the future."

"Can you expand on that?" Norian asked. He was learning respect —or at least offering it grudgingly.

"Not at this time. I believe that offering your services to the new President of this country will not go amiss. Especially since your agents did such damage on your watch while you ignored them."

It's not exactly his forte to take responsibility like that, I sent to Kaldill.

"How, exactly, could I help him? I have little knowledge of this world," Norian said.

"I can show you an empty facility in Nevada, where rogue Lyristolyi wrote *fuck Earth* on the ceiling while they were clearing it out three months ago," I said.

Norian went still. "Yes," he nodded after a moment. "Lendill and I should definitely stay."

~

"You said the magic words," Kaldill beamed at me before kissing me on both cheeks. "The Lyristolyi have been on Norian's list for a while. He knows they're up to something, he just hasn't found sufficient evidence, yet. He will do anything to prove their guilt."

"They hide behind Sirenali," Valegar said. "But we have learned that a mundane investigation may work much better than one fueled by power."

"Then perhaps they need assistance from more mundane sources here," Kaldill suggested. "I must go—many things require my attention. I hope to see both of you in the future."

"I hope so, too," I nodded. "I'm glad we met."

"If all goes well, we will do so again," Kaldill raised a hand. "Peace and joy to you," he said and disappeared.

"Sun and sleep," Val said. "Immediately."

"I'm all over that," I yawned.

I discovered later that Val bent time once again, to ensure that I had enough sleep before going back to work at the White House the following day.

I had coffee and a doughnut with James and Auggie before James drove me in. Auggie intended to bring Norian and Lendill up to date on what we knew about the Lyristolyi, but most of it revolved around the attack more than a year earlier and their suspected presence at the Nevada facility.

I didn't have time to worry about them—I had more work to do and was worried enough about Graye Sanders' situation with a fake former president. At least Graye and Amelia Sanders were childless—I'd be more worried if kids were involved.

"You're being reassigned to the President," Kyle Lakin announced when I arrived in his office. He announced it so the other employees would know what was going on.

I heard more than one person grumble and one say outright that it was because I was young and pretty. I forced myself not to give him indigestion. The applause at my apparent elevation was sparse and begrudged.

I had a feeling the Chief of Staff was going to hear complaints from his remaining staff all day long.

When I gathered my things and hauled them in a small box to the Presidential staff office, I found the Falchani twins guarding the door to the Oval Office.

Good morning, Drew grinned. I saw through the disguises he and his brother wore; to me, they wore leathers and had their long hair braided tightly down their backs. Everyone else saw two men dressed in dark suits who certainly didn't look like twins.

Good morning to you, too, I said. I realized that the real Laura Quimby would likely have to retrieve the things I placed in drawers and atop the desk I'd been assigned, but that would happen later, when this mess was resolved.

At least I hoped she would. Even with Norian Keef and Lendill Schaff now focused on tracking errant Lyristolyi I felt uncomfortable, bordering on fear. Something was in the works; I just couldn't determine what it was.

Notes—Colonel Hunter

"When Norian meets me again in the future, he won't recognize me," Mack Walters said. He'd already told me he was born a werewolf and was originally from Earth. I was beginning to feel a small amount of jealousy—that some were chosen for a higher purpose. He and I stood in a corner of the emptied facility in Nevada while Norian Keef and Lendill Schaff used advanced equipment to search for clues.

"They left fingerprints and DNA behind," Lendill said as he shut off the small tablet he carried and walked toward us. "Definitely Lyristolyi, and the fingerprint belongs to one that the Prime Potentate of Lyristolys claims is dead."

"No doubt he didn't bother to clean up after himself, thinking that Earth wouldn't have a clue about him," I said.

"And he's mostly right," Lendill agreed. "You're fortunate that you have two Larentii willing to help."

"More than you know," I ducked my head. "My question is this—how did they get away so cleanly with everything inside this facility? A lot of equipment and furniture was left behind."

"Moved it out initially by truck, I think," Mack said. "I smelled diesel outside. I don't know how far they drove it, though, since the presence of at least one Sirenali is blocking the information."

"What do you smell in here?" Lendill asked.

"At least six scents that are fresher than any others," Mack shrugged. "One of them definitely Sirenali, in humanoid phase."

"What?" I turned to him swiftly. "Cori and Val say the ones from here likely don't know how to turn humanoid. We've only seen their scaly counterparts."

"You have the one you captured in Okya-hama," Norian snorted. "He was humanoid at the time."

"He wasn't even here three months ago, from what Val says," I replied. "Gerrett would have said something, I think, if he'd been involved in this mess. And it's *Oklahoma*." I didn't add *you nitwit* at the end of my statement, although I wanted to.

"I'd like to speak with him," Norian began.

"He's mute and only communicates through mindspeech," I said. "Cori and Val talk to him all the time, and he's become friends with Bekzi," I stated.

"Bekzi?" Norian's interest was piqued.

"Cori says he's a reptanoid."

"What's that?"

"Ask Cori—or Bekzi. He's heard of you before," I said. "He wasn't complimentary." Lendill turned away to hide a smile.

"Where is he now?"

"In Canada, helping to keep things on an even keel," I said.

"What does a boat hull have to do with," Norian began. "Never mind. I'll save that discussion for later."

~

Corinne

"We have to make plans to attend Amelia's funeral," President Granville stated as two other staffers and I stood before his desk. The Chief of Staff sat in a chair beside me, nodding at the President's words.

Things had happened so quickly after her death that I hadn't had time to mourn for her or consider the inevitable—the elaborate service expected for a President of the United States.

I'm sure that the real Phillips and the real Askins would have been doing a jig about her demise, but I took satisfaction in the fact that they'd died before she did. I was now worried about their clones, wherever and however many of those there were.

I'd like to see her body first, before it's placed on display in the capitol rotunda, I sent to the President.

A slight shake of his head negated my request.

All of us were invited to sit while the plans for a state funeral were made.

~

Personal Record

Lendill Schaff

"Why do they call this the ugly building in Arlington?" Norian asked after our introduction to Justin Griffin. He was tall—taller than Norian, with dusty-blond hair, blue eyes and a ready smile.

"I didn't name it," Justin flashed a grin. "Want coffee?"

Mack, the werewolf who'd transported us to and from the facility in Nevada, snickered as he helped himself to a cup of the dark brew.

"Do you have tea?" I asked.

"We do." Justin turned to retrieve a cup from the cabinet behind him. In seconds, a cup of fragrant tea was brewing in front of me while Norian accepted a cup of coffee.

"We've been reassigned as your transportation crew," Justin said. "Gavin thinks the enemy may be planning an attack from multiple fronts."

"Gavin?"

"You haven't met him," Mack said, his dark eyes glinting with humor. "Old. Vampire. Grumpy. Need I say more?"

"No, thank you," I pulled the small tea bag from my cup and sipped. "Good," I nodded. I only knew about vampires because my father had taught me about them. Werewolves, too. I felt comfortable with the young werewolf who stood nearby. A vampire could be another story.

"My dad's a vampire," Justin grinned, causing me to choke on my tea.

Rather than ask how it was possible for a creature that was sterile by nature to have fathered anyone, I apologized for coughing and went back to my tea.

"Did the vampire happen to say where these multiple fronts could originate?" Norian tasted the coffee and stopped for a moment to determine whether he liked it or not. "This is good," he acknowledged.

"I put cream and sugar in it," Justin said. "It's how I started drinking it years ago. Now I just avoid wasting time and take it black."

"Gavin doesn't know exactly where the attacks will originate, he just expects them to come from multiple directions," Mack shrugged. "It's what he would do, if he were in charge. Divide the enemy—that's what he said."

"The first attack could be the weakest," Justin nodded as he lifted his coffee cup. "It will draw our attention while they plan to hit us harder elsewhere, in more strategic and vulnerable spots."

"What does a vampire know about strategy?" Norian played the skeptic.

"Well, he was in the Roman army back in the day, if you're familiar with this planet's history. Then, he was the Vampire Council's elite assassin for a long time before he became what he is now."

"An assassin?" I lifted an eyebrow at Justin's remark.

"The best they had," Justin grinned again.

"Perhaps he will consider working for the ASD after this," Norian suggested.

Mack and Justin burst out laughing. While I failed to understand exactly what they found so humorous, I couldn't help but smile.

Captain Brett Walker

Jen and I had gone out with Captain Finch the day before. We examined the Snow Cat used to launch the missiles responsible for the blast site in Quebec.

The vehicle was a burned ruin, now.

The identification numbers had been destroyed before the vehicle was used for its final purpose, although we did find wires and a metal box, which didn't belong. "That remote controlled," Bekzi nodded toward the remains of the box I'd set on the kitchen island. My job was to look through it for any type of identifying markers, which could lead us to its maker or seller.

"Yeah," I shook my head. "I'm looking for something that could tell us where it originated."

"Look for reason these so intent to catch Sergei. Katya. Friends of Sergei and Katya," he responded.

I know I stared at him for several moments while that germinated in my brain. "Good question," I said eventually. "I don't have an answer."

"Think I do," Bekzi murmured. "Need to see Corinne and Valegar."

"What's going on?" Dr. Farrell walked into the kitchen. "No worry," Bekzi said. "We looking at remote control device," he nodded to the pile of junk in front of me. For some reason, he didn't want to talk to Farrell about what he and I had just discussed.

That concerned me, and I was already concerned greatly about Dr. Richard Farrell.

Corinne

I spent the afternoon listening to people talking about the matched black horses to pull the caisson carriage at the funeral, plus the one to be used as the riderless, caparisoned horse.

It hit me then—so hard I wanted to destroy the Oval Office with the buildup of energy coursing through my body. We shouldn't even be talking about this. It shouldn't have happened. Everything the drug touched had been adversely affected.

Dearest, excuse yourself, came from Val. *You must release your anger elsewhere.*

I didn't excuse myself. Instead, I left a replica of myself sitting in the Oval Office while I folded space. I needed a place where I could scream my lungs out.

Neaboria was beautiful, wild and uninhabited except by plants. It bore the brunt of my anger as I shouted at people, most of whom were already dead.

For the first time, too, after I'd finished shouting where none took note, I returned to the Oval Office and replaced my mock-up with myself, with nobody the wiser.

~

Graye

I have to attend the funeral—there is no way around that. I have to pretend to mourn, too, when I feel nothing. I was forever saddled with the name Graye Sanders, when I would have preferred something else.

He says it will open doors for me. I didn't ask him which doors he meant. I feel his answer will be political in nature; therefore, I do not wish to know.

I understand he is not former President Phillips—he is only an echo of the one who was. Hal worshipped the original. Always said he was a genius. Regardless, he is dead and a shadow takes his place.

I worry that this one may not possess the genius of the original. I worry that all our deaths could come as a result.

He says not to worry—that all will be well and we will take the country back.

I wanted to tell him we already had much of it while Amelia Sanders occupied the White House. The wealthy moved and spent at our command. Armies and assassins followed our instructions. The people were oblivious. I failed to understand why this pretender thought it necessary to stand in the full light of day and open himself to possible criticism.

After all, if you make a target of yourself, someone will surely aim in your direction.

So much better to be the force behind the target, allowing them to take direct hits while you remain safe.

Yes, some would say that is cowardly.

I call it wisdom.

Hal and my assistant had taught me well.

Just get through the funeral, he said. *Afterward, you may hide as much as you like. I will deal with everything past that point.*

I told him that's exactly what I wanted.

"Your tea, sir," my assistant handed the cup and saucer to me. I accepted and thanked him before I drank.

Notes, Colonel Hunter

"Matt Michaels is on the phone," James appeared in my doorway. I'd barely seen my office in several days, yet here was another interruption.

"I'll take it," I said, lifting the receiver of my desk phone. Briefly, I wondered why he hadn't bothered to call my cell. This call could be recorded.

I learned quickly that recording it was exactly what he wanted.

"We need to get to Bethesda," he said. "They found something in the autopsy."

"What the hell?" I demanded.

"I'm telling you I just got a call, and they found something. Looks like Madam President may not have died of natural causes."

"Bloody hell," I cursed as I stood. "Fucking, bloody hell."

CHAPTER 12

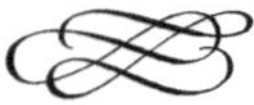

*C*orinne

I told them they should let me see the body. The answer was no. At least they wouldn't have been punched in the stomach with the news that a heart-attack inducing drug had been administered to Madam President, or that fingers were now pointing at Graye Sanders, if they had.

"I think this was their plan," Matt muttered as President Granville and I walked into the meeting room at the hospital. "She only had a year left during this term, so of course they're going to put someone forward who'll promise the country whatever it takes to get elected."

"And that someone will either be a Phillips clone or someone else with a Phillips clone's hand up his ass," I huffed.

"Dearest, remain calm," Val appeared from nowhere.

"So they're looking to discredit me however they can," the President said, sitting heavily on a chair and pulling it toward the standard, rectangular, brown, faux-wood meeting table.

"It looks that way," Matt agreed. "Whether it's foreign policy or some other, domestic debacle of their creation, they'll be aiming in your direction."

"When did elections become all-out wars?" Auggie asked. "Not just political, but physical, too?"

Nobody replied.

"What evidence do they have against Graye?" Granville asked.

"Nothing yet, but the timing, according to the forensic pathologists who've calculated the drug's path through her system, says the only person who had access to her at the proper time would be Graye— while they were alone in the bedroom. FBI is combing through the residence now, looking for proof."

Val squeezed my hand and led me to the table, where we both sat. He didn't want me to explode again, and I wanted to. I wanted to yell at Auggie and Granville both, for not allowing me the time or giving me permission to see Madam President's body.

"You know what," I stood and snapped at both of them. "Nefrigar is right. I don't answer to either of you." I disappeared before Val could stop me. My destination was the autopsy lab, and I appeared there while shielding myself from those present.

Yes, I felt ill at the sight of her body lying open on a table, but I could see her face below the opened skull.

I saw her final moments as Graye bent over her. The word *why* was on her lips as she died.

I needed to see Graye Sanders, and I needed to see him immediately. Somehow, I understood that the task could prove impossible—if my suspicions were correct, he was already dead.

"The note was found in his bedroom," the Phillips clone said during the interview. The President, just like the rest of us, was learning of Graye Sanders' death through an interview on the news instead of from more official sources.

"We have a copy of the note," the journalist claimed. "The original has been turned over to the FBI."

"When?" Granville exploded. "I've gotten no word of that."

"Sir," a Secret Service agent stepped to the President's side and handed a cell phone to him. "FBI Director on the line."

"Right." Granville rose and walked into the hall to answer.

The rest of us, along with the entire country, were exposed to the suicide note at the same time, in which Graye Sanders admitted killing his wife because, in his words, she'd told him she wanted a divorce after her term was up.

"I had no idea he had a gun," the Phillips clone wiped imaginary tears away. "No idea."

"Coming up next, we have two psychologists who deal with suicidal patients, and the Director of the National Suicide Hotline," the female journalist declared.

"Fuck," I muttered.

"Cabbage?"

Ilya had come. He sat on one side while Val had the other.

"I'm okay," I held up a hand. "I've already had one screaming fit today. I can put this one off until tomorrow."

"We must speak with Bekzi later," Val said. "Your Ilya must come, too."

"This doesn't sound good." I leaned back with a sigh and closed my eyes. "Make it go away," I whispered.

"Dearest, I cannot," Val said softly.

Former President Phillips' home

Alexandria, Virginia

"At least the snoopers are gone, now," the one posing as President Phillips sighed. "They looked through everything. We left nothing to chance—all will be as it appears, that Graye Sanders took his own life. I also appreciate your arrival on such short notice."

"It is nothing—you know I will support you no matter what," the Merle Askins clone nodded. "I am available to you at any time—you must understand this."

"I'm beginning to see that, but I worry that I rely on you too much."

"I feel we will have need of our slave," Askins jerked his head toward the wizard in the corner. "I wish we had more like him, but that will not be, I fear."

"Why can't we have others? I have been informed of the drug's use. I know how you brought me back from death, now."

"It must be the blood of an original survivor," Askins insisted. "We have taken this one's blood many times, and it does nothing." He jerked his head toward the captive wizard, who sat at a corner table, his hands shackled firmly to its steel surface.

"We keep attempting to find the original. He eludes us, as does his daughter and her husband. Our men failed to get information from Sergei while they had him—and he disappeared after his rescue. We imagined that tracking his friends would lead us to him, or at least bring him to investigate their deaths, but that effort has proven fruitless. What do you suggest we do now?"

"Are you sure there is no more blood to be had from the original?" the Phillips clone asked, his expression thoughtful.

"I am sure. There was precious little of it in the beginning. When Becker escaped, he brought what he could with him. The rest was destroyed with the mansion. I wish we had *her* blood," Askins said. He'd read all the notes concerning Corinne Watson. Before her death, she'd performed near-miracles.

"It was destroyed inadvertently, when they thought her worthless," Phillips snorted. "According to Becker, before his death. I've read the reports, too, if you remember."

"We learned never to send all our clones against an enemy at the same time," Askins noted. "The Becker clones are all dead, just like the original."

"I hear there is no available information as to who cleared out the Nevada facility. I hoped to find at least a few grains of the drug. Nothing remains. Both our caches were destroyed. If any exists, the Americans have it."

"Too bad Farrell is dead. He likely had some hidden for his own experiments."

"And as a result of his death, we may never find it."

"My question is this—why has the original not displayed any of the talents of our wizard?"

"My guess is that whatever prevents the manifestation of talent in the original may have been voided when this one suffered a blow to the head shortly after receiving the blood. He was quite combative, you understand. He is a docile slave, now, thanks to our intervention."

"Surely we could remove the chains?"

"We will take no chances with this one. He is too important, and the one whose blood he received—he can kill with only his hands."

"Ah. We will keep him chained, then."

Corinne

Bekzi didn't come to us—we went to him. I really didn't want to go back to Canada, mostly because Finch and Farrell were there, but Val thought it necessary, so there we went.

Neither Finch nor Farrell liked it that they were locked out of the meeting between us and Bekzi, but I really didn't care how either of them felt. Val studied Finch as he complained, but said nothing.

In my opinion, Finch had either been born without tact, or sold what little he had through an online auction service. Either way, he didn't possess that necessary ingredient and it showed.

Nathan shook his head behind Finch before leaving the room. I sent mindspeech to him when he left, telling him to hide for the next half hour. If he didn't, he'd be hearing all of Finch's current complaints, most of which centered on aliens and their secrets.

Once the study door was closed and Val placed a shield about the room, Bekzi began. To say that I was shocked and dismayed by his theory would be putting things in terms too mild for contemplation.

"I'm going to kill Farrell, and then go back and spit on Becker's body," I snapped when Bekzi laid out his hypothesis that there was at least one more Ilya somewhere.

Ilya, his face stony, listened carefully to everything Bekzi had to say.

"With warlock and Sirenali, they have transportation and shield," Bekzi said.

"But warlocks have to have their talent awakened," Val began.

"Look—your archives," Bekzi said. "At least three in past, have brain damage. Out pops ability. Two—murderers. One—she make dolls. Scare children. Adults, too."

"All three are long dead," Nefrigar appeared in our midst. It was obvious that Val had either sent information or allowed his father to see and hear through his senses.

"Here's my thinking—if they had him tied down, and they probably did," I began slowly, "the Ilya I know would have woke fighting. If somebody bludgeoned him to keep him from getting away," I shrugged.

"Then that explains how some of them may have evaded the army of Lyristolyi sent to kill them," Val agreed. "He knows how to fold space, now. No telling what else he knows."

"And it's likely that he's obsessed, on top of everything else. My question is this," I said. "How much power does he actually have?"

"There is a way to find out," Nefrigar said. "But it will require opening this one's power to find the level of potential."

"I don't want," Ilya began.

"It matters not what you want," a man appeared as if he'd been called. I blinked at him. I'd read about him in the Archives. Erland Morphis, father of Rylend Morphis, King of Karathia in the future, had arrived.

"Don't worry, it's not painful, or even scary, although I've known six-year-olds who've lost their breakfast because the older ones told them frightening stories," Erland smiled.

He was perhaps the handsomest man I'd ever met. To me, however, Ilya would always be my ideal.

"Cabbage?" Ilya turned to me.

"Honey, we need to know, and this will allow you to be who you were meant to be."

"Then do it," Ilya jerked his head at Erland.

"I have to put my hands on your head," Erland cautioned.

∼

Ilya

"Fifth-level capability," the one called Erland sighed and took the offered seat at the kitchen island.

"What does that mean?" I didn't attempt to cover my accent.

"It means you can kick ass after your training," Erland said. "Most can do basic things after their power is awakened, but most six-year-olds don't have the focus the older students do. You, on the other hand," he shook his head. "I think your middle names should be focus and control."

"What are the levels, then, so I may make a comparison?"

"First is weakest, Fifth is strongest. Does that answer your question?"

"Yes."

"You don't sound pleased."

"I am most displeased that there may be a clone of me with the same power I hold," I said. "One who is obsessed—perhaps more so than I am."

"Very true," Erland dipped his head in a nod. "At least he's on someone's chain and likely to use his abilities on command, rather than going wild and causing random destruction."

"That's a rather horrible thing to say," Corinne interrupted. "Somewhere, there is a victim who is being coerced in the worst way possible."

"I understand," Erland held up a hand. "I fear for innocent lives if he isn't coerced. I imagine he is damaged in some way and no longer holds perfect reasoning. He only knows pain, if my calculations are correct. An animal in pain is a dangerous one. Would you not agree?"

"How does an obsession work with someone who is brain damaged?" Corinne turned to Nefrigar.

"Lord Morphis is correct in one respect," Nefrigar sighed. "If the damage created is not repaired, the farther this individual could sink toward his basic, instinctual level. Obsessions cannot be placed upon animals. They fail to take hold."

"So we may be working against the clock—to find this one before he goes completely mad," I muttered.

"Finding him would be best," Erland agreed. "His death should be swift—and as merciful as you can make it."

"Do we have information on his whereabouts?" Corinne asked. "And is there any other option?"

"None," Nefrigar replied.

Corinne

Somewhere, hidden by the ass-hats who used to be in charge of the American government, was a brain-damaged Ilya who could and probably would perform any misdeeds directed by his less than ethical masters.

I understood that the one acting as former President Phillips was a powerful Sirenali directing his warlock puppet. Anything could come from that unholy alliance, whether the Ilya clone intended it or not.

I understood why they were so anxious to get Sergei and Katya, too; capture them and either force them to reveal Ilya's location, or threaten their lives to bring him into the open. They wanted to make more Ilya clones. They had no idea that capturing Ilya would gain them nothing; Valegar had neutralized Ilya's blood already. There would be no more clones. To me, that spelled further obsession to do their bidding if they managed to capture him.

I'd taken a seat in the sunroom I'd created at the ugly building in Arlington, just so I could stare out the windows at the city and its suburbs beyond.

He doesn't like feeling helpless, does he? Gerrett joined me, choosing a nearby chair and flopping down on it.

"If you're talking about Ilya, then that's putting it in mild terms. I believe he is currently furious, and that's perfectly understandable."

They tried to get information from Sergei. I understand that, he jerked his head in a nod.

"They almost killed Sergei, and then intended to come after Katya," I agreed. "He's pissed about that, too."

In their hands, he would be quite dangerous, Gerrett said.

"We'll do our best to keep him out of their hands," I responded. "Katya, Sergei and their friends, too."

I understand this. However, I also know that removing him from the planet will ensure that they do not find him.

Right. I doubt any of them would agree to that.

Stubbornness. I see it far too often, he gave a mental sigh.

Yes, that made me laugh.

"I was going to offer to take you wherever you wished to go after this is over," I said.

But, he began, *I cannot think of a safer place for one such as myself than beside a Larentii.*

"Are you certain of that?" I asked. "Wherever I go, trouble seems to crop up."

Yes, but one of my kind will never control you, he responded. *Or any Larentii. I know that much, at least. My mother was quite bitter over that.*

Do you know the history of the Larentii and the Sirenali? I asked.

No. She would beat me if I asked.

The Larentii don't like to talk about it, either, I shrugged. *It goes like this, though, so make sure of your answer as to where you'd like to go after you hear this story.*

I'm listening, he nodded.

Long ago, I began, *Sirena, your home world, was ruled by one who came to the throne by assassination. He wished to take whatever he could—worlds, people, treasures. Whatever he desired.*

He understood, though, that he didn't possess anything other than obsession to gain what he wanted.

The Larentii, however, possessed everything.

Of all the races, only one was made who could slip past the shields around the Larentii homeworld. That race was Sirenali.

The king gathered his finest warriors, to attack that world and bend Larentii to their will by placing obsessions.

By the hundreds, they transported themselves. Once there, they discovered that not only could they not place an obsession upon even the youngest Larentii, they were also guilty of trespass. In the beginning, the Sirenali had signed a pact with the Larentii that they would never approach the Larentii upon their homeworld—either to destroy it or harm its inhabitants. The pact decreed that the Sirenali would be subject to Larentii judgment if that pact were ever broken.

When the first Sirenali set foot on the Larentii homeworld, the pact was broken. Once the invaders discovered they couldn't place obsession on a Larentii, they attempted to take young ones—to enslave them.

The Larentii were enraged. Their children are the most precious thing to them, and each one is loved and treasured.

So, not only were those Sirenali killed who'd attacked the Larentii, but because Larentii children were made targets, Sirena itself was destroyed. It is the only time the Larentii have ever gone to war, and it was to save their children.

The few Sirenali who remain were either offworld during the destruction, or pulled away by the powerful before it happened. The Larentii do not speak of their act of destruction—it shames them that they destroyed an entire world because a small percentage of the population attacked them.

Young Larentii are taught that seeking vengeance against the innocent must never happen again.

That is a frightening story, Gerrett shook his head. *I think I understand most of it, although I want to weep for the innocents lost.*

Me, too, I said. *That's why I want to protect you—because you deserve so much better than you have received before now.*

And that is why I wish to remain at your side—because you see me as a person and not a slave.

Notes—Colonel Hunter

Matt and I sat in the Oval office, while the President stared at his hands. Both rested atop his desk, as if he were contemplating an action he found distasteful. Finally, he spoke.

"We are at war," he said. "A war we cannot declare openly, against those who seek to overthrow our government and all the others. It was their plan last time. It is their plan again. Amelia Sanders is dead because of the enemy. While the country believes it an act of jealousy at the hands of her husband, we understand there were other motives. That makes me—and this office—their next target."

"What do you suggest we do, then?" Matt's unblinking gaze leveled on Granville.

"I want a team of assassins gathered, to attack Phillips' compound. I've had it under surveillance since Graye Sanders was invited there. I only have information as to employees leaving to run errands and then returning. The forensics team that went through Graye's suite found little, but they supplied information as to whom they saw there. I have their reports if you'd like to go over them."

"I assume this attack will in no way be associated with the White House?" I asked.

"An organization will take responsibility," Granville huffed. "A manhunt will ensue. If you want, we have intel on a cell of insurgents hiding in the country. We can haul them in for questioning."

"I'm not sure I like this idea," I stated flatly.

"You won't be involved. Neither will Matt. Hold all your people back—I'm handling this one."

"And when they retaliate?" Matt asked, his voice soft.

"I'm hoping there won't be anyone who realizes the terrorist attack is false," Granville replied.

"Until you realize that Phillips was in league with that bunch since before he left office," Matt snapped, standing abruptly.

"There's an offshoot of that group," Granville began. "They've made some threats."

"I'm aware of that. What if they're in this up to their hairline?" Matt shook his head in disbelief.

"They've stated that they want all Americans dead. I assume that includes former Presidents, too."

"I stand with Matt on this," I said, rising to my feet. "I also understand you're not willing to listen to our advice, since this plan is already in the works. I think it best that we leave now. I have people I'd like to speak with, to see what the potential fallout will be."

"I don't want you to discuss this with anyone," Granville snapped.

"Tell that to Corinne, who will see it in my face. I don't have to open my mouth," I said.

Granville cursed while Matt and I walked out the door.

Corinne

"Cabbage?" Ilya walked into the kitchen, where I watched Gerrett devour a massive omelet. Auggie had called moments before, telling me my work as a White House staffer was over. In fact, President Granville had dismissed all the Saa Thalarr guards we'd brought in to protect him.

I understood without asking that Granville's PTSD had kicked in and he was declaring his own war. Those who'd volunteered to guard him and the White House would naturally disagree with his methods and tactics, so he'd sent them away.

"We lost our help," I muttered. "Those who came to guard the White House have been dismissed by the President."

"Because he wants to wage his own war, rather than relying on others to protect him. Foolish," Ilya shook his head.

"I'm worried that he hasn't thought this through. We know what the enemy is capable of doing. I doubt he fully understands. He could end up dead and hand the country right over to those he wants to keep it from."

"The bigger bomb," Ilya sighed. "Your weapon may be able to protect you from your neighbors or petty thieves, but it will be ineffective against the bombs dropped from overhead. You—and your gun—will be destroyed."

"Yeah."

"My love?" Valegar strode into the kitchen. "I just came from the meeting with Gavin and the others—Father invited them to the Archives after their dismissal," he said.

"What did they say?" I asked.

"They say things are not good," he replied. "If I thought I could convince you, I would take you and those you wish to bring with us and leave this world behind. Father says it is too important to abandon. I understand this—from his perspective. From my perspective, it frightens me to stay."

"I feel as if the ground has shifted beneath our feet," I said. "But it hasn't dropped from beneath us. Not yet. We have to stay, honey. You know we do."

"I am concerned about the terrible things to come," he dropped his gaze.

"Honey, terrible may not be a strong enough word."

I still here, Bekzi sent mindspeech. *You need, I come.*

Thank you, I returned. *For now, keep an eye on Farrell. I'm concerned about what he may do if the President pulls Jen and Brett away.*

You think this may happen?

They're his to command, so yeah, I think it could happen. He doesn't have control of us, remember, and he realizes that we won't involve ourselves in all his hastily made plans. Jen and Brett are still military and he can order them to do whatever he wants.

Not good. I think on this.

Yeah. Let me know what you come up with.

I will.

"Bekzi's still with us," I said aloud. "I don't think he'll leave until we do."

"Perhaps we should turn our attention to other things, then, since the President no longer desires our help," Ilya suggested.

"Honey, remember, you're still part of the Program, too," I pointed out. "He'll call you in with Jen and Brett—count on it."

"I dislike this greatly," Ilya growled.

"You'll have to be our eyes and ears on the inside, then," Matt and Auggie walked in, both looking grim and out of sorts. "Colonel Hunter just got a call from the President, asking for all three members of the Program, along with Dr. Farrell, to be sent to the White House."

"I quit," Ilya declared.

"You're in it for life," Auggie muttered. "Remember the agreement you signed? The only reason he isn't trying to order Cori around is because he knows he can't."

"What happened?" I asked. "Why is he suddenly running scared? He had ample protection. He sent them away." I flung out a hand.

"I think he's having control issues," Matt suggested. "He doesn't like what he can't control, and he couldn't control them—not really. All he could do was ask. He can't control Phillips—not openly. So he's employing what he does have control over."

"He's going to get people killed," I snapped. "You know it'll happen."

"We understand he isn't taking the long view on this," Auggie said. "If you'll recall, he and Phillips have bad blood between them, anyway. He was in Phillips' cabinet, remember? They disagreed on almost everything."

"So he's settling old debts by doing the worst thing possible, now? I don't believe this," I said.

"He feels threatened by Phillips. You understand Phillips—or the one posing as Phillips—will do everything in his power to take over the country. Granville wants to destroy Phillips using his own methods and on his own terms."

"He'll find himself on the losing end of this, mark my words," I snapped.

"Cori, we're not disagreeing with you," Auggie rubbed my shoulders.

"Then what do you suggest?" I asked. "Wait for the fallout and attempt to do damage control?"

"That may be all we can do at this point," Matt said.

"Fuck. Ilya," I turned to him.

"What is it, Cabbage?" he asked.

"You need a crash course in warlockery one-oh-one," I said. "Beginning with how to fold space so you and anyone you care about can get the hell away from a dangerous situation."

～

Ilya

By the end of the day, and before I was called to the White House, Corinne and Valegar taught me how to fold space. I also learned how to level power blasts, melt metal or plastic, burn anything combustible and *Pull* anything to me that I could focus my mind on.

Unlike my Larentii tutors, however, I could not control atoms. I couldn't create or destroy the same way they could. Whatever I blasted that afternoon, they rebuilt with barely a thought so I could destroy it again. An advanced spell might do the same, but I didn't have enough time to learn it and it wasn't the same as commanding atoms, anyway. It was merely reconstructing the bits and pieces left after an object's destruction.

Still, I hoped to learn it, someday.

"Time to go," Colonel Hunter walked warily into the basement where I practiced my new skills.

"Here," Corinne held out a hand and ensured that I was dressed appropriately in a dark suit and tie. "Wouldn't do to go see the Prez looking like you just reduced a wall to rubble, you know."

"What if they won't allow me to return here?" I asked.

"You can fold space now, remember?" Corinne said. "Send mindspeech. I'll let you know where we are. I doubt we stay here—there's no reason for it."

"All right. What about Brett and Jen? I understand the meeting is so late because the President was waiting for their flight to arrive."

"You can take them anywhere with you," Corinne said. "If they want to come."

"What about Katya and Sergei?"

"Bekzi will keep them safe," she said. "Count on it."

"All right," I said, straightening the cuffs on the suit I wore. I could tell by the feel that the fabric was expensive and of the highest quality. Corinne had dressed me like royalty. "I am ready to go," I nodded to Colonel Hunter. "We will get this over with quickly."

CHAPTER 13

*N*otes—*Colonel Hunter*

"Thank you for coming on such short notice," the President said. I wanted to laugh—these four didn't have a choice but to appear at the President's bidding.

Ilya wore no expression—he waited to see what the President's command was. Jen and Brett—they had no idea what was going on. Farrell sat nearby, undisguised anger marring his features.

"I received a note yesterday," the President said. "From former President Phillips. I've made copies for you to see," he said, pushing four sheets of paper toward Jen. Trust him to expect the woman to act as secretary and distribute the notes to the others. I also noted that I wasn't included as a recipient. I also wondered at his reason for withholding this information from Matt and me earlier.

It's because he didn't have it earlier, Cori's voice whispered in my ear. Once again, she was in the Oval Office, shielded from sight. The information she provided made me want to shiver. *It's fabricated,* she confirmed. *I've already told Ilya,* she added.

"This is a threat against you and your office," Brett set his copy of the note on Granville's desk.

"Yes it is," Granville agreed. "I am taking steps to eliminate that threat. This is where you come in. As members of the Program, your assignment is to assist in the search for evidence at Phillips' home in Virginia," he said. "It is my plan to wait until he is away. You and my special unit will get inside, take evidence, make it look like a break-in and get out. We need to know what his plans are, you understand."

Until they discover that Phillips isn't gone and he and his goons either become dead or make Granville's team dead, Corinne said. *My bet will be on the latter. Granville has no idea what he is facing, including Sirenali who can command them to shoot themselves or each other, to a brain-damaged version of Ilya, who is a loose cannon.*

At that moment, I wished mightily for mindspeech. Granville had gone off the deep end, in my opinion.

He wants to be able to point a finger at Phillips—for Amelia Sanders' death, Graye Sanders' suicide and conspiring with the insurgency. I doubt he'll get the evidence he wants, Cori said. *I think he wants the path smoothed for his election and get rid of an old enemy at the same time. He's been thinking about this ever since he first sat in that chair.*

I guess the old saying was correct—*power corrupts*. It certainly looked that way from where I was standing. I realized, too, how precarious my position had become. Matt's too, when it came down to it.

The President could replace either or both of us, on a whim.

"Why am I here, then?" Farrell demanded.

"I think you know why," Granville turned to him with a smile. "I have a feeling you know where more of the drug is. Don't you?"

Corinne

Richard Farrell did know. Just as he'd kept blood from Maye and Nick, he'd kept a stash of the drug left over from the experiments on himself. I'd ignored it, since my life had been saved by a second dose of the drug early on. I considered it insurance, in case Ilya needed help.

Well, that time had just passed. Granville wanted to bring back the experimentation. He wanted to deepen his resources. Make his own Sirenali and who knows what else?

Farrell, I sent, *Tell him that the drug and any remaining blood has been destroyed. As of five seconds ago. By me. If he doesn't believe you, tell him to check for himself. All of it has been neutralized.*

You didn't, Farrell snapped back.

I did. He's not going to do this a second time. If Phillips doesn't kill him, the Lyristolyi will.

"I know where it is, but its effectiveness has been neutralized," Farrell informed the President stiffly. "I can tell you where it is, but it won't do any good."

"How was it neutralized?" Granville became angry immediately.

"Corinne," Farrell said. "She said if Phillips didn't kill you first, then the Lyristolyi would if you used the drug for more experiments."

"Then tell Corinne that she is no longer welcome in the United States," Granville hissed. "I have no control over other countries, but she needs to get off American soil."

"Your wish, my command," Corinne dropped her shield. "If your ass needs saving again, don't look to me to help you." With that, she disappeared. I listened while Granville cursed a second time that day.

～

Ilya

I'm in Canada, Corinne informed me. *For now. Is it all right if Val and I use the villa in Italy?*

Of course, my love. Please, take Sergei and Katya with you. I want them to be safe. I fear that Granville will want to ensure my cooperation with this mad scheme he has concocted. Taking them hostage will be first on his list.

I'll take Bekzi and their friends, too, she responded. *Finch can continue his witch-hunt here in Canada without us. I think the enemy is much too smart to leave anything useful behind for him to discover.*

If there were something, I feel we would have found it by now, I agreed.

Yeah. Well, you know where I'll be, she said. *If you want to get away.*

That may be sooner than you think, my love.

187

I love you, too.

I know this. Stay safe, beloved.

~

Corinne

"Leo, you should come with us. Is it possible for you to take Nathan along—as an assistant?"

"With Matt's permission," Leo agreed. "I think we can get that with little argument."

"Good. I just didn't want to leave him here to listen to Finch," I said.

Leo Shaw and I stood in the kitchen while Val shielded us—I didn't want anyone else to hear while I explained what happened in the President's meeting. Leo understood what I didn't say, too—that Auggie and Matt could lose their jobs just by pointing out the flaws in the President's plans.

"Something has caused this mental break—this acute stress disorder," Leo said. "Perhaps due to the pressure suddenly placed upon him, coupled with the fact that he is likely marked for death—at Phillips' earliest opportunity. You saw how easy it was to get President Sanders out of the way."

"I understand that part. What I don't understand is dismissing the best protection he'll ever have, just so he can go after Phillips on an ill-conceived whim."

"And if he were thinking clearly, he would realize these things. He is not thinking clearly, and as he holds the highest office in the country, he has the power to enforce his ill-conceived whim."

"This is insane," I whispered.

"Not insane, just in desperate need of help, which is something he isn't getting, that's obvious," Leo said.

"Leo, it's insane in the fact that he can cause World War Three if he isn't careful and right now, he doesn't understand that."

"Let me call Colonel Hunter and Director Michaels. We can

continue this discussion in Italy, once we have permission to take Nathan with us."

∼

"Cori, I want you to come for James," Auggie said over the phone. "I know you have Nathan there with you, and since things are so dicey here, well, you understand what I'm saying. I'm approving an extended leave of absence, and I've sent Laci to her sister's."

"Yeah." I did understand. Auggie was worried about anybody close to him. When Granville's plan went into action, then anybody could become fair game if the Phillips clone survived the attack.

I was also beginning to worry about Norian Keef—we hadn't heard from him or Lendill Schaff in a while.

"I'll be right there," I said.

When I arrived in Auggie's office, James stood beside a packed suitcase and threw his arms around me when I appeared.

"Honey, Nathan's waiting for you," I kissed his cheek. "Stop worrying, okay?"

"Cori, keep him safe," Auggie said. "No matter what happens."

"You know I will," I said. "He's my son."

That caused James to hug me harder. "Come on, honey, let's go. I think we can get you some dinner from Carano's before they close."

Leo had already gotten takeout when I set James down in the villa's kitchen. Nathan lifted him up and gave him a generous smack before setting him down again.

"I think I got four of everything," Leo grinned as James and Nathan took seats at the table. Katya, Sergei and their friends were already seated and waiting. "Wine, too," Leo added. "Want anything?"

"No. Go ahead. I think I just want Val to take me somewhere sunny so we can feed."

"I watch and eat, too," Bekzi declared as he scooted a chair back. "Go. Get sunlight. We be fine."

Val, who'd watched everything with half a smile on his face, offered me a full grin before transporting me to Australia, where the sun was shining the following day.

"I guess I'm a woman without a country, now, since the President kicked me out," I said. We sat on a private stretch of beach, both of us naked and shielded. Val wrapped his arms around me while I leaned my head against his shoulder.

"He has no control over you, my love. You must understand that. It is that which he fears—that he has no control. Therefore, he acts irrationally, to exercise the control he can. To him, the world is spinning away from his grasp, making him fear for his life. He knows not how to deal with that."

"Should we go find Mister Norian and company, after we feed?" I asked, closing my eyes.

"Sleep now. When you are rested, we will hunt for him. I will bend time if necessary, to ensure that we find him."

"Awesome," I mumbled and allowed sleep to claim me.

"May we come with you?" Sergei asked when I explained that Val and I were going to look for Norian Keef the following morning. Val had let me sleep through our feed and then got me in bed at the villa without waking me. I felt better, at least, after the tiring events of the previous day.

"Val?" I turned to him after Sergei posed his question.

"I think it will be all right—if you wish it," Val nodded.

"Sure," I shrugged at Sergei. "You may get something interesting for lunch, but what the hell?"

"I've had interesting things for lunch before," Sergei flashed a grin. "I'll tell Katya."

Half an hour later, we were in Nevada again, where Val worked to coordinate Norian's movements.

"This is how my brothers and I learned to track those important to history, and detail the events surrounding them," he said, closing his eyes and employing his *Looking* ability to search for Norian's next stop. "Las Vegas," Val opened his eyes and smiled. "We will go to the hotel where he stayed."

The hotel Norian chose wasn't on the strip and didn't house a casino. I assumed he paid cash for his room—I doubted he had any credit cards. "Only one night," Val said as we studied the room. "I must *Look* again to find his next destination."

"Can you not just use your talent to find where he is now?" Katya asked.

"We don't know where he is," I informed Katya. "He and Lendill dropped off the radar days ago."

Unofficial communication from:
Geethe Cheriss, Prime Potentate of Lyristolys
To: Outland Commander Fisk Boralus
Subject: Capture
I am unsurprised by Keef's shapeshifting ability—he reveals the serpent I always imagined him to be. Condolences on the loss of two of yours from their wounds in capturing Keef. Keep him unconscious as much as possible. Threaten the death of his companion if he fails to cooperate. You understand the importance that their bodies be found elsewhere—I do not wish to have another conversation with Deonus Wyyld. I suggest you implement your plans quickly—I want this situation resolved very soon.

Morrett read the message a second time—quickly, before Fisk came back. It would be destroyed, just like all the others. Fisk's footsteps at their hotel door in Paris caused Morrett to retreat to his corner, where the comp-vid he was allowed to read lay waiting.

When Fisk arrived, there was no evidence that Morrett had ever moved from his corner. With hooded eyes, he watched as Fisk erased the message from Geethe Cheriss before stuffing the comp-vid in a trouser pocket.

Morrett knew some of the plans Fisk had for Earth.

They terrified him.

Fisk was about to unleash the first wave of attacks, and many would die. Morrett huddled farther into his corner and searched desperately through his comp-vid for a favorite story to read.

~

Ilya

Someone I didn't know had been placed in charge of our group. He was CIA, but claimed he worked for Matt Michaels.

That was a lie.

The name and title he gave—Lead Agent Milton Smith—also a lie.

We were scheduled to infiltrate the grounds surrounding former President Phillips' home in Alexandria at midnight. Lead Agent Smith told us Phillips was out of town.

Another lie.

Did he not know with whom he was dealing?

I wished for Corinne, however, to read in him exactly what he knew and what his intentions were. I also wished for the opportunity for a quiet word with Jennifer and Brett. Lead Agent Smith didn't want that, as he had someone with us constantly while we waited at a facility located in Silver Spring.

Most of the day, Smith's agents worked all around us, checking their weapons, studying the layout of the property and examining the architectural details of the home. Much discussion was had in order to determine the best place to breach the security in place—both electronic and human. The three of us were neither consulted nor offered weapons of any kind.

What did they expect us to do if we ran into trouble? Yes, I could likely take care of myself and Brett—well—I assumed he could, too, if he chose his other shape. Jen—I had no idea whether Maye's talents in martial arts had transferred to Jen. She'd certainly never mentioned it if they had.

I suspected that the agents going in with us knew that Phillips would be in residence, and that deadly force was not only permissible, but required. I had no idea whether they'd been instructed to kill anyone they found, but found myself concerned about the possibility.

After all—Phillips had a Secret Service detail assigned and always would—as long as he was deemed alive. Wherever he was, they would be, too.

I disliked the fact that they could be considered collateral damage, without first determining whether they were involved in the Phillips clone's machinations.

In that respect, Corinne had certainly influenced me. In my early days, it wouldn't have concerned me much. After my son's death and my relationship began with Corinne, things had certainly changed.

I love you, Cabbage, I sent to her.

Honey, be careful, she replied. *Things are looking rather grim from where we are, and I doubt you're in for a picnic, tonight. Don't forget—you can get yourself out of there if you need to, and take Jen and Brett with you. Don't wait for the worst to happen.*

I understood what she meant, although she hadn't said it. If I hadn't hesitated to kill the original Phillips, he'd never have placed his obsession.

I will, I promised.

Call if you need me, she added.

I will.

I love you, too. Don't ever forget that.

I will never forget.

Notes—Colonel Hunter

"What is it?" I asked. "In English," I added. Shaw was on the phone, talking psych gibberish while I attempted to decipher what he meant.

"Farrell may blow this all to kingdom come," Shaw snapped. "I just got off the phone with him. He doesn't know I'm out of the country, and he's threatening to go to whomever or whatever, to force Granville to remove Jen from tonight's plans and bring her to him instead."

"What the bloody hell is happening to everybody?" I shouted. Frankly, I wanted to put a fist through one of my office walls, but that would place me in the same rubber room with Farrell.

It was during the brief moments it took to dial Farrell's cell phone —I intended to tell him to stay put until I could send someone to pick him up—that it actually happened.

Of course, the news didn't reach us until half an hour later, but when it did, it was devastating. I'd seen video of events from the past where the course of our nation and that of the world was changed forever.

This—this could be the death knell. I knew it. I hoped the President and every other world leader understood that, too. Sarin gas, in a widespread distribution, had been dropped by near-silent drones onto the streets of Paris, especially those crowded with night tourists.

Thousands of deaths were given as an early estimate, and I imagined that the toll would increase dramatically with the rising of the sun. The city was in chaos, as hospitals were filled with those affected. Many dead were left lying in the streets as others ran to get away from the deadly, odorless killer.

Matt Michaels removed the phone I held in nerveless fingers as I watched the news on my computer screen with horror. "Come with me," he said. "We've been summoned to the White House."

"I was trying to reach Farrell—he's gone off the deep end," I babbled as Matt drove like a maniac through D.C. streets.

"I heard. The President hasn't been informed. I think it's idiocy that he still wants to go after the Phillips clone tonight."

"Is everybody nuts, now?" I asked. The visions of the unedited image feed I'd gotten from Paris continued to slice painfully through my brain.

"The President got word that the insurgency is claiming responsibility for this," Matt said.

"What? I figured they'd just fire those missiles they have and be done with it."

"Not until they have a way to fire them undetected," Matt snorted. "Which may not be impossible, if what I'm thinking has happened. I have Opal on it now; I'm just waiting for her to report her findings."

"What the hell are you talking about?" I snapped.

"The technology to deliver the sarin gas? Those silent drones? Right now, our technology is good, but not that good."

"So the insurgents got ahead of us."

"That's not what I'm saying."

"Fuck. I'm getting a headache." My cell phone rang while I rubbed my forehead to relieve the tension.

"What?" I said. No, that greeting wasn't civil, but then I wasn't on the same planet as civil at the moment.

"They've hit Berlin. Sarin again. Same thing as Paris."

"Who is this?"

"Colonel Hunter, this is Nathan. Bekzi has us hooked up to direct satellite feeds here at the villa," Nathan explained. "James is here, but he's taking notes and sending them to you in an e-mail. You should probably check it when you get the chance. We're worried they'll hit London and Rome, too, before the night's over."

"Holy fuck," I muttered and dropped the phone, which lodged between the seat and the center console of Matt's car.

"I hear that," Matt said and pressed the accelerator. The car lurched forward as Matt wove in and out of traffic to get us to the White House.

Corinne

Low-flying drones, silent as the killer they carried, destroyed hundreds of thousands before dawn arrived in Europe. Paris, Berlin, London, Rome and Madrid were all hit, in an effort to cause as much death and chaos-induced fear as they could. Almost as an afterthought, Moscow was also attacked. At least ten thousand died there, most of them while they slept.

The insurgency claimed responsibility for all of it.

Val and I—we knew that wasn't the case, but those in charge of the insurgency preened like peacocks at the news—they were proud to be blamed for so many deaths. Images of them were shown quickly, hiding their faces as usual and waving signs proclaiming the U.S. was next.

I'd heard from Ilya that the President called off their mission the night before—Granville went straight to the bunker and stayed there until dawn. They were scheduled to go again at midnight, tonight, unless another chemical weapons attack was launched.

For now, every nation on Earth was desperately searching for an answer to sarin gas. People were locking themselves inside their houses and taping plastic on windows and doors.

Val and I—we were nearly at a dead-end in our search for Norian Keef and Lendill Schaff. We were now backtracking, looking for clues in out of the way places, just to see if they could have been spotted by one of our enemies there.

I suspected the Lyristolyi, but since Phillips' cronies had Sirenali, I couldn't point a finger with certainty, yet.

"I worry that we may have to bend time to a specific place, just to follow them discreetly," Val said. I looked at Katya and Sergei, who sat at a corner table at a coffee shop while Val and I ordered at the counter for them. They were worn out from going back and forth, searching for clues.

They knew about the attacks on Europe. Disheartening would be putting their reaction into mild terms. Both were terrified.

"I think we should take them back to Bekzi," I said as Val lifted two coffee cups to my one.

"I agree, but their wishes must be considered."

"Yeah. I know."

"Corinne, is there some way you can take Papa away from that madman?" Katya lifted her eyes to mine as Val set a cup of coffee in front of her.

"Honey, I'm not sure about that—not yet, anyway, and yes, I really would like to get him out of there, just to keep him safe. He has a choice in this, too, you know."

"Katya, he will be fine. He always is," Sergei wrapped his arms around her shoulders. I wanted to weep with her when she leaned her head on Sergei's chest and sobbed.

The frustration I felt at that moment was a crushing weight. The longer our search for Norian Keef lasted, the more worried I became that he was not only being held hostage by one faction or another, but that he could either be dead already or marked for death—at a more convenient time.

His death wouldn't—shouldn't—happen for centuries. Too many things could change in successive timelines, and that could prove disastrous.

Lendill Schaff, too—if he shared the same fate.

Val and I had been concentrating our resources on hunting Norian, to the exclusion of everything else. Yes, the intent to release drones in major cities to kill the innocent had been hidden by Sirenali involvement, but I chastised myself for shutting everything else out. In other words, I felt guilty as hell about it.

Yes, I knew the insurgency had Sirenali at their disposal, so the planning of this mass killing would have gone unnoted.

I suspected, however, that the insurgency hadn't considered this method of destroying lives. They were more in the *Let's blow everything up at the same time* camp.

While they were happy to take the responsibility assigned to them for this carefully planned genocide, I doubted they'd had a hand in it.

Meanwhile, governments across the globe were once again planning meetings—teleconferences actually, since they were still wary after the last mass world leader destruction in D.C.—to discuss what to do about the insurgents who'd killed so many people already and likely had more targets in their sights.

In my mind, World War Three had a strong foothold already, and that was likely due to outside influence.

Fuck Earth. The Lyristolyi had written that on the ceiling of the abandoned Nevada facility, after they'd scraped every grain of the drug out of it. "The Lyristolyi did this," I said, setting the cup of cold coffee I still held on the table. Katya, whose eyes were dry, now, watched as my hand shook when I released my grip on the paper cup.

"Dearest, you have been unresponsive for several moments," Val said softly beside me.

"The Lyristolyi have Norian and Lendill—if they haven't killed them already. I want to see the drones used in the attacks," I added.

"Dearest, they cannot die; their deaths will destroy the timeline," Val said. His voice now sounded far away, drowned out by the sudden noise in my ears. Visions were coming—of everything that could be affected. A new term—*God Wars*—echoed in my mind. This was the past. Something important could unravel in the future. A victory could become a disastrous defeat.

All could be lost. The panic overwhelmed me, until Val took matters in hand and placed me in a healing sleep.

Ilya

I'd spent the night in a guarded bedroom, with no communication devices available—those had been taken early on. I'd attempted to send mindspeech to Corinne, with no reply.

That frightened me. *Valegar?* I sent.

I am here, he replied immediately.

Corinne?

She had a severe panic attack, he said. *I was forced to place her in a healing sleep. Things, as you likely know, are not going well at the moment. I realize you may not understand what I am about to tell you, but the timeline into the future is crumbling.*

Where are you? Are Katya and Sergei safe?

I have brought Corinne, your daughter and her husband back to the villa, he said. *Corinne is still sleeping. Katya and Sergei are huddled with their friends and discussing the sarin gas attacks with Bekzi and Dr. Shaw. Gerrett, James and Nathan are preparing lunch for the others.*

I've heard very little about the attacks, I admitted. *They are keeping us away from outside communication.*

They are fools, Val said. *Lying fools, intent on performing at the direction of one whose reason cannot be relied upon.*

I agree completely, my friend, I said. *They have lied to us from the beginning, and I worry that tonight the attack may commence.*

Tread carefully, then, Val said. *Do not risk your life. I understand you feel responsible for getting Jennifer and Brett away if things go badly, and that is why you remain where you are. You must protect yourself, too. You are important, in ways you cannot begin to fathom.*

I took a moment to process his words. I had no ready reply for them, after all. *Take care of Corinne,* I said. If I'd spoken aloud, my voice would have been thick with emotion.

I intend to do so, he acknowledged. *When she wakes, we will continue our search for Keef. If his timeline ends here and now, things will not go well in the future.*

Does this mean the odds are against us? I asked.

The odds are certainly against us. I worry that desperate measures will be considered, merely to salvage what we can.

Will you ask Corinne to contact me when she wakes?

I will.

Thank you.

~

Personal Notes—Dr. Richard Farrell

If Corinne had left any useful drug behind, I'd have retrieved it. The original attack had been postponed, at least—after Sarin was dumped on major European cities, resulting in countless deaths.

Yet Granville wanted to send Jen into that hellhole with a Phillips clone. Yes, I often called her Maye in my mind, and a part of me understood how wrong that was. It no longer mattered what her name was—she was everything to me and merely a pawn marked for death by the idiot occupying the White House.

Granville had separated us, too—I no longer had access. Jealousy ate at me—was she sleeping with that bastard, Brett? Her phone and other methods of communication were turned off—likely at Granville's direction.

Yes, he was at the bottom of all my concerns. I no longer cared that he was President. If anything happened to her, I couldn't predict my actions afterward.

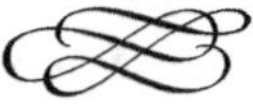

CHAPTER 14

*N*otes—*Colonel Hunter*

"You're saying there was some sort of antidetection device on those drones? That nothing we have could detect them? Where did that technology come from? Somebody's ass?" the President shouted.

Matt and I sat in a meeting with the President and the Joint Chiefs, where blame-laying and finger-pointing prevailed and sensible discussion hadn't been invited.

I understood quickly that the President didn't want to hear what Matt and I had to say—he wanted to mire himself in mundane, Earthly excuses for the attacks instead of considering where they'd likely originated.

The presence of technology that had nothing to do with what could currently be produced on our planet failed to interest him.

"Right now, it doesn't matter where it came from," Navy pointed out. "What we have to do is a study to determine how to prevent an attack here."

"How long do you think that study will take?" Air Force broke in. "Months? We don't have months. Hell, we may not have hours, the way things look to me."

"I say we go in and bomb the hell out of Iraq and Syria to put an end to this once and for all," Army snapped.

"Because that's your answer for everything," Marines countered. "You just want to make a mess that my boys will have to clean up."

"I've already got my people watching the coastline for suspicious or unusual activity," Coast Guard said. "It's the best I could do with the limited time I've had."

"That's the best thing I've heard so far in this meeting," Matt said. "What are the rest of you doing—or plan to do? I'm coordinating with Homeland, the FBI and state officials across the country. They're looking for any unusual activity, now. They could probably use some help, too."

"Mr. President, the country is waiting for you to make a statement," I said during the ensuing lull.

"Yeah—I'll get to that," he waved off my suggestion.

I watched Matt rub his forehead—the country was terrified and the President was having a psychotic episode. A perfect pairing for chaos. "I've had requests for interviews," I added. "I can't do that without official word from the White House as to the plans put in place to combat this potential menace."

"Just tell them we're employing every resource to keep the country safe," the President mumbled.

"Mr. President, those journalists will want specifics," Matt tapped a finger on the table. "They want us to spell out exactly what we intend to do to keep the people safe. You have resources in this room that can help with that. They're just waiting for you to tell them what you want to do."

"Put together a plan of action. All of you. Meet me here tomorrow at the same time. We'll hammer out something then." I watched as the President rose from his chair, forcing the rest of us to our feet. He walked out, leaving us to glance warily at our neighbors.

The leader of our country was disintegrating before our eyes.

"Well," Coast Guard sighed, "this is my question. What would Amelia Sanders do?"

"She'd call Corinne," Matt said cryptically.

I jerked my head in a nod.

~

Corinne

The world hadn't improved any while I slept. When Val woke me, I had a request to contact Ilya, a request to contact Auggie and Matt, Keef was still missing and everybody on the planet was waiting for a press conference from the White House, which still hadn't happened. Meanwhile, hundreds of thousands were still just as dead across Europe.

"Cori, what are we gonna do?" James whispered as I shuffled into the villa's kitchen. Gerrett, who stood nearby, nodded a greeting to me.

"Honeys," I went to pull both into a hug. "We'll try to sort this out, okay?" I leaned away and peered into both faces. "Because we have to."

"I hear this," Bekzi agreed as he walked past, carrying two bags of groceries. "You sit, we cook."

It was then I realized that lunchtime the following day had arrived, while I'd slept nearly round the clock.

Ilya? I sent.

I am here. We are on for tonight—the President retired early last evening, he said.

Thank goodness, I replied. *I just woke up and nothing is better,* I added.

I know. If they didn't have me under surveillance every moment, I'd get away for a short visit.

Yeah. I raked hair away from my face, only then considering my appearance. *Do you know how Brett and Jen are?*

They're keeping us apart, he said, *so I cannot say for sure. They're probably worried we'll conspire to escape. I confess; that has crossed my mind many times.*

I understand. Do they not even allow you to eat together? A mental hmmph met my question. *I guess that's a no, then,* I said.

Correct. It concerns me that the President has become so paranoid, he added.

I think Leo can add a full list of psychological disorders behind that one, I said, my sending dry. *Hold on, I'll Look to check on Brett and Jen—okay, got it,* I said as the information came. *Brett is feeling like a caged wolf—no surprise. Jen is concerned over the lack of communication, and she's working on crossword puzzles—somebody gave her a book of those and a pen.*

At least one of us can be distracted, then. Tell me what else is happening.

I told him what I knew, which really wasn't much. He considered each piece as it dropped into the puzzle we'd been given. There were still far too many blank spaces to hazard a guess at the full picture.

The President is destroying his chances for the next election, Ilya pointed out when I explained about the lack of information and cooperation from the White House.

If he were completely sane, he might be worried about that now, I responded. *As it is, I think we whizzed by that stop long ago. He was worried once, but I think he's sunk too far into revenge and self-preservation at this point. You know, I miss the good old days when all I had to worry about was Becker shoving me into the mud.*

I should have killed him for that, Ilya said. *I wanted to.*

Well, he and all his clone buddies are dead. Not our problem now, I said.

True. We merely have a much larger, more troubling set of problems.

Yeah. Look, I need to call Auggie. Let me know how things progress.

I will. I miss you, Cabbage.

I miss you, too.

~

Notes—Colonel Hunter

"He said I wasn't welcome on American soil," Corinne said. "This tile was made in China." I watched as she pointed to the floor of my office. Instead of calling me, she'd come herself—and Valegar with her.

I didn't blame her for leaving James in Italy, where he was guarded by a watchful Bekzi. She was right all along—Bekzi deserved all the medals I could throw at him for staying the course and keeping people safe.

"I'm not surprised the tile is Chinese," I sighed. "The President is delusional," I added.

"I know."

"I don't know what to do about it," I said. "We're supposed to hand him an action plan in a meeting this afternoon. Matt and I worked ours out together, but the others," I shrugged. "So far, only the Coast Guard has really done anything useful."

"Look, if they have a way to transport that stuff around that doesn't involve the usual methods," she said, "then even going house to house, looking for terror cells won't help. They can pick a spot, land there, release their drones and zip out again. Easy."

"Cori, please don't muck up my plan with your confounded relevance and common sense," I muttered. "The President doesn't want to hear about extraterrestrial involvement. He wants this to have originated here—on this planet."

"Because he has no way to combat the unknown," Valegar offered. "He has also alienated anyone who could help with it."

"You and Corinne." My words were flat. They sounded dead, even to my own ears.

"Auggie—we're at a tipping point," Corinne warned. "If a few more things go wrong, then everything could be destroyed."

Somehow, I got the idea that she wasn't just talking about Earth anymore. She was talking about *everything* everything.

Yes, I'd fallen into the two-word, repetitive explanation category. It did nothing to improve my mood—or increase the effectiveness of the proposal Matt and I had put together for the President.

"Auggie, it doesn't matter," Corinne said. "Just—do the best you can, okay? We have things to do, so let's hope that the nut-jobs behind this aren't ready to attack the U.S. yet. I'm worried they may have something worse up their sleeve."

"Cori, you can't get much worse than this," I smacked a hand on my desk.

"Colonel Hunter, I assume you understand how foolish that statement could become," Valegar warned. "We will keep in touch."

I stared—for a long time—at the empty space where he and

Corinne had stood, giving me a warning that the apocalypse was about to happen.

Some people would be disappointed that zombies didn't appear to be involved.

Frankly, I was grateful we didn't have rotting corpses to combat while we dealt with everything else.

~

Corinne

"Val, what is the weight of everything in the universe?" I asked.

"All of them?" he countered.

"Never mind," I waved a hand. "I merely wanted to know how much we were carrying around, that's all."

"Dearest, let us concentrate on the immediate problem. We can discuss weights and measures at a later time."

"What was it Auggie said about relevance and common sense?"

"It applies," he nodded. "Shall we begin our search again for Director Keef?"

"I should have sent his snaky ass back to Wyyld when I had the chance," I muttered. "We wouldn't be hunting him now if I had."

"We cannot always foresee when things will take an errant turn," he advised. "We are hunting him now—to save him. This is more than any other Larentii has been allowed to do since the beginning."

~

Personal Record

Lendill Schaff

Norian attempted to fight our kidnappers every time he was allowed to wake. As a result, he was covered in cuts and bruises, and likely still had internal damage from the pistol blast that sleeping hadn't cured.

I watched as his head lolled toward me now; we sat against a rough wall in a hunting cabin—that's how the Lyristolyi referred to it, anyway. "They won't kill us here," I hissed as he blinked at me.

I was surprised he could still open his eyes; the bruising around them was so severe. "They don't want anyone hunting them after this, you can count on it," I added. "We'll die elsewhere, or at least that's their plan. Stop fighting, get your strength back and we'll get out of this mess eventually."

I was hoping to already be out of it, if truth be told. I had no idea why Father would leave me in such a way—unless something prevented him from knowing I'd been captured. I attempted to sort out that conundrum. After all, my father was the one person who could find just about anything, if he put his mind and talent to it.

"Your breakfast," one of our captors walked into the room, set a plate of food on the floor and slid it toward us. They'd started this tactic the day before, when Norian almost gained the strength to change.

Until this mission, I'd never guessed he was a shapeshifter.

Many things made sense, now, but I couldn't dwell on those unraveled mysteries—I had to form a plan of escape, knowing that Norian would be able to escape with me. With a hand still chained to the wall, I gripped the edge of the plate and drew it toward me.

I'd studied shapeshifters when I was young—my father had seen to that. I understood their elevated metabolism. Norian needed most of what they'd given us; I intended to see that he got it.

It had become Morrett's duty to empty the slop bucket. He understood that going in after meals was the proper time to do so—he felt less afraid, then.

Only one of the men used the bucket; the one his masters had shot and beaten after he'd become a large snake and bitten two, killing them quickly. Morrett had no words to explain to Fisk that the other man—the one with deeper eyes and paler hair—didn't need the bucket.

Immortal whispered in Morrett's mind. He only knew that because he'd read it somewhere—his mother certainly hadn't taught him anything. His captors weren't immortal, however. Yes, they resembled what he could become when enraged, but the resemblance stopped there. Somewhere in the timeline, they may have been related.

Morrett wanted to claim no kinship with them. To him, they were cruel—as his mother had been cruel. He couldn't deny that when they changed to their other form, however, they greatly resembled his race, which could also change.

Morrett seldom changed—his mother had laid compulsion to never attack his masters; therefore, it wasn't worth the beating he'd receive if he did so. He had no idea where his mother was, but wherever she was, he cursed her.

Again.

~

Geethe Cheriss, Prime Potentate of Lyristolys
   To: Outland Commander Fisk Boralus
   Subject: Wymarr Belancour
   There is no need to send the wizard back and forth; keep him there with you until this is finished. I have no immediate need of his services and your successful mission is now of utmost importance. I have had word that Deonus Wyyld is quietly searching for Keef; therefore, we must eliminate him very soon. Have Wymarr transport you and any equipment you need—send him back to me when this is finished.

~

Corinne

"This is where they were captured." Val's gaze settled on the wrecked duplex in Toronto. At first, I'd wondered why the owner hadn't bothered to check on the rental, but discovered he lived in the unit next door.

It was obvious he'd come to check on his renters when the noise started. He was now decidedly dead, his bloated corpse lying in a pile of rubble nearby.

That's where we stood, inside the rented side of the duplex, surveying the damage.

"Six days ago," Val surmised. "I have determined the level of decomposition in the body and translated it into local time."

"If Auggie didn't have his hands full already, I'd ask him to pass this on," I sighed. The landlord, a man in his early fifties, had been fit and in good health before the horde of Lyristolyi descended.

He'd died quickly, from a single weapon discharge.

"Ranos technology—in its infancy," Val explained. "There wouldn't have been anything left of the body with a pistol from current times. This weapon was quite old."

"Keef and Schaff put up a fight," I said. "They were better armed, at least."

"Yet outnumbered, unless I err in my guess," Val nodded. "I detect two deaths—from poisoning—Keef turned at the last. They must have wounded him badly to take him after that. I fear you were right, dearest; I also detect the interference of a wizard."

"So not all those holes in the wall were from a ranos pistol?" I asked.

"Here—see this one—*Look*, you will find no ranos burn—the residue it leaves behind. No, this blast was from a wizard's hands."

"And not a warlock?"

"Different methods," Val shrugged. "If we had time, I would return you to the places where the Elemaiya leveled blasts, then take you to the room where Ilya practiced, then allow you to compare both to these. We have not the time. I fear Keef's time is dwindling rapidly, and with a Sirenali to hide them and a wizard to transport the Lyristolyi from place to place, we may not find him soon enough."

I wanted to curse the Sirenali again, for keeping us in the dark as to where a rogue wizard could have transported the ones from this room. At least they'd taken their dead with them; I could barely look at the body on the floor without feeling ill.

"Do you think they're still in Canada?" I asked. "That they may have established a base here, since they can hide easily and get in and out with the wizard's help?"

"I believe Keef and Schaff thought they were getting close; why would they lease a temporary home otherwise?"

"Good question. I didn't understand it—not really. It doesn't make much sense."

"It makes me wonder if there were communications placed with Deonus Wyyld or with their agency regarding their decision," Val agreed. "I can contact Father about those things."

"Yeah. I think we should," I said. "This is awful." I pulled my eyes away from the dead man on the floor. I couldn't help comparing his death to that of hundreds of thousands across Europe—all caused by the same people.

"I must go, dearest, Father is calling," Val said. He disappeared almost immediately.

"Huh?" I stared at the space he'd occupied. "Damn," I muttered before transporting myself to Italy.

Sunlight on the snow surrounding their lodge almost blinded Finch. He took a moment to fumble in a pocket for his goggles. Two of his team had spent the night before and most of the current day out in the weather—they'd gone farther than they should have, looking for signs of others in the area.

He'd just gotten a garbled message on his radio, so he'd gone outside to get a better signal. "Finch here," he said. "Come in, rover."

"Rover here," came the answer. "We smelled smoke from a fire earlier. We're currently looking at a hidden cabin buried in the snow. Sundown in twenty, sir."

"Give me your coordinates," Finch snapped. "We'll be there soon. Remain undetected, do you hear me?"

"Yes, sir."

Ilya

After mindspeech with Corinne, the day crept by. Sundown was upon us, leaving roughly six hours before our planned attack. The usual knock sounded on my door, announcing the arrival of food.

At least we were being fed properly, if somewhat blandly.

"We're still on for tonight," the corporal informed me as the tray he carried was set down on a small table.

"I understand," I nodded. "Thank you." I tipped my head toward the tray.

"You're welcome, sir."

"Will you be coming with us, tonight?"

"That's the plan." He sounded excited. I made a mental note to attempt to protect his life, too. I doubted he had any idea what we would encounter when we arrived at Phillips' compound.

"I will see you then," I said.

"Yes, sir."

~

"There's no movement sir. Inside or outside that cabin," Finch's Lieutenant reported.

"Let me see." Finch took the binoculars to check for himself. "You're right—I don't see a thing, and the smoke isn't very thick. The fire may be dying. Do you suppose they've abandoned the site? Are you sure they didn't detect you?"

"No, sir. Nobody's left—before or after we arrived."

"Then let's go in and check it out. If this is where our bombers have been hiding, we'll know soon enough."

"Yes, sir. Who's guarding the perimeter, sir?"

"You come with me. You two," he pointed at two others, "stay back and watch for their return."

"Yes, sir."

"Come on, we have a cabin to search." Finch moved forward, his boots crunching softly in deep snow.

~

"We don't have to change the original paint or wording, we merely have to remove what was added later." Fisk tapped the outer shell of a purloined missile. "We want to blame the original owners, not the more recent ones, after all."

Wymarr Belancour studied the missiles he'd whisked away from their hiding places—the newer paint was ridiculously easy to separate from the aging lettering of the original.

Two different languages—neither of which he could read. He cared not—his job paid quite well and allowed him comforts he'd never received in his brother's home—the same brother who'd kicked him out when the first notice was released by the ASD, telling everyone there was a bounty on his head for a few minor misdeeds.

Marid could fuck himself—Wymarr had done quite well on his own. Lifting his hands, he prepared a spell to remove the designated paint.

Nearby, and almost undetected, Morrett dropped to his knees and shuddered.

~

The moment Finch crossed the invisible perimeter, he knew it—for approximately two-thirds of a second, until the cabin exploded in a huge fireball, taking everything inside the perimeter with it.

From the hill above, two men were on the radio quickly, asking for help as debris rained about them.

~

Corinne

"Norian's dead. Schaff, too," Val said. He didn't conceal the weariness in his voice as he spoke after his arrival.

"I know. If I'd known to look for a window where the Sirenali wouldn't have been present to hide their location," I shivered.

"Dearest, you can't take blame for this," Val said. "Father worried that something like this would occur. I was meeting with him and Kalenegar when this tragedy happened."

"The worst part?" I looked up at Val, whose eyes were deeper and sadder than when I'd seen them last. "The worst part is that Finch set off the perimeter spell, causing everything to blow up. Courtesy of their wizard, no doubt."

"No doubt," Val agreed before sitting heavily beside me. "I understand only two of his team are still alive."

"I heard from Auggie shortly after it happened, but I already knew," I sighed. "I didn't want to go—word is there isn't much left to see."

"Yet the President is still insisting on sending Ilya and the others into that trap," Val muttered. "Word has not reached Deonus Wyyld, as yet. If he hears that Lyristolys is responsible for Keef's death, he will oust them from the Alliance."

"Is that a bad thing?" I asked.

"In some instances, it could prove to be quite detrimental to all involved. Lyristolyi tend to be a vindictive people—as you have witnessed. Without the Alliance laws to hold them in check, they can willfully cause much damage. Look at what they have accomplished here, with only a handful of their people."

"Good point," I mumbled. "Val, I feel numb. Like it's not real one minute, and that it shouldn't have happened the next. I don't know what to do, right now."

"That is an understandable reaction," he soothed. "When did you last feed? Come, I will take you elsewhere."

Ilya

The van we rode in dropped us off half a mile from the wall surrounding the estate. Agent Smith led us in; Brett, Jennifer and I, followed by four others. At least they'd given us weapons at the last; I worried that we'd be forced to go in unarmed.

We'd been provided body armor, too, but I was concerned it

wouldn't help us against what we might meet inside Phillips' home. Getting over the wall went well enough; it was what came after that changed everything.

～

Captain Brett Walker

Smith had taken the lead, with Rafe right behind him. Jen and I came next, with Smith's agents following. Rafe should have been in the lead—I recall thinking that. He appeared to be better prepared and more knowledgeable than Smith, who took a circuitous route toward the house.

We'd almost arrived at the designated door when the impossible happened—Smith turned as if to signal the rest of us, but instead, he hit Rafe in the head with the butt of his gun.

Rafe fell, unconscious, while weapons were poked into Jen's and my back. "Keep quiet or we kill him," Smith snarled, jerking his head toward Rafe, who lay unmoving on the ground.

The door—the one we'd targeted, opened, and former President Phillips stood there, the light at his back, smiling at Smith as if he'd been expecting us all along.

Turns out, that's exactly how it was.

Our weapons were taken away and Jen and I were forced inside the house while Rafe was dragged in by two of Smith's agents.

"I don't want him damaged too much," Phillips chuckled as the agents dumped Rafe on the tiled floor of the kitchen. "I need him, after all."

Guns were still pointed at us—and at Rafe while he struggled back to consciousness. I witnessed something then that I never want to see again—when Rafe's eyes blinked open, and before he had time to do anything else, Phillips placed a command.

"From now on, you will only do what I say," he snapped.

I'm sure it was the wolf in me that detected the waves of power in that command—I doubted my previous human self would have recognized it.

Somehow, too, the wolf knew better than I did what to do. I turned in the kitchen and fought my way through it, getting two bullet wounds for my trouble.

Yes, I should have known better.

Whatever that power was that Phillips had, he turned it on Jen, next, ordering her to do the same thing. What came next defied logic and would have made me ill, if I'd been human.

~

Notes—Colonel Hunter

Matt and I sat at the bar in a restaurant not far from my office. He'd been the one to tell me that Granville had sent the team in early. Therefore, we'd chosen a public place to drink, imagining that we'd be called to account for our whereabouts at a later time—once word of the infiltration and attack on Phillips' estate got out.

As it surely would.

News of that explosion did come first—barely.

What followed left us both staring at the television screen mounted over the bar, where images were transmitted by Israeli and Saudi news crews of nuclear weapons destroying Iraq.

I found I couldn't move as we watched infrared cameras record high, massive plumes and mushroom clouds. Matt must have called my name a dozen times before I realized he was pulling on my arm to get me away from the bar.

"We have to get to the White House," he said when the roaring lessened in my head.

"Who?" I blinked at him, still in shock.

"They're going to blame this on the Russians," he hissed. "We may be next," he added. "Come on. We have to hurry." Tossing a large bill on the bar, he practically carried me away.

I didn't comprehend how Opal could be outside in a car, waiting for us to get in. The last I heard, she'd been in Europe earlier in the day.

"Buckle up," she instructed as the car peeled away from the curb.

"I've contacted Cori—she and Val are on the way. Half of Iraq is gone —six bombs hit. That only put a dent in the stockpile, so who knows what may get hit, next."

"They're getting hit with the bombs—the ones given to them?" I asked. I'd squeezed myself into the back seat and now stared at the back of Opal's head as she wove her way through traffic toward the capitol.

Matt's cell phone rang. "On our way," he barked into it.

"Sir, there's a firefight going on at the Phillips estate," I heard clearly through the phone.

"No surprise," Matt said. "We'll be there soon." Opal hit the gas, forcing the car to lurch forward. Horns honked all about us that night —the night World War Three actually started.

~

Corinne

When Val and I arrived at Phillips' compound, half of it was destroyed and the other half was burning, the flames fed by an unnatural source and licking high into the sky. The roar of it joined the noise in my head, amid desperate attempts to reach Ilya in mindspeech, which were peppered with the images of a country hit by the very bombs they'd stockpiled to destroy others.

Except that's not how it would look when all was said and done.

Blame would be laid elsewhere—by design.

Treaties and agreements would be ignored or blatantly tossed aside, as fingers began to point. Ilya—there was no reply from him. That terrified me.

Those who'd taken the bombs away to drop them on unsuspecting targets would find more nuclear weapons and attack more countries. They wouldn't be forced to rebrand the next round of bombs in order to spread the lies of where the attack originated—it would already be written on the missiles themselves.

While some might be shot down—if they could see past the

technology and wizardry concealing them—there were too many to be eradicated completely.

All this raced through my mind as we frantically searched for Ilya, Jen and Brett. Wherever they were, a Sirenali hid them from us—we couldn't find them anywhere by *Looking*. In desperation, I attempted to contact Jen. After all, Maye had mindspeech.

Still nothing. Forcing rising fear and panic down again, Val and I snuffed the flames of the fire. He cooled the heated remains well enough that we could walk among them. We scanned every inch of Phillips' compound that night, and found nothing. I feared we'd find bodies of those who'd gone in with Ilya.

There wasn't so much as a fingernail left behind.

Wherever Ilya was, he was either dead or incapacitated. He'd have answered me if he were conscious—or himself.

A terrible dread came over me, then.

Phillips was Sirenali.

What had he done?

CHAPTER 15

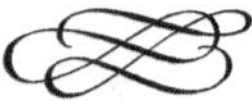

orinne

Earth doesn't sleep after an event such as this. After the initial shock and silence ends, voices rise in a demand to know why. And, in this case, *who*.

At first, satellite images of the bombing sites were all anyone could see. Radiation levels were off the charts across Iraq; clouds of radioactive dust moved with the winds while surrounding cities and nations did what they could to prepare for its arrival.

Medical teams converged on the borders of Iraq, waiting for refugees to spill over as they ran from the bombsites. Images of dying children, carried by unidentifiable personnel dressed in white protective gear, became common.

Still, there was no word from Ilya.

Auggie and Matt were practically living at the White House—I hoped Granville had enough sense left to realize what a colossal mistake he'd made, but I wasn't counting on it.

James was torn between wanting to go back to D.C. and staying as far from the troubles as he could. The U.N. had launched an investigation into the bombing, as well as the sarin-carrying drone strikes.

They'd find exactly what the Lyristolyi wanted them to find.

*The villa was supposed to be ours—Ilya's and mine—*filtered into my thoughts. I stood, a familiar cup of coffee in my hands, on the villa's terrace, gazing across the landscape. Houses and villas were strewn across the land, and in the distance, the town where we'd had our honeymoon dinner.

Everything appeared so peaceful. Benign. Somewhere, not really that far away, people fought for their lives and died, victims of an invisible enemy known as radiation poisoning.

Fuck Earth.

That phrase returned to haunt me.

Of course, many rallied to the defense of those responsible for the bombings—in their minds, it was justified retribution for the sarin gas killings.

They merely had no idea that those they pointed at as responsible actually had nothing to do with either.

Lies come back to haunt you. If it weren't so tragic, the fact that the insurgency accepted responsibility for the sarin attacks in the beginning was almost laughable.

It was too late to admit the truth of it now—that they had no idea who was responsible.

Frankly, too, alerting the media that aliens were in their midst and creating chaos on Earth would be met with skepticism and ridicule at this point. Everybody had a known enemy to blame, and was currently doing just that.

Blaming.

While it was something people usually did, the ramifications this time could destroy all of them, with or without help from the Lyristolyi.

Sales of guns and rifles were skyrocketing, too, as if a bullet could stop sarin gas or a nuclear weapon. Or a plane or a tank or any one of a thousand other bigger, badder things.

I cursed the drug, then, and those who'd created it. The foul substance was at the root of all these deaths and destruction.

I understood, too, why the Lyristolyi wanted all of it gone.

The drug could end up killing all of us, in one way or another.

~

Notes—Colonel Hunter

Amelia Sander's funeral was postponed for a second time, due to the chaos after the Iraqi bombings. I worried that the former President would never get her just due, because Earth would be destroyed beforehand.

Granville's aide ordered Matt and me into another meeting—one where Richard Farrell was also commanded to attend. Farrell knew Jennifer was missing. I feared not only his instability, but the President's as well.

That's why I asked that Farrell be checked twice for any weapons before he was allowed into the meeting room.

With a glare in my direction that could melt steel, Farrell strode into the meeting room, jerked a chair away from the table and sat before turning his angry gaze toward Matt.

Matt pointedly ignored Farrell, as did Opal, who sat beside Matt. My cell phone was outside with the Secret Service, or I'd have called Cori on the spot. Perhaps she could defuse this situation—I was fresh out of tact at the moment.

"Good morning," an aide announced as she walked into the room. I suppose it was then I noticed it was Laura Quimby—the real one and not Corinne in disguise. Two Secret Service stalked in on her heels, bringing us to our feet for the President's arrival.

Granville looked even more haggard than the last time I'd seen him. At that point, I wished for Leo Shaw's presence—perhaps someone would listen to him as a licensed physician and psychiatrist.

Whatever troubled Granville now, it didn't look good. A swift glance in Matt's direction showed me something I hadn't seen before —he looked pale. Beside him, Opal appeared ill.

They knew something already.

I merely waited to learn what it was before sinking farther into terror and depression than I ever thought possible.

"We have video," Laura announced, and I noticed then that she looked queasy. "The President wants to show you this before discussing our next course of action."

The following ten minutes proved to me that some things can always be worse than your most terrible imaginings.

I will never forget Phillips' grinning face in that video, while he ordered an obsessed and subjugated Ilya to behead Jennifer. I couldn't keep my eyes open to watch the horror as her blood spattered everywhere.

In the background, an unmistakable wolf howl sounded.

Farrell went crazy, trying to get his hands on the President. Two Secret Service agents fired at the same time, while the video continued to play in the background. Farrell was dead, bleeding out on the carpet in a meeting room. Jennifer was already dead, her blood pooling on a tile floor somewhere in the past, the President was crazy and, in my mind, responsible for both deaths. As for Ilya—his eyes had been blank as he dutifully carried out Phillips' commands.

Corinne

I think Auggie had to calm down before he called me. Still, he was upset when he spoke—as he should be.

"We're pretty sure it was Rafe and not the doppelganger," Auggie's voice shook.

"How?" Val took the phone away from my shaking hands.

"We saw a hand of the camera operator," Auggie said. "Matt did everything he could to identify him from what we had. Turns out, Granville's trusted Agent-in-Charge wasn't so trustworthy. That, or he was obsessed early on and was following Phillips' commands."

"I regret saving Granville's life," I said. The words sounded dead—foreign, even.

"Cori, you can't second-guess everything," Auggie began, his voice sounding small and ineffective from such a distance.

"Sure I can," I said. "Has any of this leaked to the media?" I realized

I was trembling. I doubted we'd get Ilya back from this—and there was evidence he was guilty of murder, even if we could remove the obsession.

"Not yet—Phillips doesn't want that, I don't think, although this is as sure a way as I know not to be invited back to the White House," Auggie replied.

"Then why would he do it? Auggie, tell me," I stuttered.

"Do you remember the real Phillips' plans, dearest?" Val turned to me. "Perhaps this one has his sights set on larger things after all."

"The U.N. is calling for Russia to prove that all their stockpiled nuclear weapons are accounted for," Auggie said. "According to the most recent treaty."

"And since the U.N. was never notified that some of those weapons were handed over to insurgents," my lips felt numb as I said the words.

"Exactly. The remnants of the insurgency are already issuing death threats against Russia," Auggie confirmed. "For killing their country with nuclear weapons."

"They were doing a good enough job on their own," I whispered. "Are they complaining, now that somebody else did the job for them?" Yes, I was scrambling—mentally and verbally—to keep from *Looking* to glean the images from Auggie's brain. Images that showed Ilya—*my Ilya*—doing a terrible, terrible thing.

What would he be commanded to do next?

Who would he be told to betray?

Would Phillips understand enough to know I meant him harm if Ilya revealed the Larentii to him?

Once, on the Larentii homeworld, the Sirenali had attempted to bend Larentii to their will.

Would another Sirenali, without the benefit of knowing that history, attempt to do the same thing? Would Phillips' clone do blackmail, or offer things he didn't intend to give, in order to control a Larentii?

"Some things are worse than death," I said aloud.

"What?" Auggie strained to hear what I'd said, since I no longer held the cell phone.

"Colonel Hunter, we will be there in a moment," Val said and ended the call.

~

High Council Meeting

Larentii Homeworld

Breanne

"Now we see why Larentii do not interfere," one stood and spoke.

"Yet the Wise Ones are here, and they say to stay the course," Kalenegar responded. It surprised me that he'd listened to the Wise Ones in this matter. His father, Ferrigar, would have blown them off as he often did.

Turning my head, I studied the five Larentii in question. All were resolute in this—as was I. A part remained to be played and as sad as it could be, it would likely prove necessary.

Too many outcomes depended on it. Outcomes that had already happened once, but as these events were taking place in our past, it could affect our present as well as our future.

Even as we stood here, discussing it.

Stephen Hawking said, *"The past, like the future, is indefinite and exists only as a spectrum of possibilities."* He was right.

Only one here knew of my presence—Kalenegar. The others—it was best they didn't know. Kal and I—we'd already had a discussion, and at the end included Nefrigar and Valegar.

Too many things were uncertain, and Kal's word would be final in the matter. I was merely present to see what the others had to say.

I wanted to sigh, too, for the hard, hard road that lay ahead. Not just for us, but for others.

Six months had passed since Wisdom had approached me to make his suggestion.

Yes, many of those gods already dead in our current existence had left their own version of landmines behind, to trip us up. I suspected the drug was a part of that, in addition to other, less obvious things.

Wisdom had pointed to one such. I'd been surprised by his suggestion, yet saw the sense in it before long. Little did I know, then, how it would become intertwined with our current dilemma.

Together, he and I—Wisdom and Love—had exerted our power.

What had been designed to destroy now held a desire for the opposite. We couldn't erase the rogue god's influence from the whole of the intended weapon, but we'd neutralized as much as we could.

That made me smile. Wisdom and I—we'd laid claim to it. It was ours. We would protect it as much as we could, but it had become its own, guided by its own sensibilities. Yes, we felt a bit of pride from our efforts.

I merely wanted everything else to turn out as well.

I no longer knew if that were possible.

"We cannot destroy the Lyristolyi," another Larentii spoke. "It violates everything we do and have done as a race to even consider it."

Corinne

He's gone. Those two words whirled continuously through my mind as we landed in Auggie's office and I saw what Auggie had seen in Ilya's face.

No, Ilya wasn't dead. Not physically. I saw the look in his eyes, though, courtesy of Auggie's memory. Inside, Ilya was gone. I couldn't read what he'd been obsessed to do, and likely the original obsession to destroy me had manifested again.

Perhaps it was similar to fictional characters learning that the one they loved had been taken over by a monster, or had become a zombie.

Either way, the result was the same.

Either way, that one was essentially dead.

Val attempted to massage my neck. I moved away from him. Panic threatened to overwhelm me for a moment as the image of Jen's death settled in my brain. A useless, pointless death.

Phillips merely wanted to stretch his credibility. He understood how much he could influence the current President by showing how he could command anyone to do anything.

Since he was Sirenali, there wasn't any way the strongest and most talented among us could find him, either, unless we found a way to track him by mundane means.

"We took bloodhounds to the site," Auggie said as if reading my mind. "Phillips and company didn't leave in any of the usual ways," he added.

"Because Ilya can now fold space," I muttered. I'd thought to protect him. I'd done pretty much the opposite. By handing a powerful weapon to a Phillips clone, he now appeared to be on track to become as bad as the original.

Ilya is gone, ran through my head again. I should have pulled him away when Granville started down this mad path. Jen and Brett, too. Jen was dead. Ilya as good as. Brett—who knew what they'd tell him to do, or whether they'd just kill him out of hand and be done with it.

Farrell—also dead. Norian Keef and Lendill Schaff, both dead. Hundreds of thousands dead across the globe, thanks to some interfering Lyristolyi.

Fuck Earth.

"I need some time," I said, fighting panic yet again. "In the Archives. Will your father mind?" I turned to Val.

"He will not mind, dearest," Val said gently.

"Good." I bent time and folded space, traveling to the Archives of the future without waiting for Val.

In the Archives is a section that only a few have ever visited. Most don't realize it exists.

I'd found it during my yearlong stay, waiting for Kalenegar of the Larentii to decide my fate.

Perhaps my fate had already been decided, I just didn't realize it at the time.

I studied the bodies—three of them—that lay on stone slabs in this hidden portion of the Archives.

These weren't real—doppelgangers, perhaps, but certainly not the originals.

These replicas of the Three—Strength, Wisdom and Love, lay as if ready to awaken at any moment. They'd served a purpose once, and like all things in the Archives, they'd been kept, pristine and without decay, in these positions.

Strength was quite tall, with light-brown hair and a beautiful, ageless face. Wisdom was slightly shorter, with dark hair and more than handsome features.

Love was the only female, with dark hair and a pale, lovely complexion. This was how they'd look if they were to appear—those who'd defeated the enemy during the God Wars, in order to save the universes from chaos and death.

With the events happening on Earth in the past, that victory was threatened. For a moment, my vision wavered and I witnessed a change—as if the Three in reality lay before me instead of their replicas.

I had to think on this.

Ilya was gone.

Fuck Earth.

~

Captain Brett Walker

As long as I remained wolf, they couldn't work their mojo on me. I'd attacked them twice, and managed to rip an arm off one of them.

It didn't matter—they'd ordered Rafe to kill Jen and I wasn't going to let them get away with that. They'd have to kill me first.

They'd already shot me twice. I howled at them in return. They learned not to come into the room where I was; I finally killed one of the fuckers.

Instead, they had something new up their sleeves. If I wasn't going to behave and do as they ordered, they'd just send me elsewhere.

I yelped when I hit the floor inside the Oval Office. If one of the Secret Service agents hadn't stopped his buddies from firing, I'd have died immediately.

My consciousness fled before I could consider turning human.

Notes—Colonel Hunter

"So we're depending on a veterinarian to save his life?" Opal and Matt had shown up unannounced at my office to let me know that Brett had been dumped—in werewolf form—in the oval office.

Not only had he been shot twice, but there was evidence that he'd attacked some of his attackers.

I was grateful he was still alive, wolf or not. The President had called Matt, shouting gibberish after Brett's sudden appearance. Matt had gone to the White House immediately.

I still hadn't figured out how he'd gotten Brett out of there so fast.

We needed Farrell, but he was just as dead that afternoon as he'd been that morning.

"Screw that, we need Cori," I muttered.

"Corinne is unavailable," Valegar appeared inside my office. "I will heal Captain Walker for you, in her stead."

"Where is she?" I asked.

"She is thinking and cannot be disturbed. We should have considered her role as Vhanaraszh all along, instead of keeping her away from those things." Val's eyes carried sadness, and I couldn't say particularly why that was.

"What's that?" I said.

"We must tend to Captain Walker," Val brushed away my question and transported us to the animal hospital where Brett's wolf was being tended.

"Do you know where you were?" Matt asked when Brett woke. He lay on a hospital bed inside the ugly building in Arlington. Val had effected the change from wolf to human before healing Brett of his wounds.

"Hmmph," Brett snorted and named an Asian country I'd suspected all along. "I guess they think I don't recognize it when somebody speaks the language."

"Phillips is calling in his favors," Opal muttered from her seat nearby. "Toss a few crown jewels in somebody's direction and Bob's your uncle."

I'd forgotten about those, to be honest. Somebody hadn't forgotten, though.

"Tell me what happened with Rafe," Matt said.

"Agent Smith," Brett growled. "He was leading us in, his rifle in his hand, when he turned back. I thought he was going to tell us something. Instead, he knocks Rafe out with the butt of his rifle and his agents have their guns trained on Jen and me immediately. They forced us into Phillips' house, two of Smith's agents dragging Rafe between them. Phillips and several others were there waiting for us. They knew we were coming."

"Fuck," I wiped a hand across my face. Rafe had gone to protect Jen and Brett. Instead, he'd ended up killing Jen.

"The minute Rafe woke, Phillips was there, telling him he'd only do what he said from now on. It was uncanny how fast it happened. His eyes just went dead—as if he wasn't who he was anymore. When he killed—Jen, I knew it for certain."

"Did you see the other one—Rafe's doppelganger?" Opal asked.

"Dead—at least two days, if my nose was correct. Shot multiple times, as near as I could tell. Looked like he'd gone nuts and tried to destroy everything around him before it happened," Brett shook his head.

"So they were desperate to get their hands on Rafe," Matt sighed. "As a replacement. The other one went animal on them and they couldn't control him any longer."

"Has anyone told Katya—about her father?" Opal asked.

"I don't think so," I said. "This will kill her."

"Maybe she shouldn't know—it's not his fault. It isn't him anymore," Brett said and stared at his hands. "It happened so fast—nobody expected Smith to turn on us like that."

"Who is this Smith guy?" I asked. "Matt, do you know?"

"Not one of mine," Matt said. "If the President had any sense left, I'd ask him. As it is," he shrugged. "Smith could be anybody."

"Do we have any images of this guy?" I asked.

"Probably from somewhere," Matt nodded.

"Good. You get them and I'll ask Cori to take a look—the next time we see her."

"I will transport the images to her," Val offered. He'd been so quiet, I'd almost forgotten he was with us, still.

"Give me a few minutes," Matt said and loped out of the room.

~

Corinne

"Dearest, I hate to disturb you," Val appeared at my side. I stood on a porch designed after a Greek temple, which was connected to an outside display at the Archives.

"You're not disturbing me," I said, turning toward him.

"I have this," he handed a photograph to me. "Colonel Hunter says this is the man who betrayed Ilya. He calls himself Milton Smith— Lead Agent Milton Smith."

I went still for a moment, before reaching for the photograph with shaking fingers. My gaze raked across Smith's features many times, as if willing them to change. When I handed the picture back to Val, I understood much more than I had earlier.

"Tell Auggie that he won't be able to stop this one," I said. "No human can."

I knew Val wanted more information, but I couldn't give it to him. I wiped tears away and struggled to keep my sobs under control. How had I not suspected this? I'd read so many things in the Archives.

"What shall I tell Colonel Hunter to do, then?" Val asked gently. He attempted to place his arms around me, but I moved away from him.

I'd never felt so empty, before. Even when Ilya's obsession was to kill me, at least I knew he lived.

What he was now—Ilya was gone. An automaton had taken his place—one who would murder anyone on command. I considered bending time, but there were so many things to correct, so many things I wanted to do—or that needed doing, that the sheer magnitude of it was overwhelming.

I understood, somehow, that Val or Kalenegar or the Larentii as a whole would find a way to stop me before I was even halfway done. Perhaps some things I could get away with, but it wouldn't bring me any closer to righting the whole of the wrong.

As for destroying Agent Smith, well, I doubted any Larentii could do it.

Smith was a rogue god, after all, in a time before all the rogues had been destroyed.

Yes, I knew his name.

I also knew he had a weakness.

I saw it in his face. I wondered at the fact that I could read him, but then I'd always been able to read Opal and Matt, too. Perhaps it was a side effect of the drug.

Perhaps it was something else—whether blessing or curse, I couldn't say. Hugging myself, I turned back to the view off the porch. Did Phillips even know what he'd recruited to his cause?

I doubted that. Phillips, even as a clone, imagined himself to be in charge.

He wasn't.

Liron, the rogue god, was.

"Dearest, I know you are in pain. Allow me to help," Val spoke softly.

"I need to be alone for a while longer," I said. "I'm sorry. I just—have to work through this on my own."

"Call if you need me," he said. "Never forget that I love you."

"I won't forget," I whispered. "For as long as I live."

~

Notes—Colonel Hunter

"Val says we can't destroy this one—that no human can, according to Corinne," I handed the photograph back to Matt.

He and I sat in a small meeting room at the White House, fidgeting and waiting for another appearance from the President.

At times, I wondered if I shouldn't just go to the most respected journalist I knew and tell him everything, so the world would know that we were being led by someone in serious need of psychological help.

That would not only brand me as a fellow lunatic, but a treasonous one, too.

"We have intel," the President swept into the room, poor Laura Quimby almost running to keep up with him. "Those fuckers are in New York," he said. "They want to kill the entire city."

~

"Does he expect us to believe this?" I fumed.

We'd driven to Matt's office—it was closer to the White House—to discuss the evidence the President had given us for the insurgency's presence in New York.

Since Matt and I knew the sarin attacks weren't initiated by the insurgents, we doubted they'd have the gas or the drones necessary to launch an assault.

Yes, we had photographs, but those could be faked easily enough. I was just about to say that when Opal magically appeared in Matt's office.

I stopped breathing for a moment.

"It's time you knew," Matt sighed. "This has gone beyond what we signed up for."

"What the hell are you talking about?" I demanded, once I got my breath back.

"He's saying the insurgents aren't in New York—well, there may be a few, but they're still in hiding, too afraid to peek out of their shells," Opal huffed. "If anybody is in New York to kill people, it'll be the Lyristolyi—who, unwittingly, may be playing into another's hands for the worst end-game imaginable."

"Whose hands?"

"Agent Smith's, or so he calls himself. Corinne didn't identify him and we don't know his real name; he's relatively new in this part of the equation."

≈

James

We knew something was wrong. Katya was on edge all the time, which unsettled Sergei. Dr. Shaw did his best to calm both down, but he felt it, too.

Nathan said everything was under pressure—as if we were locked inside an airless space in which the breaths we drew felt like our last.

I couldn't disagree with him—I wanted to talk in whispers, like someone was listening that shouldn't be.

We hadn't seen Cori or Val for more than two days. I didn't know what to make of that, either, and wished for the trick she had of speaking mind-to-mind.

Bekzi—normally he and Gerrett were smiling or cheering up the rest of us. Both had succumbed to whatever this was. Neither could explain it, either. Whatever conversation they had, it was done mentally and the rest of us weren't included.

≈

Corinne

As a Larentii, I had a talent for making lists in my head—I could even visualize each list and add to or subtract from it. The lists I worked on now—were morbid in nature.

They held the names of the dead.

One list held the names of those who'd have died, regardless. Some of those names shocked and saddened me—to the point of depression.

The other held the list of names that shouldn't be dead. Their continued existence would have held the future together and helped keep chaos from becoming triumphant.

Norian and Lendill were on that list.

I hesitated before adding Ilya's name to that one. This was something I had to do quickly, before the histories recorded for the Archives shifted.

Yes, it could happen. Had happened—in lesser circumstances—already. I'm sure Nefrigar would have been happy to discuss it with me.

I didn't have time.

Nobody did. Not really.

I'd compared the lists so many times the names were burned on the cells of my eyes.

One name was missing from both lists.

One name could resolve nearly everything, when combined with the proper actions.

Holding out my arm, I studied it for a moment. As a Larentii, I had perfect, blue, flawless skin. Reaching out with my other hand, I *Pulled* away the tiny chip that Kalenegar had placed inside a wrist bone. This allowed them to track me, wherever I went. They'd said it in the beginning—I was an unreadable and impossible to track unless I sent mindspeech or expended certain types of power.

I intended to expend that power.

I merely didn't intend to wait this time for them to show up afterward.

Forming a replica of myself, similar to those of the Three in the Archives, I placed the chip in the wrist of my doppelganger and bent time.

CHAPTER 16

otes—Colonel Hunter

"James, stop worrying—the President is overreacting," I said over the phone. "Yes, I know the President has declared a state of emergency and ordered that D.C. be evacuated, but I'm pretty sure we're safe, here. He's doing the same thing to New York City, when there's really no evidence to support his claim that they'll be attacked with sarin."

"Colonel Hunter," Leo was now on the phone, "I hope you take all warnings seriously. I am becoming quite concerned over the state of affairs across the globe."

"Shaw? What the hell are you talking about?" I demanded.

"Don't you feel it?" he asked. "That you're in a pressure cooker that's about to blow?"

"Hell, I'm up to my eyebrows in worry that the President will send nukes into every nook and cranny, to take revenge on anybody who's ever looked at him wrong," I exploded. "You're safe where you are—or at least that's how it looks from where I'm sitting," I added.

"Do you want me to schedule a flight home?" he asked.

"No. Hell no," I shouted. "Just stay the hell away, and keep the others with you."

"Katya wants to know what has happened to her father and Corinne," he said.

That settled my hash in a blink. "Damn," I muttered and pinched the bridge of my nose.

"What happened?"

"Rafe—he's, well, he may as well be dead," I mumbled. "The enemy has him and he's—been obsessed again. Only this time, it's much, much worse. Corinne is in mourning. Val says that to the rest of us, Rafe *is* dead. Phillips is using him as a weapon, for who knows how much death and destruction."

"Fucking hell," Shaw cursed.

~

Corinne

There was one person I wanted to tell about my plan, and he was currently obsessed so deeply there was no reaching him. It involved him, after all, in addition to many, many others.

I sat at a small table at the coffee shop in Vancouver—the one Ilya and I had chosen during our search for Baikov. For us, that may as well have been a lifetime ago. Ilya probably didn't have the memory any longer—in my estimation, the obsession the Phillips clone placed was similar to those I'd seen in others the original had taken for slaves —they had no will of their own. Only Phillips' will mattered, and it consumed them.

Sure, I could pick a time to go back—to find Ilya and explain matters to him. There were several problems with that option. First, I'd be crying and holding onto him so hard, he'd know something was wrong right away.

Second, I'd be tempted—too tempted—to blow everybody else off and just disappear with him. I could fix it so we'd never be found, after all. That, of course, would leave everybody else in the cesspit that Earth had become, and the future would crumble just as surely as it was crumbling now.

That's what I wanted to fix in all this—the future. Fix it so the major events wouldn't be altered and the rogue gods would be just as dead. At this point in time, many of them still lived, and someone had called at least one of the hidden rogues out and set him on Earth to destroy everything.

Liron has a weak spot.

I reminded myself of that. I merely had to figure out how to exploit it, in order to convince him to leave Earth alone. Everything else in my plan hinged on that.

❧

Notes—Colonel Hunter

"You should beef up your security," Matt said. "If you intend to stay here."

"I thought this whole, crazy idea the President has didn't have merit," I blustered.

"But what if he's captured the attention of the Lyristolyi by attempting to evacuate everybody? Wouldn't it be perfect and serve to panic everybody if they manage to kill people while they're trying to escape from D.C. and New York? You've seen the gridlock on the news. It's prime time for them to act. Who do you think will start lobbing missiles first if they see hundreds of thousands drop dead while they're stuck in traffic jams on the streets?"

"Granville," I mumbled. "Who would he target first?"

"I think he'd consider a two-prong attack—the Middle East and Russia. If he wants to toss China into the mix," Matt went silent for a moment.

"And we have more than enough missiles to destroy them and every other country on the planet," I added for him. "All while they launch a counter-attack, and that will be all she wrote."

"It's what the Lyristolyi want—you can bet on that. They launch the initial attacks, then sit back and watch the rest of us destroy ourselves. To all outside interests, we will have destroyed ourselves. The Lyristolyi will remain blameless in this action. Except we know better. That's why you need to beef up your security. They'll be coming after anybody who can point a finger in their direction, you know. You're vulnerable—more than you realize, Colonel Hunter. Find some guards. Look for a way to get out if you have to. It may be the only thing standing between them and total destruction."

"Holy, fucking shit," I muttered. Right then, I wanted Corinne. And Rafe. The Rafe we knew, and not the one who may as well be dead. Those two I would trust with my life.

"What about Laci?" I asked. "Will they look for her, too? She's still at her sister's house."

"Anything's possible."

"Just when you think it can't get any worse," I sighed.

"Worse? That's coming," Matt said and ended the call.

Corinne

I'd determined that I couldn't talk to Ilya—not the present me. The past me—I'd already done that. It meant revisiting the past and concealing myself to hear the conversation between us, but I did it.

It was painful.

"Cabbage, all of us face terrible things. No matter how good we are, we cannot prevent all of them from happening." The sheets rustled as Ilya shoved them back and worked himself into a sitting position beside me—the me from the past.

"Will you answer a question for me, then?" she/I sighed.

"Always."

"What if," she began and then stopped.

"What if what?" Ilya said when she/I hesitated.

"Ilya, I love you more than anything," she said.

"And I you."

Watching from my hidden vantage point, I wept while dampening the sound. I still loved him more than anything, yet things had gone so far awry he couldn't be brought back from it.

"But what if—what if I'm faced with a choice—of saving you from something awful, or letting the enemy get away?" she said.

"Cabbage, listen to me," he said, pulling her face around so his eyes met with hers/mine. "Get that piece of excrement. No matter what. I have been taking care of myself for a very long time. Let me worry about me in that situation. Take the bastard down."

"Then you do the same, Ilya," she said before kissing him fiercely and drawing away to speak again. "No matter what my situation is, kill him if you can."

"I have never had a love such as this," he declared. "We understand one another."

"I've waited for you my whole life," she said and kissed him again.

I was sobbing as I folded space. We'd made a promise. I'd kept it once. I was about to do it again.

Winkler

"Dad, I'm not doing this." Wayne flung out a hand. "It's suicide—on your part. The Pack could turn on me immediately after, and where will all your grand plans be, then?"

"Look, I'm old," I pointed out. "It's only a matter of time before somebody comes to make a challenge. The Pack and the business needs to remain in Winkler hands, not somebody else's. This is to protect you, your sister and the children that will come. You understand me?" I gave him the sternest look I could muster.

The truth was, I had no idea how my father had done this. I was just as belligerent about it then as Wayne was, now. Inwardly I was quaking—I knew I'd have to throw the fight, and any wolf would realize how difficult that would be.

The instinct is strong in favor of preservation. Wayne was correct —it was suicide. He, like me, would be scarred the rest of his life because of it. Because of his role in it.

There wasn't any other way, though, unless I wanted to hand the Pack and everything else I had to a victor who'd have no mercy for my son. This was the only way.

"Son, you'll do this because I love you. I'll do it because you love me. That will never change," I said. "Remember that when I'm gone and you're Packmaster—that there was love between us, even at the last."

"Daddy." He came to me then and wrapped his arms around my neck.

"Hush, son, it'll be all right," I said and held him tight.

~

Opal

As it turned out, I'd been right about the rogue god. The trouble was, he had a Sirenali, which meant Matt and I had no way to get to him, or to tell how powerful he was. We'd pretty much screwed up by not taking things more seriously than we had.

I told you so wanted to come out of my mouth so badly, that I had to physically stop my words from forming. Matt misinterpreted my frown.

"I know I wasn't supposed to say anything to Hunter—it won't matter in the end," Matt snapped as I sent him a questioning look. "He'll just have a heads-up when they come to the door," he added.

"Right. So he'll have time to worry and be afraid beforehand," I retorted. "The timeline is fraying. Only a few more things to happen before it all turns to shit and we're on a battlefield again, only this time, it'll likely go the other way."

~

Gerrett

Corinne? I'd finally succumbed to my fears and attempted to contact her directly. Bekzi, who stood with me on the villa's patio, sighed and looked away. He knew what I was doing. He didn't try to stop me.

Honey, I can't talk right now, she returned. *Will you do something for me, though?*

Anything, I promised.

Ask Bekzi to make sure that you, James and Nathan are kept safe.

I will.

Thank you.

That was the end of our conversation. It was something I'd replay in my head in the future, but I failed to recognize the importance of it now. Instead, I relayed her message to Bekzi, who blinked at me with eyes that weren't quite humanoid before nodding.

"I do this," he confirmed aloud. "For her."

Notes—Colonel Hunter

"I think you may be in danger, too," I pointed out. Brett walked beside me, limping slightly since one of the bullets that hit him had been removed from his left leg. Valegar had healed the wound but it was still sore—that's what Brett said when I went to the ugly building in Arlington to collect him.

"Then why didn't they kill me when they had me before?" he asked.

"Because they wanted to make a point, and were probably counting on the Secret Service shooting you the minute they dropped you in the Oval Office," I said. "They want the President to know that they can now show up wherever, whenever. They want us all to know that nobody's safe. If that agent hadn't been a werewolf too, you'd be dead, now."

"At least the President has one good bodyguard, then," Brett huffed. "Where are we going?"

The winter sun was bright in the afternoon sky when we left the building, heading for the SUV I'd borrowed from the motor pool. I'd gone over it myself before settling in the driver's seat, and checked it again before allowing Brett to climb in on the passenger side.

Matt's call had spooked me—that's for certain. I had no idea whether there was a safe place for any of us, now. I sure as hell didn't want to go back to my office; it was the first place they'd look for me.

"We're going to a safe house," I said. "One the enemy doesn't know about."

I hope.

~

Morrett watched as Wymarr blasted the last of the personnel at the missile silo. According to Fisk, this was their last act—there was no need for anything else. They could leave the planet, knowing their goal had been accomplished.

When Wymarr sent these missiles toward their targets, there wouldn't be enough firepower to destroy all of them.

The countries in question would certainly retaliate.

More missiles would be launched—from everywhere.

Morrett had the vision of them crossing paths as they flew toward their intended targets. Nobody would be spared. Those who weren't killed by the bombs in the initial attacks would be subjected to a slow and hideous death as the poison destroyed them in swaths.

Fisk would make sure that he and his crew were far away when that happened. Fisk was upset that he couldn't retrieve Keef's body—it had been cremated in the blast set off by the intruders.

Morrett wondered if Deonus Wyyld knew his ASD Director was dead, yet. At first, he'd hoped ASD ships would come and deal with Fisk. He'd lost that hope soon after it formed.

Earth was too far from the Reth Alliance, and the doings on that remote planet held little interest for most of the Alliance's inhabitants. It was a lost cause, now. Morrett wanted to weep for lives lost, past and future, at the hands of Fisk and his crew.

Fuck Earth.

He recalled clearly what Fisk's underlings had written on the ceiling of the facility—the one where drug experimentation had been carried out.

Similar messages had been scrawled across walls on other worlds —just before Fisk and his crew destroyed them.

Morrett's obsession said he couldn't harm his masters. It didn't say he couldn't hate them. He hated Fisk with a passion equal and opposite to his love for books. He hated Fisk just as much as he hated his mother. Sliding down a wall in the underground bunker, he turned to reading as a distraction while Fisk's technicians disabled the archaic firing and guidance protocols, attached their own guidance systems to the missiles and then programmed them.

~

Larentii Archives
   Private files of Nefrigar
   Chief Archivist

"We knew this would happen," Kalenegar stood beside me as we gazed upon the construct Corinne had left in her place. The chip was even located properly in the wrist, just as Kalenegar had placed it.

"She will *Change What Was* as necessary, before returning to us," Kalenegar continued. "It will only require bringing Kccf and Schaff back, and perhaps a few others," he shrugged.

"We have already decided that her other mate is irretrievable," Kalenegar added. "His death may be painful for her. If she is unable to bring it about, Matt Michaels is prepared to do this, after Ilya brings the deaths of a few others, you understand. When that occurs, then he will be hunted across the globe and Matt's agency will take credit for destroying the monster he has become."

"Do you think she knows that more deaths are coming at Ilya's hands? This could send her in a dangerous direction," I observed.

"It won't matter," Kalenegar gestured, dismissing the information. "She is Larentii. She will know when it is wrong to interfere."

I studied the Head of the Council for a moment before turning to my son. There was a hesitation in him as his eyes met mine. As if he considered speaking and then thought better of it.

As did I.

Corinne was the Vhanaraszh; her part no Larentii could predict. I refrained from pointing that out to Kalenegar. Things would go as they would, with no interference from me. I merely worried that my child—and his mate—could be harmed emotionally before this was over.

~

Captain Brett Walker

"I'm not the best cook," Colonel Hunter confessed. "I can do grilled cheese. Bacon and eggs. Nothing fancier than that, I'm afraid. Laci is an amazing cook, as is Corinne. Damn, I wish Cori were here."

I understood he didn't want her here to cook. He wanted her here because she spelled safety for both of us. After my brief stint in captivity, I'd never felt so unsettled and unsafe.

Control is something you never understand until you don't have it. That's when you realize that it was never really yours to begin with. It's an illusion, at the best of times. Colonel Hunter and I stood at the stove in the safe house's kitchen, studying the contraption in order to determine how to get it to work. At the moment, we didn't even have control over household appliances.

That's when the doorbell rang. We froze. I pulled the pistol I carried from my waistband and followed Colonel Hunter to the door. He peered through the peephole to see who it was.

"A kid selling cookies," he turned to me with a grin. I replaced the weapon in my back waistband while Hunter opened the door.

"Surprised?" The girl morphed into Rafe Black, whose grin was nasty as he fired three times at Colonel Hunter, the last shot hitting him in the forehead from close range. Rafe disappeared before I could fire my weapon.

~

Personal Diary—Laura Quimby

It was supposed to be an ordinary afternoon, which would be followed by an ordinary evening at the White House. President Granville was scheduled for meetings all afternoon, and I'd arranged his schedule to fit in a short break between his four and five o'clock.

Secret Service Agents began running into the Oval Office as the President sipped the soft drink I'd carried to him.

"Colonel Hunter is dead—shot by Rafe Black, sir," one of the agents reported. "We have to get you to the bunker. You're in danger."

I watched as the President stood—almost in slow motion. Two agents grabbed him and attempted to lead him toward the exit. The dark-haired man appeared with an assault rifle in his hands.

No matter how many times the agents surrounding the President fired at the intruder, their bullets bounced off some sort of invisible shield around him. One of those bullets ricocheted and hit me in the shoulder while I shouted into a phone that the Oval Office was under attack.

I barely remember falling afterward; I watched the President die as I bled onto the rug—the one that depicted the President's seal. My head lay on the eagle's breast, but it offered no protection or comfort.

The President fell beside me, his eyes already losing their light as I gazed into them.

~

Opal

By the eleven o'clock news, Rafe's photograph was splashed on every television screen across the globe. Images were shown from cameras placed in sensitive areas across the globe—including the U.S.

Colonel Hunter's safe house was equipped with a camera, and the footage showed a grinning Rafe pumping bullets into the Colonel before he disappeared from view.

Eyewitness accounts from the Oval Office said the same thing about President Granville's death—the assassin was identified as Rafe Black by a White House aide.

In all, Rafe had been directed to assassinate Granville, Hunter, the President of France, the Prime Minister of Great Britain and the leaders of sixteen other world countries, including Greece, Russia, Japan and Australia.

Matt, I sent. *I think it's time you got the hell away. I figure I know what's coming next.*

What about you? he returned.

I think Bree will want a first-hand account, I replied. *I'm a big girl. I can take care of myself. Say hello to your mom for me, okay?*
Will do. Call if you need me.
I will.

Corinne

I knew what Ilya had done. I also knew that Katya and Sergei wept because of it. The images were everywhere, after all, of Ilya murdering world leaders.

My vision blurred after a moment; I realized I was weeping, too.

I was still sobbing when the missiles launched from a U.S. silo that ended up obliterating Russia and the Middle East.

Gerrett

Bekzi made sure I understood the languages on the news programs, so he wouldn't have to interpret them for me. All of it was terrible, and Katya suffered most from seeing her father listed as a murderous assassin on every major continent.

I understood what had happened—perhaps better than anyone else at the villa. I carried an obsession, after all. Rafe—he carried many. They'd taken away every scrap of will he had and replaced it with their own—this nameless, faceless Sirenali.

I clenched my fists in fury as the images played across the screen. This one, whomever he was—he was like my mother. Conniving. Hungry for power and wealth. Using others as tools to get those things while accepting no blame themselves.

"The words—they die with Elemaiya," Bekzi murmured.

I turned to him quickly and blinked.

How? I sent.

"I know they use words—transfer you to new master," Bekzi said.

"Those words—they dead now. With Elemaiya. You free. Corinne— she make sure," he said. "When time to go, I take you, too."

I didn't say it, but in my heart, I wanted to go with Corinne. No matter where she intended to go. She pulled at me in a way I couldn't deny.

Bekzi snorted. *I feel same*, he sent.

$\sim$

Corinne

There is a star system less than sixty light-years from Earth, with an inhabited planet. Yes, they'd discovered coffee there, too, only they served it much darker and stronger than most of Earth's continents did.

I'd employed power to dilute it first, then added hot milk and vanilla syrup before attempting to drink. I sipped coffee while extending my vision to witness the destruction of Earth.

Yes, I still felt like crying. The remnants of humanity attempted to dig out of the rubble left behind, while many of them sickened and died of radiation poisoning. The climate had been altered, too, so that poisoned rain fell, killing plants and animals alike.

I was surprised that I hadn't heard from Val or any other Larentii, but I probably would soon enough. I had a game plan, now, and my first action would draw an outcry from anyone with blue skin.

I wanted to send an "I love you," to Val, but that could reveal my whereabouts. I couldn't take any chances from now on; the plan was about to be activated and I wouldn't be able to stop once it was in motion.

Draining my cup, I rose with a sigh and placed a credit token on the cafe table. The server would never know I'd altered their coffee to render it drinkable to me. They'd also never realize that a Larentii sat at their table, casually considering how to rewrite history with the fewest strokes possible.

Taking a deep breath, I bent time to arrive at a certain missile silo in the U.S. No, I didn't intend to stop the first wave of missiles. Or the second or third, for that matter.

No.

I needed to find the Lyristolyi, and I knew where and when they'd be at the silo. I intended to read them, before bending time again and making them very, very dead. They—and the one or ones who sent them, had become my first targets.

CHAPTER 17

*C*orinne

I found I'd arrived a few minutes early. Shielding myself from the sight of silo personnel, I watched as they busied themselves with routine checks and communications.

Until the Lyristolyi arrived and put a stop to it by killing all of them.

It won't matter, I kept telling myself as shots were fired and blood spilled.

One member of the Lyristolyi team—one I did and didn't expect—kept himself away from the violence and huddled against a wall before pulling out a comp-vid and avoiding the massacre by reading a book.

His name was Morrett, he was Sirenali and I sympathized with his plight.

Like Gerrett, he was mute. Like Gerrett—they were kin. Brothers. Gerrett had never said the name of his brother. I knew it now, just by looking at him. Reading him.

Forcing my eyes away, I turned to the wizard employed by the Lyristolyi.

Wymarr Belancour.

Grasping.

Ambitious.

I'd feel no grief allowing him to die with the others.

Just not yet.

I turned to Fisk Boralus, then. He was operating under the direction of Geethe Cheriss, Prime Potentate of Lyristolys. There were no rogues, here. These were undercover agents who knew exactly what they were doing.

They'd done it before, after all.

They were experts in making it look as if worlds had destroyed themselves, when in actuality, they'd initiated conflict and let nature take its course. There was nothing noble in them or their cause—what they'd accomplished so far could have been done easier and with far less bloodshed.

What I searched for last was dates and times—when they'd appear at a convenient place for me to meet up with them.

All part of my plan.

The only one I'd allow to live afterward was Morrett.

I merely had to decide where to send him, so he'd be safest and most effective. *It'll come to me,* I promised myself and folded space.

Opal

"You're just as safe here as anywhere else," I said. I'd folded space to arrive at the villa for breakfast, bearing bags of groceries.

Food that was untainted by radiation would be hard to come by in the near future. In one way, it was fortunate that Earth's population had taken such a hit. It would be difficult enough to feed the few survivors.

Still, there'd been no word or actions from Corinne.

I was beginning to worry.

After all, I understood that Rafe was still out there, doing his master's bidding. I wanted to laugh humorlessly at the fact that Phillips' bid for world domination would be over a shrinking, dying world.

He'd be in charge of poisoned fields and mountains of rotting corpses.

In other words, he'd be a despot in charge of nothing. It would be laughable if so many hadn't been sacrificed. What good would crown jewels and an alliance with an Asian dictator do him now?

He'd been played, just like the rest of Earth's population.

That's when I felt the first tremor.

Yes, I, like many others who held power, expected Corinne to *Change What Was* for a handful of people. To be there at the right moment to restore their lives.

Nobody would blame her if Ilya were among that number.

Nobody expected something of this magnitude.

Lyristolys

Grand Chambers of the Prime Potentate

Corinne

Only a Sirenali, a Larentii—or a god or godling—can hide themselves so thoroughly from those who hold power.

Geethe Cheriss was alone in the Grand Chamber—he'd sent his aides and servants away.

He was expecting company, after all. Company that wasn't supposed to exist. Company that would brand him an outlaw if they and their deeds were revealed. I waited just as Geethe did, for their arrival.

I'd made preparations and I intended for everything to go without a hitch.

Of course, I expected an outcry from Kalenegar and several others when time shifted afterward, but I was resolved now and there was no turning back.

Fisk Boralus and his crew arrived, courtesy of Wymarr Belancour. Well, Wymarr and his half-talented family had dabbled too often in the wrong waters. They would continue to do so, but without Wymarr's assistance.

The time had come. Employing power, I locked all the doors leading into the chamber and placed a shield to prevent Wymarr's escape.

Then, I *Pulled* in my weapon.

He was hungry.

Dinosaur Boy had a feast that day; eventually Wymarr grew too weary to fold space away from him and his spells and blasts just bounced off DB's tough scales. Eventually, when DB tired of the game of chase, Wymarr was also devoured.

No, I didn't turn my eyes away from the carnage. Not after the visions had come to me of children turned to dust by nuclear weapons, or babies dying afterward quickly because they had no defense against radiation sickness.

Fisk and his crew never turned a hair or felt a moment of guilt over the deaths of innocents. Morrett, on the other hand, did feel sorrow. I'd sent him away before DB began eating—there was no reason to inflict further trauma on him. I'd finally figured out what to do with him and imagined how surprised he'd be when and where he'd landed.

I also imagined that he'd be safe enough there, and he'd end up keeping those around him safe from the predations of those intending harm.

Yes, a root of history had just been destroyed. I was about to destroy more of them. Peeling myself away from the wall, I studied the Grand Chamber for a moment. DB had been neat in his table manners—for the most part. Only a blood-slicked floor remained of Fisk, Geethe, Wymarr and company.

Nice work, I sent to DB before neutralizing his blood and sending him to the planet where he should have been born. There, the oceans were filled with his kind. He'd learn to communicate with them and live his life as he should.

What in the name of the Three are you doing? Kalenegar's voice snapped in my head. I folded space before he had time to follow those words with his arrival.

~

Opal

"What's happening?" Katya quavered. She, Sergei and their friends were terrified. James and Nathan had arms wrapped about each other after the quiet settled.

"Time in limbo," Bekzi explained. "Course change. More coming, I think."

"What does that mean?" Leo Shaw whispered.

"It means that someone powerful is affecting the timeline," I whispered back. There really wasn't any need to stay quiet, but the entire planet had gone still and shadowy. Even the lights overhead flickered and went out, leaving us in darkness.

~

Corinne

My next stop was a gamble. This one—it could kill me. There was a danger in that—to the one who might raise his hand against me. I had to play my hand and play it deftly, when I'd never been a good poker player.

I'd have to see Ilya, too—the Ilya who was obsessed with killing me. I could shield myself against his attacks, including those from the warlock he'd become. Those would have to be muted so Agent Smith, AKA Liron the god, could hold a conversation with me.

I had to do something no Larentii had ever done before, and it felt painful.

I knew Liron's weak spot. I knew *why* he had a weak spot.

After all, few artists want to destroy their masterpieces. He'd been tasked with creating a world. He hadn't known why he was given that task, but took it with joy and a great deal of planning.

The planet Ranos had come into being under his skilled hands, and there were two races that lived upon it; the Ranali and the Avii. Then, Liron's taskmaster came to explain Ranos' purpose. The swiftly evolving population would build terrible weapons, and the planet itself would harbor an all-consuming poisonous creature.

Ranos was doomed from the start.

Liron had been so intent in his purpose that he failed to notice what his superior was planning.

Liron loved both races he'd created—with an all-consuming love. When the poison his superior planted in its core devoured the planet and killed most of its inhabitants, Liron moved the survivors to another world.

Sadly, some of the poison moved with them, and he needed a way to contain it. The Avii he moved were charged with protecting the humanoids from Ranos, and instructed on how to force the poisonous creatures to become dormant. He called it the *First Ordinance*, and they were bound to keep his commandments.

I was about to upset his applecart, by threatening the remains of the races he'd created. He couldn't kill a Larentii; if he did, the legend said the One would come and retaliate. If the One appeared now, all hell could break loose.

Literally.

The One would come, but it couldn't be now. This wasn't the proper time.

I was about to play a dangerous, dangerous game with a god.

No, I'd never played craps or any other dice game. The stakes were huge and I was about to risk everything on beginner's luck at rolling the bones.

The Dictator's palace may as well have been empty—I walked through it unseen and unheard, heavily shielded while I made my way toward the blank spot in it. I knew I'd find Phillips' clone there, hiding what he didn't want revealed to anyone else with power.

I understood that Liron would be with him, too; Phillips was Sirenali and Liron couldn't find him either, should he manage to get away. Liron, therefore, would remain in close contact with Phillips, in order to pull Phillips' strings when necessary.

Yes, I knew Auggie was dead.

As was Granville and dozens of other world leaders. Ilya had accomplished that for Phillips, but likely at Liron's urging. Rogue gods wanted to destroy Earth. I had suspicions as to why, but those would have to remain what they were; as suspicions only. I had no time to dedicate to their unraveling.

When I walked into the antechamber of Phillips' suite, I found Ilya.

A bowl of uneaten rice lay on the floor close to his feet—he was chained in the corner without benefit of a chair or bedding. In a slow, steady rhythm, he knocked his head against the wall.

Some spark in his brain, as small as it might be, wanted to escape.

I had no time to weep for his plight. I couldn't even send soothing mindspeech—he'd likely been programmed to alert his master if that happened. I didn't want to fall into a trap; everything hinged on my taking those in the next room by surprise.

No, I didn't intend to kill Phillips.

Not yet.

It wasn't time.

No, I had to convince Liron to leave and then stay away. Turning away from Ilya, I stepped toward the door—the one leading deeper into the suite. Phillips, Liron and who knew what else waited for me there.

Larentii Archives

Nefrigar, Chief Archivist

"It is written into our laws—you cannot force a Larentii to act against his mate," I said. "Even if his mate has done wrong."

"She is my mate, too," Kalenegar shouted. Yes, in that respect, he was much like his father, Ferrigar.

"You did not declare openly," Valegar pointed out. "Whereas I did. I refuse to act against my mate. I have to trust that she understands her actions and has thought them through completely before employing them."

"These are not actions," Kalenegar thundered. "This is a violation of our laws. She has gone to a meeting between Cheriss and his hidden operatives—before they ever arrived on Earth. She caused the timeline to shift because of that. We all felt it. If she comes to us now and confesses her actions, she will be punished but not too severely. The Council is calling for her separation now."

"That has not been done for hundreds of thousands of years," I pointed out. "I feel it foolish to rush to that sort of judgment now."

"We must bring her back. The Council must be made to understand that she acted in a moment of weakness. She will be confined, but that is all—if she returns now."

"She is the Vhanaraszh," I said. "The prophecy says that she will travel her own path and wondrous things will occur."

"They were talking about Breanne," Kalenegar snapped. "Who is also the Mighty Heart, lest you forget. This one," he snorted and shook his head. "This one was created by the drug and we are seeing the detrimental side effects of that now. If she wishes to keep her life, she must return now. I will see that she learns what is necessary to become a proper Larentii."

"And if she fails to return? If she continues to alter the timeline greatly?" Valegar's voice was soft. I knew he was angry; Kalenegar did not.

"Then she will be separated. I cannot help her past this point. That is why I came to you—to ask for your help in bringing her back. I see that you do not wish to cooperate. In doing so, you may as well sign away her life."

"Her life is her own," Valegar stated flatly and disappeared.

~

Corinne

The reason time hadn't flowed backward to before the missiles were fired was because they'd been scheduled to fire anyway. If Fisk and company hadn't done it, then Liron intended to see it done. Therefore, those events hadn't changed. The cause had merely shifted to another set of shoulders.

That's why Earth was still a smoking ruin after nuclear Armageddon had arrived. The situation was tricky enough—that fact made it worse. Those humans who'd survived were huddled in the safest place they could find, praying for deliverance. I wanted to weep for all of them. Tightening my resolve, I stepped through the door.

I found the Phillips clone, a Hal Prentice clone and a Merle Askins clone, ironically playing poker with Liron, who was still disguised as Agent Smith. I released my shield, becoming visible to all present before lifting a hand and freezing Phillips, Askins and Prentice inside a tight shield.

"I can release them, you know," Liron tossed away his disguise. I admit, the fact that he had white wings threw me for a moment.

"I'll separate their particles," I shrugged, feigning indifference. "I know you can't bring back the dead. Only a handful can do that. You're not one of them."

"I can destroy you," he said. I noticed his eyes were a pale brown and his hair matched his eyes—for the most part. Strands of gold, copper and silver threaded through his thick mane, making him more than unusual. That, combined with his white wings, made him appear to be a creature from a myth or fairy tale.

"You know what will happen if you destroy a Larentii," I retorted, attempting to force my anger to the surface. "Your life won't be worth the dust on your feet when the One shows up."

"Hmmph. You think I care about that?" He was calling my bluff.

"What you should care about is the people of Fyris," I upped the ante. "I know about them. Hell, there's a whole section in the Larentii Archives about them. The Avii, too. I see you made the Avii in your image." I inclined my head and pretended to give him the once-over.

"Larentii do not interfere," he snorted and started to turn away.

"This Larentii already has." I sent images, then, of me bringing DB into the Grand Chamber of the Lyristolyi—in the past. I'd wiped out an entire root of the timeline tree when I'd done that. "Didn't you feel it? I sure as hell did. It's why you had to launch the missiles yourself."

"That was you?" He turned back to me quickly.

"That was me," I jerked my chin down in a half-nod. "This is what I have planned for the races you've created, if you don't get the hell away from here and erase your existence from Earth's timeline. *Any* of Earth's timelines."

I showed him Siriaa—the planet where the Avii and the Fyrians resided. I also showed him the images of it withering and dying, people, animals, everything.

"You wouldn't—Larentii do not," he began, before stopping and blinking at me.

"I know about the poison," I said. "How do you think the Alliance will react if they learn you're growing that foul mess in Fyris, waiting for the day when your superior asks for it? You know it was designed to destroy everything. It already destroyed Ranos. How about I send mindspeech to everyone in the Alliance, telling them where to find Siriaa? How long do you expect your people to last when that happens?"

"No," he held up a hand and backed away.

"Remove yourself from Earth's timeline. I know you're powerful enough to do it. Hide yourself if you want, but I'd go back in time far enough to fool your superior. You seem clever enough. I'm sure you'll come up with something."

"You won't kill my people," he attempted to call my bluff again.

"Try me," I said. "I have nothing else to lose at this point. You leave or they die. Choose quickly; I'm tired of waiting."

I saw images flit through his mind, then, of possible answers to the dilemma I presented.

No, he didn't want to die—especially at the hands of the One. He also wanted to ensure the safety of the two races he'd created. I threatened them.

Without a word, he disappeared.

Yes, I waited and *Looked*, to make sure he'd left the timeline completely. Another jolt came—a bigger one, this time, and I watched as his place at the poker table disappeared.

I felt beyond weary, then, and knew I'd have to recharge. Just before Kalenegar arrived to take me into custody while he shouted in mindspeech that the Council had declared my death sentence, I released Phillips, Askins and Prentice before folding space to get away.

~

Larentii Archives

Nefrigar, Chief Archivist

Valegar had hidden himself among the stacks and shelves containing Earth's history. Parts of it were now dark; other parts flickered, as if in flux.

They were in flux, I reminded myself.

Corinne had been declared a rebel and an outcast by the Larentii Council. Kalenegar had aligned with them.

Valegar tasted the bitterness of depression and regret, choosing to do nothing to reset certain levels in his body to reject those things. I worried about my son. If things became worse, I intended to call his brothers.

With all of us working together, we would set everything right.

For now, however, Val and I mourned.

We mourned Corinne, who could be destroyed by any Larentii the next time she was found.

We mourned for Val's unborn child, too, who should have had Corinne as a mother. Someday, perhaps, Val could locate a found mother—one the Wise Ones thought suitable. I found it strange, however, that the Wise Ones had refrained from passing judgment on Corinne, remaining silent instead on her deeds as well as her future.

A part of me wondered at that.

The other one we hadn't heard from was Breanne—or any of the Mighty.

Sighing, I sent comforting thoughts to my son and walked away.

Corinne

The next part of my plan pivoted on timing. Everything had to be just so, in order to achieve the proper result. A miscalculation at this point could allow the drug and some of its recipients to slip through, only to create destruction on Earth again.

I couldn't let that happen.

D.C. was my next stop, after I fed.

Opal

I had a shield in place around the villa, or it would have been affected, too. Outside, the sun blinked on and off like a pulsar, as time ran backward. Tentatively, I *Looked*, testing the waters outside our small island.

Lives, buildings, countries—so many things fell and rose, died and lived in the strangest planetary disco anyone could imagine. It hurt to look at it after a few seconds.

"Stay in the house and draw all the curtains," I told James and Nathan, who'd wandered onto the terrace. "If you don't, it may cause madness."

"Don't look," I snapped as both attempted to turn and do just that. I ended up folding them inside the house and slamming shutters and curtains closed on every window. Earth was now a runaway horse heading for a cliff. I hoped there wasn't a sudden stop waiting for us at the end.

"Corinne, please be right," I muttered as I locked the villa against escape by its inhabitants.

Corinne

I'd been forced off-planet to feed—I hadn't realized what would happen when two timelines were destroyed, one right after the other. At least the wild disco had stopped by the time I'd fed and slept on Tulgalan.

Before I went back, I'd been forced to determine the day for me to appear—a day when I was assured I'd have time alone with the real, original President Phillips. The one who was neck-deep in his nefarious plans, but not so far into them that the drug had been given to too many and before the clones he'd ordered practically covered the earth.

Eventually I made a choice—I knew just the day.

The day before my husband and I had walked into the Louvre, thinking we were going to see famous works of art we'd never seen in person.

The real Phillips still sat in the President's chair at that time; it was by his command that I'd been given the drug.

All I needed was a short amount of time to see what he knew, who he knew was involved with the drug and where, in both Russia and the U.S., it was hidden. If all went well, I intended to take care of those things.

If you continue with this madness, Kal's voice hissed in my mind, *you will set things in motion that you cannot comprehend.*

I love you, too, I replied and folded space.

Opal

When the dust settled, I unlocked the doors. All of us walked outside. James carried his cell phone, which was now tuned to a U.S. news program.

Everything appeared normal.

"Can we go home, now?" Nathan asked.

"Corinne isn't finished," I said. "You need to wait a little longer."

"Cori's doing this?" James whirled to face me.

"She's trying to make it right."

"Will it be right?" Leo Shaw asked.

"Only history will say for sure," I shrugged.

Corinne

He—Phillips—sat at his desk, reading a bill and acting perfectly normal. He hadn't become Sirenali, yet. I studied him for nearly an hour as he turned pages, scanning the thick document.

That's when the real Hal Prentice wandered in and settled on a guest chair.

"Everything's in place for tomorrow—those paintings may as well be ours already," Phillips said without looking up.

"Will he keep his end of the bargain? We need those weapons designs sent to the proper location. His people will do the testing for us and make sure everything works before we go into full production."

"Don't worry," Phillips turned a page. "It's all taken care of."

"Minimum loss of life at the museum?"

"You can't make an omelet without breaking eggs," Phillips mumbled. "We have to make this look real. Without those deaths, it won't look real. Everyone will think those paintings destroyed, and on live television, too. As for the crown and other things, those are already in our possession. It's what he wanted, to ensure his cooperation."

I'd heard enough.

"Well, hello, boys," I said, revealing the taller, bluer me.

"What the hell?" Prentice scrambled out of his seat and backed toward the President's desk.

"Oh, I'm a drug survivor—from your future," I replied. "Except it won't be from your future, now." Before Phillips could fire the gun he'd drawn from a desk drawer, I separated their particles.

I may have laughed while I did it. I can't really say.

That afternoon and evening, I lost count of the people I destroyed. Either by separating particles or by remote killing, the talent I'd had in my first incarnation. For those who'd received the drug that I didn't want to kill, their blood was neutralized. I didn't want Nick or Maye clones running around anywhere.

As for Becker, he was still a bully. The autopsy report claimed his death was due to an unusual blood clot in the brain. I didn't waste more time on him than that.

Richard Farrell, though, I had to think a long time about him. He ended up being the only one I went back to the beginning for. I neutralized the stash of drug he had to experiment on himself.

That meant he was very, very old where and when I was at the moment.

Every jolt that unsettled the timeline after I interfered—I received angry mindspeech from Kalenegar. I knew what he wasn't saying, though.

He wasn't saying that I was marked for death if any Larentii found me. I'd known all along it would come to that. I already had a plan in place, just as Phillips did.

Like Phillips, too, nothing would stop those he'd paid to show up at the Louvre the following day.

It was my final act—before the curtain closed.

I figured Kal would eventually figure it out and show up to take me. That's why I had to maneuver around him. I still had something to do and nobody was going to stop me.

I'd never gotten to see the grand works of art in the Louvre—the attack had happened shortly after our arrival. We'd arranged to be included in a guided tour, so we and those poor souls with us had already been marked for death by Phillips and his horde.

This time, I'd taken a private tour while heavily shielded, just so I could see the things I hadn't before. I'd already viewed the *Mona Lisa* and many, many other things. The painting that caught my attention, however, was *The Funeral of Phocion*, by Nicholas Poussin.

I stood feet away, studying it. Phocion, a politician often known as Phocion the Good, had lived a frugal, quiet life as an Athenian Statesman. Eventually, however, he'd fallen out of favor and been sentenced to death by a new regime.

He'd been ordered to drink hemlock, after which his body was denied burial in Athens. At that moment, I felt a kinship with him.

In the painting, his body was being carried away from the city by two slaves. There were no mourners present to mark his death— everyone else in the painting is going about their business and take no notice of his passing. Even in death, Phocion had been banished from the city he served for so long.

Pulling my gaze away from the image, I went in search of those who were gathering to attack the Louvre. They'd formed an elaborate scheme to steal works of art and a king's crown, to feed the desires of an Asian dictator.

Kal would come to the museum at the time allotted for them to begin their killing, thinking I would appear then.

He would be too late.

Those employees on the inside, who'd accepted a bribe to let the assumed terrorists in? They were already dead inside an office. They'd be discovered later.

Folding space to a nearby building, I held my anger in check as I released the particles of eleven would-be killers.

At the Louvre, it would just be another day.

Except for one thing.

I folded space to the museum, shielding myself from view.

If this were a movie, then someone would put music to this scene —something sad and nostalgic. For what was and could have been, and what everything had come to in the end.

Instead, there was nothing but silence as I stared across a marble floor at myself. There, the former me, aging and standing apart from her husband, blinked right back.

I even heard tourists talking about the many, sudden deaths of people scattered across several continents. News programs had repeatedly spoken their theories concerning the disappearance of President Phillips and his Chief of Staff, too. Everybody was scratching their heads, wondering who could have kidnapped the American President with no sign or appearance of a ransom note.

The attackers were already dead—there would be no blood on marble floors today.

Elsewhere, the attackers' contacts, cohorts and conspirators were also dead. I'd made a note of all of them when I'd read the attackers. That, combined with information garnered from Phillips, Askins and everyone else, ensured that Mary Evans and anyone she worked with was dead.

She'd been in charge of the Paris operation. I had no sympathy for her.

As for Baikov and the Russian President? They'd be found dead in the same room at the Kremlin, their deaths attributed to some strange malady.

In this time, Ilya had never met me.

In this time, we'd never had the chance to fall in love and marry. I wanted to weep for my—our—loss. I couldn't; I had something to do.

It was time to complete my plan.

This—this last act—was all that was left.

Good-bye, Ilya, I sent, knowing he'd never hear me.

Cue the music.

Lifting my hand (the one that Ilya's ring had disappeared from) and realizing what would happen when I exerted power, I released the particles of my former self across the room, knowing that I would disintegrate right along with her.

Across that distance, just before we both disappeared forever, I saw her nod in acceptance.

CHAPTER 18

Personal Notes—Kalenegar of the Larentii

    I arrived too late. Yes, I realized the irony of it. I was set to release her particles. By the time I learned what she intended, it was to see the last of her—and her previous self's—particles spread and wink out of existence.

I kept myself shielded as I dropped to my knees and sobbed.

At the end, she'd fixed everything. She'd turned rebel to do it, but she'd accomplished the impossible.

Then, at the end, she'd left us all, completing her self-imposed mission.

She'd planned this so carefully, down to the minutest detail, and on another day, I would marvel at her skill.

But not today. Today, I would mourn my mate, as was proper.

Opal

"It's over."

Bekzi and I were the only ones left at the villa, now.

In the last wave of changes, our guests had disappeared, some in a group, others by themselves. Poor James—he'd shouted and wept when Nathan disappeared first.

"This," Bekzi swept out his hand, indicating the villa, "It belong someone else, now."

"The original owner," I agreed. "We're a few years earlier than when we started out. Earth's history—some of it, will take a detour and go down a different road."

"Yes." Bekzi nodded. "Still," he added, "I make promise. I keep." He disappeared.

~

Larentii Archives

Nefrigar, Chief Archivist

I followed Valegar as he gently carried the replacement body Corinne had left in the Archives. I thought perhaps he'd lay it on a pedestal in the same room with those left behind by the Three.

Instead, he carried it toward the section of Earth's history that had gone dark. There, he fashioned a glass box for Corinnelar's duplicate and set it carefully amid the chaos that this particular section had become.

In all of it, the replacement body looked beautiful and pristine. I watched as Valegar's tears dropped onto the glass before he stepped away.

Mourning is never simple.

Or easy.

It is a painful, solitary journey that we all take, at times.

I love you, child, I sent to him. *As do your brothers. We will stand with you in the days ahead, no matter what comes.*

~

Dublin, Ireland

Katya, the message began,

I regret to inform you that your father, Ilya Kuznetzov, passed from this life earlier today while still in prison. My condolences to you and Sergei for this terrible loss.

Ambassador Bespalov

Katya wept.

~

One Year Later

Notes—Colonel Hunter

I read the message on my phone for the fifth time. Laci knocked on my study door again, telling me we would be late for dinner with the President and Secretary of State. I understood that newly elected Amelia Sanders was looking to fill her cabinet. What I failed to understand was why she might consider me.

After Merle Askins' sudden death, the Joint Chiefs had resigned, leaving a gap that Madam President would have to fill quickly. Shaking those thoughts away, I turned my attention to the message on my phone.

James was dead. James, Lieutenant Nathan Cross, James' companion, and two others had been killed in a diving accident off the coast of Hawaii.

I couldn't comprehend that James was gone. The media had the idea that he and Lieutenant Cross were together and were reporting them as a couple. I always imagined that James would tell me someday, but not like this.

"Come in, sweetheart," I said when Laci knocked on the door again. "I have bad news," I added.

~

Le-Ath Veronis

Queen Lissa's Private Journal

"What is it?" I asked. Renée Coffin, my third personal assistant, walked into my study with a cream-colored envelope in her hand. I froze.

I knew that stationery.

What the hell was Charles up to now?

"It says," Renée began, "To Queen Lissa, from Corinne Watson."

I didn't draw a breath for several seconds.

Corinne was dead—she'd separated her own particles in the past. She'd learned, however, the trick the Larentii had for delivering messages at a specified time in the future. Instead of mindspeech, however, she'd taken another tack, making sure I'd sit up and take notice.

Smart woman.

Well, Larentii. I held out my hand, willing it not to shake.

Renée handed the envelope to me.

Hello, Lissa, the message began.

I was hoping to be there in the past, when Winkler decided to hand the Pack to his son by deliberately losing the challenge. I was supposed to be there, I think, but things got in the way.

What this means, really, is that if you love your werewolf, then you need to go now—don't delay—and save him from himself. I know you hold the power and talent now to do it, whereas you didn't in the past.

Go save your love. I would have if it were possible.

Corinne

Without stopping to blink, I bent time and folded space. There wasn't any way I would ever not love my wolf, and I would save him now because, as Corinne so deftly pointed out, it was necessary and she couldn't. Belen would get a surprise visit from me afterward, but it was possible that he wouldn't be so surprised after all.

Karathia

"It's a boy," the healer smiled at the mother. The boy's father, Braxlin Ironsmith, stood nearby, nodding proudly. The labor had been long and intense. The mother's eyes closed in exhaustion and she slept while the healer settled the baby at her breast.

Braxlin had a son—his first child and a warlock to add to the family. He was more than proud and smiled fondly at wife and child.

"The name? For the records?" The healer asked.

"His name will be Ilya," a woman appeared.

"We wanted to name him Brylin," Braxlin snapped, his voice stiff. "Who are you? Why are you interfering here?"

"Braxlin Ironsmith, this child's name is chosen by the Mighty," the woman snapped back, her body glowing softly in the early evening light.

"I have no faith in the Mighty," Braxlin hissed.

"No? Your son will," she retorted. "His name will be recorded in Karathia's history as Ilya Rafael Ironsmith. The birth name has already been reported to the King. If you don't believe me, check for yourself."

With that, she disappeared.

~

Matt Michaels, AKA Jayson Rome

I sat on a comfortable chair on a balcony outside SouthStar's palace while Hank Bell strode around me. Criminals in an interrogation probably felt less intimidated. Every time he looked at me, smoke drifted from his nostrils.

He was pissed. I got that.

"Corinne did your work for you, and died for it." Hank wasn't mincing words.

"She separated her own particles," I attempted to defend myself.

"What choice did she have?" Hank hissed. "If she hadn't, Kalenegar or any other Larentii would be obligated. She merely relieved them of that responsibility. This shouldn't have gone as far as it did," Hank snapped. "If you'd killed the Lyristolyi who appeared in that meeting, it would have gone a long way toward preventing this disaster. With bodies to prove to the idiots still out there that neither you nor Colonel Hunter were responsible," he flung out a hand.

"Then," he went on, "if you'd tagged those fucking Elemaiya before they left the White House, or had Keef and Schaff followed or any number of other things, all that could have been avoided. Somewhere along the line, you'd have figured out that a rogue god had arrived and was pulling strings if you'd done those other things and paid attention."

"I know." I did know. I was supposed to be in charge, and I couldn't say how many times Opal wanted to argue with my actions—or lack thereof. She'd been there through it all, while I'd left Earth faster than a rabbit chased by a hound.

"I'm relieving you of your duties there," Hank said.

That caused my head to jerk up immediately. "But," I said.

"You will retire the minute you return. You will make appropriate arrangements and fake your death from some disease or other, then remove yourself from the planet."

"But who will," I began. He intended to leave Opal in charge—I just knew it.

"Opal will decide for herself. I have other plans in place," he informed me. "Your services are no longer required."

Reth Alliance

Ildevar Wyyld, Founder

"I detest state funerals, especially when I detested the planetary leader the state funeral is for," I muttered as I studied my formal robes in the mirror. "At least I only have to focus on an elaborate burial box the entire time. It's such a shame that the creature ate Geethe and his companions, after all."

"I've identified everyone in those images," Norian responded. "One of them—Wymarr Belancour—I still can't figure out what kept him inside that chamber. We've had a bounty on his head for a while. Fisk

Boralus—same thing. He was wanted on Lyristolys, too, so I can't imagine why he was meeting with Geethe."

"Perhaps we will learn those things in the future," I sighed. I had a very good idea why Fisk and Wymarr were meeting with Geethe—but I kept that to myself.

"Geethe always was a particularly sharp pain in our posteriors," Norian observed. "Lendill is already there; he says the guest suite at the Potentate's palace is free of illegal devices and your stay will be a safe one," he shrugged. "I don't envy you in any way, although the food is good on Lyristolys."

~

Morrett—Private Journal

I may never understand how or why I found myself in a long line of people waiting outside a castle door to be interviewed for employment at the castle. I had little to recommend me, after all, and as for explaining what I was—that was better left unsaid. The phrase hadn't been spoken, handing me from one master to the next to ensure my unwilling cooperation, and I hoped it had died with Fisk.

At first, I'd stared in disbelief at the date and time on my now-ancient comp-vid. I'd been flung more than four hundred sun-turns into the future. Yes, I'd double-checked, asking the man ahead of me by tapping my question on the comp-vid. He'd verified the date.

It stunned me at first—that revelation, but then the woman had achieved impossible things before, in order to deliver me from Fisk and the others. Therefore, I felt like a free man where and when I stood, and that meant I required employment to feed and house myself.

Perhaps they would allow me to work in the kitchen or as a castle servant who cleaned chambers and hall. Those things I could do well enough, and perhaps I could find a way to buy new books with my earnings—my comp-vid was now tucked tightly in a pocket and I didn't intend to let it go.

Whomever she was—the woman—had decided to let me live. I would do my best to justify her faith in me.

"You—what's your name?" a man at the door barked.

I made the sign—the one that indicated I couldn't speak. Then, pulling my comp-vid from its pocket, I tapped my name on it for the man to read.

"Morrett?" he pronounced it by rolling both Rs. I shrugged—that was good enough. "Come with me," he beckoned. "I think the Prince would like to see you."

Little did I understand at that moment that Prince Amlis would not see my inability to speak as a disability. As it turned out, he'd had a silent servant before.

"You understand Alliance common?" the Prince asked. He used a normal tone, knowing my hearing was fine and that there was no need to shout as if I were deaf, too. I nodded.

"You carry a comp-vid," he nodded toward my device. "Do you like to read?"

I nodded again—with much enthusiasm.

"I need help with my library," he said. "I need to stock and replace most of it. How would you feel about doing that? Are you familiar with history, geography and other books of learning and lore?"

My breath caught in my throat. *Yes,* I tapped on my comp-vid. *I have many such in my comp-vid's memory,* I added, tapping the words as swiftly as I could.

"Perfect," the Prince declared. "I name you Chief Librarian to the Prince. Rodrik will outline your duties and arrange for funds to buy books. Mind you, I want physical books as well as those you store in a device's memory. Every Prince should have an actual library, don't you think?"

Joy, such as I'd never known, swept through me and I wept from the intensity of that unfamiliar emotion.

James

I felt as if I were opening my eyes for the first time. All I recalled was the accident and the panic that came with it—before Nathan disappeared in murky water and my eyes went dark.

"You awake. This good," someone spoke. I blinked, discovering I was on dry land instead of a boat.

Nathan, his hand grasped in mine, lay next to me. I watched his eyes open before turning my gaze on our companion, who sat on the soft grass nearby. Below us, the green-carpeted ground dipped and fell away, revealing rows upon rows of trees, all of them covered in the sweetest-smelling white blossoms.

"Who?" I croaked. "Where are we?"

"I Bekzi. I keep promise to protect," our companion shrugged. He was young—and old—at the same time. How I knew that, I couldn't say.

Someone else appeared in my field of vision, walking up the hill toward us. He flashed Bekzi a wide grin. "That Gerrett," Bekzi stated. "He come to help."

"Jamie?" Nathan turned his head toward me. "Are we dead? Is this heaven?" His hand gripped mine tighter.

I couldn't deny that what I saw above and below us could be categorized as heaven—the sky was so blue I couldn't put a name to the color of it. Wisps of white clouds floated past that deepened the blue and gave me a shiver, it was so perfect. The air was so pure, too, that I couldn't fill my lungs fast enough.

"Not heaven," Bekzi chuckled. "This—is Avendor."

EPILOGUE

BREANNE

The crypt was dark, but spelled against damp and mold. No dust settled on this coffin; a warlock had seen to that.

Sometime in the future, the beautifully carved and bejeweled box would be altered and its true contents hidden. I smiled at the thought before breaking the spelled seal and pulling up the lid with power. Weak light shone about the warlock's body, which was protected against decomposition.

Yes, I could scent the mundane kinship between us.

I wanted to laugh, then.

This one—he'd shown his weakness.

Holding out a hand, I separated the particles of his body. No warlock's spell could defeat the power I held. I felt the sadness of it, however—that the drug had interfered and altered the timeline to prevent this warlock's daughter from being born.

I intended to rectify that matter.

A handwritten book and another small object remained after the body disappeared. I would leave them there; they would be dealt with —for good or bad—in the future.

Instead, I focused on settling the body I'd brought with me inside the elaborate box—the body I'd placed in stasis to preserve it until the proper time arrived. Closing the coffin lid, I sealed it with a spell similar to the original.

Someday, it would be opened.

Someday, someone would be quite surprised to find the one I'd placed inside.

Most fortunate it was that I could *Change What Was*, no matter the circumstance.

Most fortunate, indeed.

The End